ENTRIES IN THE M.M. DIARIES

1929 – 1945

In this engaging, suspenseful, and powerful document, Ron Kaufman explores events that emphasize the extremely valuable lessons of recent world history. The historical detail is thorough and comprehensive and provides a lens that can be applied to present political/ideological campaigns that, much as they did in the past, are threatening current democratic principles and the foundations of "civilized" culture. Read about Moses Mendelssohn's work on rocket guidance for Germany's war effort and his simultaneous efforts to sabotage its progress.

Moses Mendelssohn's voice is one of reason amidst chaotic and barbaric circumstances. It bears witness to the atrocities of Moses's time and emphasizes the need to do anything one can to undermine and defeat the agendas of corrupt leaders. His sabotaging of the V2 rocket's guidance system is heroic and serves as a contrast to the shamefully prolonged "non-involvement" of powerful government officials and religious leaders...those among the Allied powers included.

ENTRIES IN THE M.M. DIARIES

1929–1945

RON KAUFMAN

Published 2022
Printed in the United States of America
ISBN (Print: hard-cover): 978-1-7359377-7-9

For information: Ron Kaufman, c/o The Ron Kaufman Companies, 1 Lombard Street, San Francisco, CA 94111

INTRODUCTION

This book is a fact-based fictional diary about one man's view of Germany in the 1930s and 1940s until the end of World War II in Europe. Moses Mendelssohn is that man, the writer of the diary. It is the companion piece to my forthcoming novel titled *The M.M. Diaries*, which has Mendelssohn as the main character. In the novel, Mendelssohn is a German rocket scientist who is not a Nazi, whose life and those of his family are nonetheless severely affected by the Nazi regime and its policies. The diary pages here serve as an introduction to this story. It is the result of my fifty years of thought about the history involved, the resultant story, and its content.

Although history may not repeat itself, you can easily delete the name "Hitler" that occurs repeatedly in this diary and insert the names "Napoleon" or "Putin." These men have followed a similarly dark playbook. The diary and its companion novel help us understand the past and show how it can shape the present.

—Ron Kaufman

1929

January 10, 1929

I am Moses Mendelssohn III, an 18-year-old great, great, great grandson of Moses Mendelssohn, the famous Jewish/German philosopher and intellectual. The Mendelssohn family became wealthy, highly educated, and culturally assimilated Germans. My intention is to keep a diary so that I can remember and record the events of my life and so that, if I have a family, they will read these diary entries and better understand my life and remember the events that made me the man that I am.

I sense a need for the Jewish people to have a home, and being "at home" in Germany in the 20th century is an illusion.

My older brother Kurt was born in 1906 and is already, at the age of twenty-two, a distinguished physicist with an interest in low temperature research.

There is a rising tide of anti-Semitism in Germany, including blaming Jews for the humiliating German loss in World War I, and the very harsh peace terms. These terms contributed to inflation and economic hardships that have made Germany a breeding ground for hate politics. My inner conviction is that I am Jewish…but due to the poisonous environment in Germany, I must keep that a secret. I am "Jewish Christian." Therefore, the confidentiality of this will be guarded at all costs. I owe what I am to a Jewish heritage, and that influences my thinking. To better understand the Mendelssohn family, I have researched some of my illustrious ancestors and believe it is necessary to note some of this research.

In order to understand me, it is important to understand my history, my values, and why I am both blessed and cursed.

My personal, family, and scholarly influences date back to Moses Mendelssohn (1729-1786) and are colored by a 1000-year history of virulent anti-Semitism in Germany, a highly sophisticated and cultured German society, and a dark side of irrational behavior that was reinforced by the churches. It is delusional to assume that converting to Christianity will make a family acceptable to Germans, in spite of legendary achievements.

Moses Mendelssohn was born in 1729 in Dessau, Germany and died in Berlin, Germany in 1786. He was the most important Jewish philosopher of the German enlightenment. As a poor youth he studied Torah, migrated to Berlin at 14 and self-educated himself in German literature, many languages, mathematics, and philosophy. Moses eventually became a partner in a silk factory and a successful merchant. He published numerous essays, edited a magazine, and was granted the privilege of a "protected Jew" by the King, which allowed him unlimited residency in a very restricted Germany. He continued to publish numerous acclaimed books.

When Moses was challenged by Pastor Lavater to convert to Christianity, he proudly asserted his loyalty to Judaism and dedicated his energy to integrating Jews in German society. He advocated the separation of Religion and State. Moses Mendelssohn was committed to his faith but unafraid of modernity. However, four of his six children practiced Christianity, as did his famous composer grandchild Felix Mendelssohn. Many of Moses's children and grandchildren became very successful in banking and business. For example, Paul Mendelssohn and his cousin Alexander raised the Mendelssohn Bank to new levels of affluence. Paul produced a distinguished lineage. Felix and his wife died at an early age and their four surviving children became young orphans. Their son Carl became a history professor and their son Paul was a scientist who founded the chemical firm Agfa. Agfa became a vast enterprise and eventually part of the LG. Farben. Felix's daughter Marie married an Englishman and established a Mendelssohn Bank branch in England.

Felix Mendelssohn has been an inspiration to me. He was born in 1809 into a wealthy Jewish family, later baptized as a Lutheran, but was known to have had strong Jewish ties. His family even took the last name of Bartholdy, which Felix refused to do. This musical prodigy had early successes and traveled throughout Europe, writing symphonies, operas, concerts, and piano music, and also performing. Felix encountered anti-Semitism in a Europe that had experienced Jewish discrimination for many,

many centuries. I wonder if I too will experience this vile form of prejudice because I carry a famous Jewish name? I know that soon after Felix's death in 1847 at the young age of 38, Richard Wagner wrote an anti-Semitic diatribe which began almost a century-long effort in Europe to downgrade Mendelssohn's music and reputation. Wagner set out to damage Felix's reputation and, sadly, to a great extent that happened.

Learning, excelling, and achieving were basic family principles that I admire. My education will be focused on rocketry and that guides me in my pursuit of rocket guidance accuracy.

January 12, 1929

Germany is desperate to recover from the very harsh WWI extractions and retributions. The Communists and Socialists have become very vocal and much stronger. I fear that deep down the majority of Germans hate the WWI settlements and also fear the dramatic changes to their lives that a Stalin-Lenin-style government might bring. Therefore, there is the risk that extreme opposition to the government will rise in appeal and "intoxicate" the German people with the myth of right-wing power and glory.

January 14, 1929

In the 1920s, Germany has gone through economic and monetary convulsions that have surely influenced politics and created a fertile environment for political turmoil.

In November of 1923, war debt bonds that had been worth billions were reduced to pennies due to the depreciation of German currency. The roots of this problem date back to Germany unleashing a war in 1914 and both sides setting in motion an inflationary whirlwind in order to pay the enormous costs of the conflict. This eventually affected the world's economies. A substantial percent of German taxes has gone to pay WWI reparations, which had to be paid in gold for hard currency, even though Germany printed money to create a boom and spur exports. The finance minister Matthias Erzberger was brutally murdered by a right wing hit squad. Then, a huge French Army invaded the Ruhr to extract coal. This was like an act of war. The German Mark totally lost its value and Germany was disintegrating. Somehow Germany survived and Britain and the US tried to contain the French.

A combination of hyperinflation, then depression and deflation, has given a big boost to the ranting and raving of the Nazi Party.

January 18, 1929

Although my field of study and discovery is and will be the physics of rocket guidance, I am also a great believer that every person should strive to obtain a historical perspective of events that have influenced—and will influence—our lives. Germany has had continual conflicts with its neighbors, which led to WWI. I believe the Versailles settlement imposed on a defeated Germany accelerated the rise of National Socialism and the competing Communism. An overriding theme by right and left has been anti-Semitism as the scapegoat for the ills of the European Continent, which includes Russia. This makes me all the more careful to hide this diary.

January 31, 1929

The Russian Politburo has had power struggles and Stalin has been at odds with Leon Trotsky. Trotsky has just been expelled from Russia and has fled to Turkey. Germany has a significant Communist element so that these developments in Russia are being closely watched in Berlin.

February 9, 1929

Litvinov's pact for renunciation of war was concluded in Moscow. It will be presented to Latvia, Lithuania, Estonia, Poland, Turkey, Persia, Romania, and to the League of Nations. This pact appears to impose peaceful, nonaggression obligations on its signatories. Maxim Litvinov is a Russian diplomat who believes in collective security and good relations with France and Britain.

April 1, 1929

The government of neighboring Austria has had conflicts internally and has fallen. I sense a certain instability in Austria. We must remember that it is

Austria that started the First World War as a reaction to the assassination of Archduke Ferdinand by a Bosnian Serb. The result was Germany gladly joining Austria, the end of the century-long Austria-Hungary Empire and devastating defeat for Germany. And that was just 15 years ago.

June 8, 1929

Yesterday the Vatican became a sovereign state. It is small but represents an influence over hundreds of millions of Catholics in Europe and worldwide.

June 27, 1929

Today a very significant event occurred when our German president Paul von Hindenburg refused to make payments on German WWI debt. We shall see how Britain, France, and the U.S. react. Von Hindenburg is a war hero from WWI and a senior, respected politician. My guess is this may embolden political parties in Germany, especially the Nazis and the Communists.

July 7, 1929

The Vatican has recently become a sovereign state. It is reaching out to countries with Catholic populations to sign concordats to accept the regimes in the various countries to ensure the church can pursue Catholic interests. The Vatican does not care if the countries are run by dictators, as long as the church is not bothered.

July 17, 1929

The USSR has immense territory and lengthy borders. In the Far East, the USSR has had conflicts with China and has now broken diplomatic relations with China. This has meant Russia must keep a large Army in Far East Russia.

July 23, 1929

Italy has succumbed to control by fascists, who are now banning the use of foreign words. This seems minor but may be a prelude to more harsh fascist measures.

August 8, 1929

Germany has been prohibited from making "war material" due to the WWI defeat and Versailles Treaty. Nevertheless, research in aeronautics and rocketry is taking place. The German airship, Graf Zeppelin, began a world tour today. I am continuing my studies in physics and aerodynamics to become an expert in rocket guidance systems. Some of my papers have been published and attracted public attention.

August 24, 1929

I have secretly tried to follow the (minor) Zionist movement to establish a homeland in British? mandate Palestine. Actually, it is the site of ancient Israel and, in spite of a brutal Roman dispersion of Israelis in 70 AD, there has been a continual Jewish presence in Israel. Arabs came many, many centuries later and more recently only when Jews started to clear the swamps and began to revitalize a land that had been abused by the Turks.

Yesterday Arabs attacked Jews in Palestine. Perhaps this is because recently the Jewish Agency for Palestine became official and is the Jewish government for a future Jewish country. Privately I am elated that there is a Jewish Agency, but must say nothing publicly due to the poisonous anti-Jewish atmosphere now in Germany.

August 25, 1929

Because of my Jewish heritage I am sensitive to the plight of Jews in Germany and around the world. Jews have lived in Palestine for almost 3,000 years and with the revival of Zionism, there are thousands of European Jews immigrating to Palestine. The Arabs are attacking Jewish settlements and farms and are attacking Orthodox Jews in Jerusalem. The British control Palestine by WWI mandate and do not seem capable or willing to stop those attacks.

September 17, 1929

Britain is withdrawing troops from occupied Germany. They have been there since the end of WWI and the withdrawal may open the gates of

German rearmament. Many believe this is caused by economic problems in Britain.

September 30, 1929

My interest in rocketry and the influence of missile guidance systems is intensifying with each passing month. Fritz von Opel, the Opel auto maker, actually had the first rocket plane flight. This is an amazing accomplishment considering that airplanes are recent inventions. The Opel flight was short, but it will open the door for more advanced rocketry research.

October 24, 1929

The stock market in the U.S. has had some very bad days and just today has "crashed." My fear is that this will spread to other countries. Germany has experienced inflation and currency devaluation and I fear that economic problems will create a volatile political environment. The Mendelssohn family has been prominent in German banking since Moses Mendelssohn's son Abraham started a bank. Abraham was married to Lea Solomon, a member of one of Europe's most distinguished Jewish families.

Because Germany is very unstable and the future so uncertain, I can never be sure who is going to control our government. That means there could be questions about speech and writings.

That is why my diaries continue to be kept hidden and as a guard against being confiscated.

November 10, 1929

Germany is experiencing mass unemployment and is still pinned down by massive foreign debts, all of which spells political crisis. Democracy in Germany is bound to pay the price.

November 17, 1929

Stalin in the Soviet Union has continued to tighten his grip on the Politburo and has thrown out Nicolai Bulganin. Stalin has exposed continued anger with China and stated that more Soviet troops will be sent to Manchuria.

November 20, 1929

To understand the factions and mood in Germany today, one needs to understand what has occurred in years that followed the Great War and leading up to the present. In order to finance a war that Germany had unleashed in 1914, an inflationary economy was set in motion which eventually affected much of the world. In February 1920, the US Federal Reserve hiked interest rates, and other nations soon followed. This caused a slump in 1920-21. In Germany at this time there were clashes between the Communist left and private groups to the far right that may be related to the economy.

In 1919 the Treaty of Versailles worsened Germany's chance for normality with a substantial percent of German tax revenues going toward reparations. Germany's "printed money" and German exports continued so that reparations could be paid in "hard" money. In the spring of 1920 prices dropped and the exchange rates strengthened. However, by 1921 the final reparations bill came and confidence in the economy collapsed. One of Germany's most reliable political figures, Matthias Erzberger, was murdered by the right-wing. To add more pressure on Germany, in January 1923 the French sent 100,000 troops to extract coal reparations, which were perceived as "an act of war." This caused the mark to devalue so much that Germany began to disintegrate.

Both the Nazis and the Communists planned a coup, but the other political bodies rallied around Gustav Stresemann. Spending was cut and taxes rose, and a new currency was floated. The U.S. and Britain were able to contain the French, and by late 1924 Germany stabilized.

When the Wall Street Crash hit in this year (1929), Germany was caught with huge foreign debt. Mass unemployment has started along with political crisis. However, it is my hope that the German parliamentary system will keep us calm.

Decemberb15, 1929

Since boyhood I have been very interested in rocketry and have written numerous papers about my experiments in rocket-guidance systems. These papers have caught the attention of Germany's preeminent rocket scientist Wernher Von Braun.

Wernher Von Braun has approached me to join his lab as an assistant and I will be working closely with him. This is like a dream come true since I can also pursue my university studies in physics, astronomy, and weather, while simultaneously continuing studies of European diplomatic history. I am convinced that no matter what field a person chooses we must understand the past and acknowledge this past, so we can grapple with recent conflicts and make realistic plans for the future. This understanding of historical events will help give me confidence and knowledge for making important decisions.

Von Braun has assured me that I will be privy to all communications to and from his lab. He has attempted to be apolitical and enjoys the support of all the parties since they believe this rocketry is the world of the future for long-range warfare and space exploration. The Nazis seem particularly interested and are subsidizing the Von Braun research in arming a rocket with a war head.

One of Wernher's colleagues is Hermann Oberth, who has launched his first liquid-fueled rocket. This has caused a lot of excitement in the lab and solicited words of support for more advanced research.

December 20, 1929

As a student interested in diplomatic history, I must realize that countries and their leaders fall into a continuous cycle of aggression, defensiveness, suppression of freedoms, and territorial claims.

This happened frequently in the 19th and first part of the 20th century, and I predict that in the latter 20th and into the 21st century this will continue to occur. This will be especially prevalent where countries are led by dictators, monarchs or elected officials who are insecure in holding their power.

1930

February 2, 1930

While continuing my physics studies and rocketry experiments, I have also tried to understand and study the destructive energies created by Europe that have destabilized and changed Europe. For example, the Russo-Japanese War of 1904-1905 shifted Russian foreign policy, realigned European alliances, and also promoted Japanese imperialism.

There was a failed Russian revolution in 1905 and thousands of Russian Jews were murdered in hundreds of pogroms. Mass movements emerged on the left and right and there was a rising tide of anti-Semitism. Atrocities were committed during the 1912 and 1913 Balkan Wars. All these were ominous events, followed by the mass carnage of World War I where hundreds of thousands of British, French, and German troops perished, and Russia lost millions. Troops on both sides of WWI violently brutalized civilian populations by execution, deportation, maltreatment, rape, and murder. Russian Cossack units advancing into Galicia deported 50,000 Jews to Russia. Armies of both sides moved back and forth in the same territories, destroying homes, farms, and woodlands.

The "peace" that followed the November 1918 armistice saw ultraviolent civil and territorial conflicts in Germany, Hungary, and across much of Central and Eastern Europe. Again, Jews bore the brunt of much of the violence: around 60,000 Jews were killed in just the Ukraine between 1918-1921.

February 21, 1930

Following a few years of economic growth and stability, Germany experienced economic crisis in 1929 that has spilled over into 1930. I worry about the increase of authoritarian manipulations throughout Europe that are giving rise to people like Adolf Hitler of the Nazi Party.

April 22, 1930

The London Naval Treaty has been signed by Japan, United Kingdom, France, Italy, and the United States. It is intended to regulate submarine warfare, limit naval shipbuilding, and to prevent a naval arms race. The size and firepower of subs is restricted to certain maximums. Cruisers and destroyers were included as to size and armaments.

It seems to me that this treaty is pure folly, since any one of the signatories can cheat while the others comply. Japan, for instance, has openly desired to be the naval power of the Pacific Ocean and may secretly build a massive navy. While Germany is still under post WWI restrictions, the bellicose Nazi Party may insist that someday Germany build a massive sub fleet; and Germany is not a party to the London Naval Treaty.

May 8, 1930

Unemployment in Germany is now four million due to the industrial slump of the Great Depression which is developing worldwide. I fear that this is a large group that will follow radical leaders on the right and the left, due to its low morale and desperate need for a charismatic leader promising a better future.

May 11, 1930

Austria's banks are collapsing and bankrupt. This is sure to influence a German banking crisis, which will accelerate an economy already in distress.

August 5, 1930

The Nazis have waged an intense campaign throughout Germany that was brilliantly and diabolically created by Joseph Goebbels. It has taken advantage of the Great Depression that increased political instability and has featured speeches by Hitler filled with promises for everyone. He says that he will "make Germany strong again, end payment of war reparations, tear up the Treaty of Versailles, keep down Marxism, and deal harshly with the Jews." Jews are not armed and are prominent in Germany, so they are targeted and will be easy prey for the Nazis.

August 7, 1930

One of the most influential Nazis is Alfred Rosenberg, who has deeply anti-Semitic views. He has repeatedly expressed this hatred in far right-wing publications that helped form the Nazis' platform. He has just published a book, "The Myth of the 20th Century," which along with Hitler's "Mein Kampf' (1925) has become a bible for Nazis. Rosenberg has a very close relationship with Hitler and has influenced Hitler. The Nazis also claim that Rosenberg is an expert on Russian Communism. As a person who considers himself to secretly be a Jew, I have been highly offended that Rosenberg has also promoted the "Protocols of Zion," an anti-Semitic forgery first published in Russia in 1903. The "Protocols" supports Rosenberg's bizarre idea about a Judeo-Bolshevist world conspiracy. Russia has had a long history of anti-Semitism under the czars, so the "Protocols" was used by the czars to justify extreme persecution and restrictions on Jews. This resulted in a wave of Russian Jewish immigration to the U.S. in the early 1900s.

September 15, 1930

Elections occurred yesterday and Germans elected Nazis in numbers that made the Nazis the second largest political party in Germany. This stunning victory will entitle Nazis to 107 seats in the Reichstag. Why did Germans vote for Hitler? War reparations? Hyperinflation?

Nationalism? The Versailles Treaty? Hatred of Jews? Hatred of Communists? The Great Depression? Maybe it is a combination of all of these factors, but the Depression and unemployment certainly seem dominant.

October 13, 1930

Elected Nazis in their brown shirts marched into the Reichstag to take their seats. Nazis celebrated their September 14th victory by smashing the windows of Jewish shops and department stores. I worry that this is an obvious indication of bad things to come.

October 21, 1930

I have long been an advocate of Jews from Europe resettling in British Mandate Palestine as a way to avoid the frequent European public anti-Semitism. The Balfour Declaration provided for this right and was approved by the League of Nations. Subsequent British "White Papers" did modify the territory and number of people permissible for Jewish immigration to Palestine.

These "White Papers" are the result of Arabs putting pressure on England, threats to interrupt oil supplies, and Arab/Muslim attacks on Jews, along with other violent behavior.

December 1, 1930

Because I am privy to confidential files, I have learned that work on jet-propelled missiles is already advanced in Germany. Some leaders in rocket technology include Karl Wahmke, Rudolf Nebel, Klause Riedel, and Karl Becker. Our lab is also under the direction of Walter Dornberger, since he is in the military and we secretly are working on military applications.

I have observed that Wernher is very ambitious and seems to resent competition or other opinions. It is also obvious that the program lacks accurate guidance systems, which is good for my career as that is my area of specialty and there are no other guidance specialists. My suspicion is that this lab is meant to secretly assist rearming of Germany. Wernher has displayed exceptional ability and determination, especially regarding rockets with liquid propulsion.

1931

February 3, 1931

Klaus has convinced the Austrian government to experiment with a mock mail rocket delivery and it worked. I designed the guidance system to purposely be accurate for a 5 km landing. The capsule did not explode on impact, but this is not a safe or practical use of early-stage rockets.

February 14, 1931

Spain is experiencing political unrest and the government of General Berenguer has fallen.

March 12, 1931

Russia has been brutalized by Stalin's iron rule. Stalin has eliminated any real or imagined opposition. He's constantly purging his Central Committee. This cruel instability could affect the way Germans perceive Russia and the way Germany deals with Russia.

April 15,1931

Unrest continues in Spain, as in much of Europe. Just yesterday King Alfonso was overthrown and a republic declared. Germany was very quick to openly welcome the Spanish Republic in an effort to draw Spain closer to Germany.

June 15, 1931

Today Poland and the USSR have signed a Trade and Friendship Treaty. Poland has a history of domination by Russia/USSR and it is only after WWI that it gained real independence.

Therefore, I am very leery of this "friendship" and what it means for Germany, which is at Poland's western border.

June 16, 1931

Austria has had a weak and divided government and much stress on its economy following WWI. Just today the Eider government fell, making Austria fair game for opportunists.

August 24, 1931

In a surprise move that has upset Germans, France and the USSR signed a neutrality/no attack treaty. Both countries have been enemies of Germany, although Germany clearly promoted a Soviet communist revolution in 1917 to get Russia out of WWI. The Russians, up to that time, were a major force against Germany in WWI. This pact could influence German politicians of left and right (especially) to covertly plan to rearm.

October 10, 1931

Hitler has met President von Hindenburg for the first time. It was reported that the 84-year-old former Field Marshall was not impressed.

There is constant fighting amongst the political parties in the Reichstag, which has made for a do-nothing government. In addition, there are over 100 elected Nazis in the Reichstag led by Herman Göring. They are very disruptive and undermining democracy in Germany.

October 11, 1931

Germans on the "right" have been actively organizing. On the extreme right is the Harzburger Front, which now claims 100,000 members.

October 19, 1931

Our lab has had constant contact with the military and we have collaborated on building a liquid fuel rocket engine. We believe that the liquid fuel will be more powerful, easier to control and less volatile than solid fuel.

November, 1931

Wernher has rocket scientist rivals who had begun work on rockets before him. For some unexplained reasons these rivals met with serious and deadly "accidents." For example, Reinhold Tiling's lab exploded and he received fatal burns. Karl Wahnke was killed when his rocket exploded. Rudolph Webel was dismissed from weapons research due to his Jewish fiancée and his work with Albert Einstein, who is a well-known Jewish scientist. Hermann Oberth specialized in liquid-fueled rockets. Since he was Romanian, he was not allowed to work on the rocket program and was deported to Romania.

Walter Riedel has done valuable research on rocketry and is a valued associate of Wernher. They are working as a team. Riedel has been working on a liquid-fueled rocket engine that the military is very interested in. He has recently had a successful "fire up" of a prototype.

November, 1931

Hitler's political ambitions have been fed by the Depression, unemployment, propaganda, anti? Semitism, and anger over Germany's humiliation in the decade after WWI. The Nazis are now the second largest political party and Hitler's book Mein Kampf is selling thousands of copies.

Many industrialists are contributing to the Nazis since they think that will protect them if and when Nazis come to power. This money is fueling Nazi salaries and giving Joseph Goebbels, the Nazi propagandist, the funds to spread his "trash." The German Army is limited by the Versailles Treaty, so that the generals also support Hitler's position on scrapping the treaty's limitations and building a large army.

Hitler has had internal Nazi strife and has used Heinrich Himmler's SS bodyguards to put down a revolt in the Nazi Party. Himmler has organized a secret police and acts as Hitler's bodyguard.

November, 1931

Mussolini had seized power early in October 1922. Even though he was a dictator, he courted the U.S. and especially investment by the U.S. These investments were described in the German press as instituted by the American law firm Cromwell and Sullivan on behalf of their clients.

It is further reported that the American President Herbert Hoover has advised Italy to ignore anti? fascists in the US.

November 20, 1931

I have been dating a very talented and intelligent woman who is a concert pianist. Her name is Julia Klemper. Her father, Victor Klemper, is Jewish and her mother is gentile, and she is from Dresden. Her father is a professor of history and is known as a German hero in WWI.

We have been seeing each other frequently and have discussed a wedding next year, 1932.

December 5, 1931

The Hitler Youth organization has been building membership for years and is a clever way to brainwash young people and create a future "Army." Some local governments have attempted to ban Hitler Youth activities and publications, but they still attract thousands throughout Germany. The movement is known for virulent anti-Semitism and devotion to Hitler.

December 19, 1931

Physicists working for the military have told our lab scientists about the identification of "heavy water." It is believed that heavy water can be used to create atomic energy. Hence, this research can lead to an atomic bomb for the German military. The rumor is that Werner Heisenberg will lead this work and that it may take many years to come to fruition.

1932

January 2, 1932

Germany continues to experience massive unemployment. Perhaps six million workers or more are out of work. Our research is fully funded, in contrast to the turmoil that is upsetting German society. Therefore, our employment in rocketry development seems secure.

February 25, 1932

Hitler, an Austrian, has just become a naturalized German citizen. This means that he can now run in the 1932 election for Reich president. This is a serious situation since the Nazis have been building membership and funding a huge propaganda machine that has preconditioned millions of potential voters.

The Great Depression has brought unemployment, business failures, homelessness, and starvation. Berlin is unraveling, there is fighting and killing in the streets, and I fear that Germany is ripe and desperate for any leader like Hitler who promises them relief. So far Hindenburg is holding Germany together, but barely.

President Hindenburg has agreed to run for reelection, and Hitler has decided to run against him. Hitler has Joseph Goebbels as his propaganda advisor, and Goebbels is capable of waging a campaign of speeches, posters, rallies, pamphlets, and films that could swamp Hindenburg.

March 15, 1932

The presidential election has occurred and, even though Hindenburg got 29% to 30% of the votes, he did not get an absolute majority required by German law. So, a runoff election will take place.

March 25, 1932

Hitler is waging a whirlwind runoff campaign, with a promise for everyone. This has produced growing numbers of fanatics.

March 28, 1932

There is an intolerant attitude towards gays by most Germans and a newspaper has published that SA Chief Ernst Rohm is a homosexual. Hitler kept Rohm as leader of SA despite his homosexuality. The SS now numbers 400,000. That scares me since it is Hitler's private army of thugs. Hitler continued to campaign furiously, and Hindenburg did very little.

April 10, 1932

Paul von Hindenburg is reelected president of Germany in a runoff election. He was a World War I military leader and is revered by the people. However, he is quite old and lacks political leadership skills. The vote was 53% for Hindenburg and 36% for Hitler, or over 13,000,000 votes for the Nazis. This election is a clear and ominous indicator that the Nazis have grown powerful and popular.

May 30, 1932

Germany's Chancellor Bruning has resigned and President Hindenburg has asked Franz von Papen to form a new government as Chancellor. Von Papen does not have a lot of popularity and the turnover is worrisome.

June 3, 1932

Professor Becker and Wernher have focused on the liquid-fueled rocket being developed for the Army. Our group is committed to perform feverish research and development to perfect a military rocket.

The rocket will be 14 m long and weigh 12,800 kg, including fuel and explosives. This liquid fuel is alcohol and oxygen, the highest ceiling 97km, and it will have a velocity of 1,700 meters per second. It is designed to steer by rudders in the tail, and guidance is where I come in as an important person in the design team. I know this design will not work and have other more complicated and sophisticated guidance theories.

June 14, 1932

Until now the vicious Nazi gangs known as the SS and SA have terrorized certain segments of Germany and therefore had been officially banned. That ban has just been overturned by the Reichstag, which gives the Nazis more power and will threaten other segments of the population.

July 17, 1932

The Communists in Germany have been very vocal and in direct competition with the National Socialists. Armed Communists have just attacked a Nazi demonstration and killed eighteen Nazis. This event triggered open "warfare" in the streets of some cities, pitting Communists against Nazis. We must remember that Hitler is obsessed with hate for Jews and for Communists.

July 20, 1932

A new election has been held for members of the Reichstag and the popularity of the Nazi Party is affirmed with a gain of 123 Reichstag seats.

August 30, 1932

Herman Göring is a prominent Nazi, close advisor to Hitler, and was a German flying ace in World War I. Göring has been elected to the powerful post of Chairman of the German Senate. This is a move that gives further power to the Nazis.

October 1, 1932

It is now a year since meeting Julia and we have been constant companions. Although we are both quite young, I have asked her to marry me and continue her music studies in Berlin. The wedding is scheduled for this December and we have both decided on a simple ceremony.

Although her father is from a Jewish family and his father is a rabbi, we plan to have a judge perform the ceremony to minimize any religious exposure. I have also decided not to invite my colleagues at the Rocket Center since I am not sure how many of them are rabid Nazis, or how that could affect my high security clearance, which allows me to receive confidential bulletins.

November 10, 1932

Chancellor von Papen has been unable to form a coalition that excludes the Nazis and has been forced to resign. I perceive this political uncertainty as an opportunity for the Nazis.

November 21, 1932

There has been open dissention amongst various factions in the Reichstag. This has caused President Hindenburg to again consider forming a new government. This time he is negotiating with Adolf Hitler.

December 3, 1932

Hindenburg has named Kurt von Schleicher as Chancellor, a move that has angered Hitler and caused further turmoil in the governing body. Hitler was adamant that if his party controlled the second highest voting constituency, he should be Chancellor.

December 15, 1932

Hitler has continued to cultivate the support of bankers and industrialists. Also, former Chancellor von Papen is trying to undermine Chancellor von Schleicher by actually helping Hitler.

1933

January 10, 1933

The Nazi Party has had a minority percentage of votes in the 1920s, in spite of inflation, war reparations, and very heavy German national debt. However, the Great Depression and massive unemployment gave a boost to the Nazis in recent runoff elections. They got just enough votes to come in second, and President Hindenburg now invited Hitler into the government as Chancellor.

Hindenburg claims that appointing Hitler as Chancellor will keep the Nazi Party in check. I disagree and worry that this will have a disastrous result for Germany and therefore for the entire European continent. We have experimented with "democracy" after WWI by creating the Weimar Republic. It now seems very unstable and may be the beginning of the end of supposed Democracy in Germany.

February 1, 1933

General Erich Ludendorff, the Army's Chief of Staff, sent a telegram to Hindenburg. It is said to predict that Hitler will "plunge the Reich into the abyss and future generations will curse you."

February 2, 1933

Hermann Göring has been an active Nazi official and now holds a position of power in the German government. Today he banned Communist meetings and demonstration. Hitler met with the Army generals and promises expansion of the military.

February 3, 1933

Göring has banned the social democratic newspaper *Vorwarts*.

February 4, 1933

President von Hindenburg is limiting freedom of the press. He is old and feeble, and I believe he was put up to this by the Nazis.

February 7, 1933

A Social-Democratic meeting in Berlin has declared Marxism is dead.

February 10, 1933

The Nazis have just taken power in Germany. Joseph Goebbels is a third-rate German "intellectual" who is now a high-ranking Nazi policy maker and propagandist. He attacks Jews by reference to the Christian gospels, which I believe were created in ancient times to purposely discredit Jews in order to spread Christianity. It is common knowledge that dating back thousands of years Jews have been a defamed and dispersed people who could never be the threat claimed by anti-Semites, who used untrue claims against Jews as a way to increase their own power. Jews have never posed a danger to Christians. I fear that Goebbels will demonize Jews and exaggerate their economic importance as an excuse to seize and steal their homes, businesses, and other assets to obtain free financing for the Nazi power grab. Truly a nightmare for Germany's future. The Nazis have chosen their victims!

February 11, 1933

The Great Depression continues its strong hold on Germany. There are economic pressures that have caused unemployment, hunger, fear, and desperation. Now we have a man in charge who hates the Republic.

I personally have been alright, since my family still has many generations of wealth. Also, the rocketry lab, where I work with a brilliant team, continues to be well-funded by industrialists and the Army.

February 12, 1933

The German Vice Chancellor von Papen said that Catholics must give aid to the Nazis. Since Catholics are a significant percentage of Germany's population, this is a huge boost for Hitler.

February 15, 1933

In Hitler's cabinet are Hermann Göring and Wilhelm Frick. Franz von Papen is Vice Chancellor and he is a counterbalance to Hitler. In fact, it is rumored that Papen will use Hitler as a way to end the Republic and bring back an authoritarian government to restore German glory. Rumor has it that industrialists think Hitler is good for business, so Krupp, Farben, and others support Hitler. I think they are very misguided and underestimate Hitler's motifs and massive numbers of armed "Brown Shirts."

February 16, 1933

The Catholics warned Germans against Communists and Nazis, but now von Papen has told Catholics they must help Hitler.

February 28, 1933

The Reichstag has been burned and the Nazis claim it was done by Jews and Communists. I believe the Nazis set the fire as a way of blaming others and consolidating their own power.

February 28, 1933

I am shocked, but President von Hindenburg has abolished free expression of opinion and then Hitler disallowed the German Communist Party.

February 28, 1933

Göring and Hitler have convinced Hindenburg that he must sign an emergency decree after the Reichstag fire. This means they can easily arrest political opponents.

March 3, 1933

The Nazis are starting to persecute political opponents. For example, Earnest Thalmann is a Communist presidential candidate and he has been arrested. It is not a surprise because the Nazi Party now has a majority in parliament. They announce plans to take over state and local governments.

March 10, 1933

We learn the political enemies of the Nazis are being arrested by the thousands, detained, tortured, and sometimes murdered. This is done by Hitler's private army and police, the SA and the SS.

March 12, 1933

A detention camp was opened at Oranienburg outside of Berlin. The government is taking political prisoners there and it is a sign of repression that will threaten the very soul of Germany.

March 13, 1933

Nazi Germany now has a minister of propaganda, Joseph Goebbels. He has openly advocated the burning of the books that the Nazis do not like.

March 21, 1933

Hitler and Propaganda Minister Goebbels have staged an elaborate ceremony in Potsdam to ease public concern over Hitler's gangster-like regime. I am sure this is a hoax to fool the world.

Later today it was reported that Hitler has gotten Hindenburg to sign decrees that make it a crime to criticize Nazis, and has set up military-style courts. This follows a Reichstag meeting where Hitler made absurd promises, if only the body would pass an enabling law. The act was passed by a huge majority and it is now clear that democracy in Germany has ended, "legally."

March 21, 1933

Reports have come to our lab office that yesterday the Nazis established a concentration camp in Dachau near Munich to hold political prisoners. This shocking event is just a few months after Hitler became Chancellor, so the Nazis must have had it planned for a long time. Dachau is an old WWI munitions plant with buildings that can hold 5,000 prisoners, surrounded by electrified fences and watchtowers.

March 22, 1933
Reichsfuhrer SS Heinrich Himmler, the commander of Germany's National Police, has announced that prisoners are already arriving at Dachau. He has based the arrests on the February 27th emergency decree that Hitler tricked Hindenburg into signing an order to "protect the people."

March 23, 1933
Hitler and his Nazi Party were able to pass an enabling act which allows Hitler to pass laws without the Reichstag and gives him dictatorial power.

March 25, 1933
We are confronted by all aspects of life now being under the dictatorship of Hitler and we are all told he must be obeyed or face dire consequences.

April 1, 1933
The Nazis have blamed Jews for Germany's troubles and now have accelerated a campaign against Jews, including the boycott of Jewish-owned shops. It is obvious to me that Hitler is jealous of Jews and may want to steal their assets to fund his Nazi ambitions.

April 2, 1933
The Nazis that came to power in January are firing most Jewish government employees and judges, and disbarring most lawyers. Jewish doctors, dentists, and professors are now unemployed. My colleagues are aware of my Jewish ancestry dating back to the 1800s. It does not concern them; especially since I am indispensable for the rocket program.

April 5, 1933
We now learn that Göring's SS and his Brown Shirt SS thugs are beating people, looting shops, and terrorizing Jews.

April 7, 1933
Germans have a respect for laws. However, the Nazis are passing laws that are anti-Jewish. It seems inconceivable that an educated population will

follow such laws, but Jews are now barred, by "law", from legal and public service.

April 7, 1933

Göring has now purged the Berlin police of all opposition and sworn in 50,000 storm troopers as police with the power to arrest.

April 11, 1933

Hitler's close associate and Air Force advocate, Hermann Göring, has become the Prime Minister of Prussia. The Nazis are rapidly taking control.

April 15, 1933

Many who disagree with the Nazis are leaving Germany. While I totally disagree with Hitler, my work is so interesting, so advanced, and so protected from harassment that I do not plan to leave. I am confident that my position is secure and that my new family will remain safe.

The Munich prosecutor's office is investigating the mysterious killing of three men near the abandoned munitions factory at Prittlbach, which is now known as Dachau Concentration Camp. The prosecutor assigned to this is Josef Hartinger, who is not a Nazi and is said to be a political conservative with a sense of justice.

April 16, 1933

Hartinger has reported that the three men had been executed at short range with bullets to the back of the head. All three were Jews. Hartinger plans to bring murder charges.

April 18, 1933

Our lab is excited that a rocket is to be fired tomorrow by Gerhard Zucker. It is designed to carry mail from Duhnen to the island of Neuwerk.

April 18, 1933

The Zucker Rocket flew only a few meters and then crashed to earth. This crash was a big disappointment to me and my colleagues. I suspect the trajectory caused it to tilt and descend.

April 26, 1933

Jewish students can no longer attend school in Germany, according to a new "law." Many of our rocketry group have reacted with disbelief about the evil ramifications of such a law. Since I have already completed my graduate work and am not "Jewish" by definition, this "law" does not affect me. However, it will cause Germany to lose some of its best minds.

April 27, 1933

Göring has created a secret police and intends to use it to silence political opponents and expand his power. The police are known as the Gestapo.

May 2, 1933

Hitler has banned trade unions whose members might object to him and lean toward such opposition as the Communists.

May 10, 1933

Nazis have taken to the streets in many German cities and are burning books, especially those of Jewish authors and scholars.

May 12, 1933

In international news, it is reported that Russia has had a severe famine which is decimating the population. The Nazis are happy about this since it weakens a strong potential enemy. The Nazis hate the Communists, and Hitler can pursue rearmament without fear of Russian intervention.

May 15, 1933

It seems obvious that Hitler and the Nazis are trying to create an imaginary public perception of Jews. This is based on maybe 1,500 years of literature of the Jews "in exile," and is an attempt to brainwash the public to blame Jews for the unemployment, inflation, and all the ills of Germany. This negative image builds on Christian polemics that are "centuries deep," such as the absurd blood libels. The Nazis want people to think it is okay to discriminate against and persecute Jews by dehumanizing them.

Joseph Goebbels has proclaimed “the age of Judaism is at an end.” He is trying to create a threat that is non-existent and is building on arguments of German philosophers from another era who linked Jews to “world power” and “materialism.” Goebbels finds it useful to link Jews to the Nazis’ political enemies, and vastly exaggerates the Jewish economic importance. If I could leave Germany with my family, I would do so. However, the rocket lab has already labeled me as “indispensable,” so I can never be asked to leave.

May 20, 1933

Dateline Dachau. Prosecutor Hartinger is ready to prosecute those responsible for the Dachau murders. His objective is to force the Bavarian police chief Heinrich Himmler to stop the illegal killings.

May 28, 1933

Dateline Dachau. Himmler has persuaded Hitler to close down Hartinger’ s Dachau case and sequester all files. I fear this will mean more murders at Dachau.

June 10, 1933

The Dachau commandant Hilmar Wackerle has been replaced after being charged with murdering a prisoner. He has been replaced by Theodor Eicke.

June 14, 1933

Some of Germany’s finest minds fear Hitler and are leaving the country for good by the thousands. Among them are writer Thomas Mann, actress Marlene Dietrich, architect Walter Gropius, many symphony musicians, psychologist Dr. Sigmund Freud, and physicist Albert Einstein.

June 15, 1933

The Vatican has signed a concordant with Hitler. The Catholic Church has renounced German political activity and the emerging Nazi Germany has requested the right to maintain Catholic schools and property.

June 20, 1933

We are exposed to relentless Nazi rallies, parades, and Goebbels's propaganda. I find it sickening and distracting from my research. However, the masses appear to be buying the Nazi's thinking.

June 21, 1933

The Dachau commandant Eicke has published a set of regulations for the operation of Dachau. These regulations appear to be a blueprint for other concentration camps.

June 25, 1933

I have looked for reasons why Hitler could have success going from a lowly corporal to the head of a major German movement. There have been certain role models to Hitler, such as America's Henry Ford. Ford is a known anti-Semite and has published numerous papers that have influenced Hitler. Some German industrialists such as Fritz Thyssen have also supported Hitler. Almost 40% of Germany is Catholic, so this concordant eliminates up to 40% of the opposition to Hitler and it will make it very difficult for Jews and others to seek help from the church. The pope is supposed to be the moral leader of the Catholic world, and the current pope has made an agreement with the Nazis that will silence 40% of Germany's population. This pope will be remembered as an accomplice to the Nazis.

White Russians opposed the Communists and aided Hitler. Even the King of England, Edward VIII, has expressed pro-Nazi sympathy.

My guess is that the breakdown of democracy facilitated Nazism. There is the collapse of the economy and erosion of faith in German political leadership that made it hard for the government to function. Hitler promised to correct all of this.

July 2, 1933

Mexico followed the Vatican's orders and signed the concordat with Germany. This will have a major effect on the Catholics of Central and South America, on their countries, and on Jews living in those countries.

July 5, 1933

It now seems obvious to me that the Nazis intend to discriminate against anyone with even the slightest Jewish heritage, going back many generations. Therefore, those families that have converted to Christianity are fooling themselves to think they are immune from the horrible "disease." That means that as a Mendelssohn I am vulnerable to Nazi hatred and must also continue to be in such an indispensable position in our rocket research that von Braun and Hermann Oberth will protect me, even though my heritage is well known to them. My wife Julia's father, Victor Klemper, is Jewish, so it remains to be seen if he and/or Julia will be harmed. I have taken steps with the lab to get confidential assurances that no harm will come to them.

July 9, 1933

There are random arrests, beatings, and many murders of Jews and non-Jewish political opponents of Nazis.

July 14, 1933

To further consolidate its grip on all Germans, the Nazi Party has just been declared the only political party.

September 10, 1933

Stalin in the Soviet Union has unleashed a torrent of violence against his own citizens. Millions are dying in the Ukraine due to induced famine and millions more in Russia as Stalin purges his own party, including top leadership of the Central Committee. Here in Germany, we have the rise of Hitler and the Nazis, and it is clear that Russia and Germany might someday be on a collision course to repeat World War I history.

October 14, 1933

The League of Nations has constantly enforced post war restrictions on Germany and set rules that Hitler does not like. Today, Germany quit the League of Nations.

November 8, 1933

My brother Kurt is being forced by the Nazis to give up his research in low-temperature physics and will leave for England. This is clearly Germany's loss. Kurt is going to Oxford to work at Clarendon Laboratory. Although Kurt has the Mendelssohn name, he was just one of many experts in his field. He will be able to further his work in England and I hope we can stay in touch. I suspect there are plenty of Nazis who would like to "get me," but, so far, advancing research has been my shield.

November 14, 1933

Julia's father, who is a distinguished professor, has been dismissed from teaching at his university. He was a World War I German Army hero and his wife is non-Jewish…a Catholic. For the present he is being left alone. However, with little income except his worthless army pension, he and my mother-in law will have a very austere existence.

1934

January 1, 1934

Nazis have just passed another law "to prevent genetically diseased offspring." This can be used to stop marriages, abort births, and arrest people the Nazis say are "genetically diseased." This may mean forced abortions or the murder of newborn infants.

January 10, 1934

A younger colleague has shown an aptitude for rocket design. His name is Konrad Dannenberg and he has recently graduated in engineering from the University of Hanover. It is upsetting to me that he is a member of the Nazi Party. However, most of my colleagues say they must also join if they are to remain in this classified rocket research.

January 10, 1934

1933 has seen a wave of arrests now that Hitler has his "empowerment law." He and his henchmen are doing whatever they want to crush opposition. Many of those arrested were sent to Dachau, where the camp commandant Eicke is a sadist. I suspect some of the men imprisoned in Dachau have been tortured and even murdered. Hitler is concerned about criticism, especially from America. However, America has been very silent and Hitler has taken advantage of the American silence. Hitler is also concerned about the Vatican and will rely on the concordat with the Vatican to placate Catholic Germany. Nonetheless, there are numerous unexplained deaths at Dachau which everyone knows are murders since the victims' bodies often disappear. Internal memos seen by the rocket lab leaders claim that Dachau is being tested as a model for an entire system of multiple concentration camps. In short, there is a criminal conspiracy to use terror and murder as a political tool.

January 27, 1934

Yesterday Germany signed a 10-year, non-attack treaty with Poland. This seems strange to me since Poland does not have a strong military. This may be a trick by Hitler to prepare for an invasion of Poland if they are "off guard."

February 10, 1934

I am amazed that the Nazis have gained so much power so fast. Germany is a highly educated, cultured, and industrialized country. Why is this happening? They are playing on social and class tensions, many centuries of anti-Semitism, and hate for a humiliating World War I treaty. Add to that the Great Depression, massive unemployment, and masterful Nazi propaganda methods, and you have a society ripe for a dictatorship. In addition, the Nazis have terrorized their opposition and no one has invoked a rule of how to stop them.

Jews are now trying to leave Germany and escape the Nazi menace. Some want to go to Palestine since it has a Jewish population and has been the heart of Judaism for 3,000 years. The British-controlled Palestine has a League of Nations mandate. However, the British are worried about Arab oil supplies and do not want to anger the Arabs, so are restricting entry by Jews fleeing Hitler, and blockading Jewish immigrant ships as well. While Palestine could be an alternative for my family, I cannot be allowed to leave or stop my rocket guidance research.

There was a very short civil war in Austria that ended with the defeat of the Socialists. This indicates that Austria is fragmented and unstable. It could make Austria vulnerable to a takeover by Germany.

February 20, 1934

Envy of Jews is one of the motivating forces behind Nazi anti-Semitism. Their confiscated wealth would finance Hitler's wildest dreams in the greatest theft known in history. This corrupt envy is not only in the Nazi leadership, since there is the complicity of most of the German population, and that includes the educated elite of German society.

When I try to understand this envy, I must return to my hobby of studying history for a partial explanation. In the 18th and 19th centuries, Jews in Germany became highly educated and took advantage of economic opportunity offered by urbanization and industrialization. It was the most successful of any Jewish population in Europe, and its achievements exposed Jews as a target for German envy. This contrasted with German lethargy and resentment, and helped produce envy of Jewish wealth. It is also clear that many Germans do not believe in liberty and equality, and with a history of a long-term divided Germany, there exits an insecure national identity. German unification in 1871 was followed by social tensions, again inflamed by Jewish success and the envy by gentiles. Many Germans blamed Germany's ills on the Jews.

As I have written elsewhere, the humiliating and debilitating Versailles Treaty, the economic bust of 1929, the increase of socialism and nationalism…all these factors are being exploited by Hitler to further the Nazi Party. Material gain of Jewish property and jobs has further motivated discrimination, plunder, and even murder. To this toxic mix, Hitler has added race theory, in order to justify "cleansing" Germany of Jews. What is particularly upsetting (to me) is that the left and the right have bought into Hitler's "getting rid of the Jews." In other words, the majority of Germans. I realize that anti-Semitism was rampant in France and Russia. However, I continue to believe that in Germany war, defeat, humiliations, hyperinflation, and depression have heavily contributed to the increase in numbers of ardent anti-Semites who are exploiting the jealousy of the German masses to persecute the Jews.

March 8, 1934

German newspapers have been closely following the starvation imposed by Stalin on Ukrainian peasantry. Millions have been starved to death to promote the collectivization of mass farming. Famines created elsewhere in the Soviet Union have killed millions more. Hitler has been quoted as being shocked by Stalin and regards Stalin and Communism as mortal enemies. Hitler has also said this is an example of how an all-powerful dictator can enforce his will on his people and get away with it.

Hitler commented to the press that some Soviet citizens who resisted

Stalin's plans were deported to Central Asia or the Far North. They were crammed into cattle cars and many died in transit. My fear is that the Nazis will try to do the same.

March 16, 1934

As I feared last year, Hitler has established a concentration camp system to arrest everyone who might challenge him, such as Communists and Socialists.

Heinrich Himmler has stated that the camps can serve as a test to improve the German race and thereby take on an indefinite stature. He wants to go after alcoholics, drug addicts, homosexuals, members of minority religions, prostitutes, and vagrants. The system is planned for camps at Sachsenhausen, Buchenwald, Flossenburg, Mauthausen, and Ravensbruck.

The Jews of Germany are about one percent of the population. Hitler and Himmler have a goal to create conditions that force them to emigrate. Then the Jewish possessions and wealth can be easily taken to finance the Nazi regime in what will be the greatest theft in history.

April 11, 1934

Hitler has signed an agreement to expand the military. He has barely been in power and this move is probably prohibited by the Versailles Treaty, which he is determined to break.

April 20, 1934

Wernher von Braun has published a thesis on "The Solution of the Liquid Propellant Rocket." The German Army that controls our group has decided to classify this thesis so that other nations do not have access. However, as a member of the inner group, I have read the paper and believe it will help to produce operative rockets. The liquid propellant should be able to control combustion in such a way as to accelerate the rocket's speed at various stages of ascent and descent.

Von Braun's theories were influenced by the American physicist Robert Goddard and he even incorporated a Goddard plan in the thesis. We know that Goddard landed the first liquid rocket in 1926 and holds many patents that explain rocketry principles.

Von Braun was an assistant to Hermann Oberth, who is a "founding father" of rocketry. He has incorporated some of Hermann Oberth's theories in his thesis.

April 22, 1934

Heinrich Himmler developed a rivalry with Hermann Göring over who would run the dreaded Gestapo. Himmler and his associate, Reinhard Heydrich, have won that battle and taken control of the Gestapo.

April 30, 1934

Austria has a new constitution based on Austrian fascism. This brings Austria very close to Germany's way of thinking, even though Austria is supposedly independent.

May 7, 1934

Julia has given birth to our son. On the official records we will use the first name Friedrich as a way to avoid any attention. However, he is descended from an illustrious family and we will honor that lineage by thinking of him as Felix, the great Mendelssohn composer. Julia and I are very concerned about being new parents at a time of emerging Nazi power. However, we are determined to try to lead a "normal" life and to raise a family. We decided that after this year she will decide whether or not to resume her career as a pianist. Because she has a Jewish father and grandfather, this may not be possible.

June 14, 1934

Italy has rapidly become fascist under the iron rule of Benito Mussolini. Hitler and Mussolini are meeting in Vienna and it is a guess that their styles are close enough to encourage some cooperation.

June 20, 1934

Poland has been "re-created" since the World War. It is known that Hitler has his eye on expansion to the east if and when he can rebuild the German

Army and create an air force. I question why a non-aggression pact between Germany and Poland was signed this January. There is absolutely not a threat from Poland, so Hitler must have some hidden agenda.

June 22, 1934

There have been some factions in the Nazi Party who are not "obedient" to Hitler, and it is reported that he has purged these people in a very bloody way. The SS has imprisoned or killed hundreds of men to further tighten Hitler's control over Germany.

June 25, 1934

Nazi Bulletin, June 24, 1934: The music of Felix Mendelssohn has been discredited by the Nazis and the study and performance of his music forbidden. Since I carry the family name, there is a question of what will the Nazis do to me. However, they have given the Rocket Research Center highest priority and I am crucial to the center's success. The Nazis labeled Felix a Jew and absurdly claimed that his music implanted Jewish thought into young Christians. They plan to expunge his works from concert programs and his name from books.

June 29, 1934

The Mendelssohn family bank, which has been in existence for over 130 years, has been closed by the Nazis. It is blatant seizure of great wealth that provides the Nazis with stolen assets. This also means that my source of independent wealth is gone and I am totally dependent on the modest salary I earn at the Rocket Center.

July 2, 1934

With Hitler established as German Chancellor and his overt hatred of Jews, it is now clear that Jewish assimilation in Germany was an illusion. I fear that the Gestapo will stop at nothing and there will soon be no laws to stop them.

Germany is going to accelerate work on rockets since Hitler is obsessed with them. That is good for our rocket group and we have been promised all the resources we may need. Other nations are also working on weapons. Hungary, until recently part of the Austro-Hungarian network, has just announced that their physicist Leo Sziland has patented a design for an atom bomb. This weapon is more destructive than anything known to man. While I am ambivalent about helping Hitler's rocket program, I can accomplish a personal agenda by "controlling" the flight path and accuracy of what may be very powerful weapons. Besides as a one-of-a-kind specialist who is critical to the rocket program, I believe I can protect my wife and child.

July 5, 1934

There is a new law that urges citizens to report "candidates" for sterilization.

The Nazi German regime is promoting "racial health" policies that the Nazis claim will eliminate the "corruption" of the "Aryan" race. They are targeting Germany's homosexual men who the Nazis believe are carriers of a "degeneracy" that weakens society. The Nazis have arrested and imprisoned in concentration camps many thousands of German men in an effort to terrorize them into social conformity and to eradicate homosexuality. This effort has killed thousands, shattered the lives of thousands, and is only one of numerous perverted acts by this ruling regime.

July 14, 1934

Hitler has spoken about the threat of National Bolshevism and boasts about extermination of Communists. This presents another target for the Nazis. There are reports from Berlin of a blood bath as Hitler murders Bolsheviks.

July 25, 1934

Nazis have murdered Austrian Chancellor Dollfuss in a blatant act to destabilize Austria. It is obvious that Hitler has his eyes on control of Austria.

July 26, 1934

Another person in our group who is very interested in rocket guidance is Helmut Grottrup. We are collaborating a little in some areas, but it is very important that I not reveal to him my discoveries in "misguidance" calibrations that can alter the true flight of a rocket. Helmut is very bright and seems motivated to be a leader. He professes to be a "true" Nazi, but has also confidentially commented to me about his sympathy for some of the communist programs. In order for me to stay indispensable, I will not share certain advanced concepts with Helmut and certainly not reveal my reasons.

Arthur Rudolph is a close friend of Wernher who has been a member of the Nazi parti long before Hitler came to power. He flaunts Nazism with arrogance and sometimes creates a tension that is an overlay on the research. He has a senior position in the lab and is very outspoken that once we have an operational rocket, he will lead Germany to mass produce it.

August 3, 1934

The aging, senile, and weak President Hindenburg has died. Hitler plans to merge the Presidency and Chancellor. This will now make Hitler the sole head of state. Hitler also is now commander-in-chief of German Armed Services.

August 19, 1934

Adolph Hitler has pounced on Hindenburg's death and declared himself the Fuhrer of Germany. He has asked soldiers to swear loyalty to Adolph Hitler.

August 20, 1934

Hitler has given Heinrich Himmler more power and he is now heading the Prussian Secret State Police.

August 20, 1934

The Nazis have tightened their grip on Germany and increased control of the press in order to prevent criticism of their regime and stifle reports of brutality from reaching the outside world. Foreign correspondents are closely monitored by German authorities and threatened with expulsion, violence, and imprisonment. Recently the American journalist, Dorothy Thompson, was expelled and she went back to NYC to write for the New York Herald Tribune. It is obvious that Goebbels is the mastermind behind these strict policies of control of information.

October 5, 1934

Hitler's lawyer, Hans Frank, has proclaimed that laws serve leaders, rather than protect individuals. Frank is the author on numerous Nazi laws that have solidified Hitler's absolute grip on Germany.

October 10, 1934

Yesterday in Marseille, King Alexander of Yugoslavia and Lewis Berthau the French Foreign Minister, were assassinated. This is a byproduct of the unrest and turmoil that now affects most of Europe.

October 15, 1934

The Nazis are in control of Germany and are openly preparing for another war. Our rocket research remains controlled by the Army. Dr. Paul Schmidt has conducted jet engine research. These jets could be pilotless and are now under the control of the Luftwaffe since Airforce Marshall Hermann Göring wanted command of anything that flies. This is probably a mistake and duplication of research, but it has "kept peace" between the Army and the Air Force.

I understand the flying bomb concept. It is like a torpedo used at sea and is guided by an automatic pilot. The difference is the flying bomb is in the air and is very expensive to produce and replace. Dr. Sanger of Austria has produced an aircraft that can attain a speed of 600 mph, at a very high altitude. Göring has approached Sanger to join the Luftwaffe's lab.

Guidance of the rocket continues to be based on my research. I have theorized a system that will be 100% accurate, but will not discuss it with others. There is a way to control flight through certain calibrations and fin angles. Internally there will be a gyroscopic ball floating in a fluid sphere which can stabilize and guide the flight path. That too can be set off course by slightly altering the fluid density.

November 7, 1934

Nazi Party propaganda is creating a great deal of publicity about races that they claim are inferior to Germans. They also quote numerous sources of supposed progressives in the United States who had promoted something called Eugenics. The Eugenics advocates argued that people with certain traits must be eliminated, sterilized, or kept in asylums. It is my fear that this horribly misconceived concept will be accelerated by the Nazis in order to justify the persecution of a massive number of people they despise or whom they consider a threat to Nazi domination of Europe.

December 10, 1934

Latvia is a small Baltic nation that is close to Communist Russia. It is now ruled by a fascist dictator Ulman, who is following Hitler's lead by opening a concentration camp. I think this Latvian situation is very upsetting to Stalin.

December 15, 1934

Using Von Braun's designs, our group has launched two rockets that reached heights of 2.2 and 3.5 km. The group is jubilated at this success. Guidance of the rockets was based on my gyroscopes to determine direction and power cutoff.

1935

January 10, 1935

It appears to me that the Nazis have firmly solidified their power and are transforming their racial ideas into severe policies. Heinrich Himmler's SS is accelerating the regime's anti? Semitic policies and repressing a defenseless Jewish population. I will try to focus on my rocketry research, keep my "head down" and keep my diary entries strictly confidential.

January 14, 1935

The Saar voted 90% to join Nazi Germany. This industrialized region with a heavy German population is important for the Nazis plans. The region has considerable steel production and heavy machinery works, and it is obvious that Hitler needs that for arms production. Also, I doubt that other countries will complain about this aggressive annexation.

January 18, 1935

Nazis are dismissing Jews from public service, boycotting Jewish businesses and forcing emigrating Jews to exchange their currency for worthless notes. Anti-Semitism is becoming state policy and an excuse for the theft of Jewish property. This has included every field: textiles, department stores, etc. It is clear that by financially ruining a family they have no choice but to flee.

March 16, 1935

In violation of the Versailles Treaty, Hitler has ordered rearmament of Germany. This includes reforming the Luftwaffe, commanded by Hermann Göring.

July 7, 1935 (This is an insider memo seen by our lab leaders.)
The SS for years has been infiltrating British and French intelligence organizations and the U.S. State Department. They have also had German businesses such as Farben, Schneider, and Krupp establish business ties with U.S. industry and with influential U.S. law firms who will be paid significant fees to represent German companies in the U.S. and Europe. This plan has always been to influence U.S. foreign policy or at least neutralize it. We are all aware that one such law firm is Sullivan and Cromwell, the U.S.'s most eminent corporate law firm. Its chainnan is John Foster Dulles, who has a strong foreign affairs pedigree and many lucrative German clients. He is clearly a Nazi sympathizer in spite of Hitler's blatant atrocities since 1933. JFD's background made him an ideal target and stooge for the Nazis. His grandfather and uncle were Secretaries of State and he considered himself to be a well-connected "blue blood." The S&C law firm has created numerous giant corporations and represent them worldwide, and has been accused of being ruthless and employing deceit and bribery to get its way.

The SS has also implanted a mole on the S&C staff to report back the state of U.S. industries represented by the law firm. JFD is connected to the inner circles of American power and has international experience. He is ruthlessly effective, pompous, and very well paid.

In sort, he was a perfect ally for German interests. His German clients also know that Dulles has a hate for Communism, so they emphasize that Hitler is anti-Communistic.

We know that JFD's younger brother Allen has been very active in foreign affairs (and private adulterous affairs) and had been in Foreign Service with the State Department. Allen also joined Sullivan and Cromwell around 1926 and is considered very useful due to worldwide contacts.

Allen had met early on with Hitler, witnessed thugs beating Jews on German streets, and is very disturbed by what he hears from Jewish clients. He has expressed concern according to our S&C mole that S&C work is helping fuel German financial and industrial power. To Allen's credit, he wishes to spare S&C the stigma of collaborating with the Nazis, contrary to Foster's attachment and devotion to German clients, including collusion with the Nazis to obtain massive financing in the U.S.

The SS contact at S&C has advised his handlers that S&C partners have voted to close the S&C office in Germany, in spite of JFD's impassioned plea to keep it open.

August 16, 1935

Yesterday, Julius Streicher, a prominent ally of Hitler, spoke to 16,000 people at the Berlin Sports Palace. He spoke about "cleaning our house of defilers of our race."

September 16, 1935

Yesterday the Nazis passed the Nuremberg Laws to strip Jews of their citizenship. The German public is brainwashed to believe this draconian measure is a "law" so it is acceptable. The Nazis have a campaign of terror and coercion that has silenced all opposition. Combined with popular approval and consent, this means absolute Nazi control. The concentration camps are only a part of the apparatus of repression. Those two laws are labeled the Reich Citizenship Law and the Law to Protect German Blood. Both are blatantly racist, take citizenship away from the Jews, and outlaw marriage between Jews and non-Jews.

"Juden Verboten" signs are increasing in numbers throughout Germany.

Nazis are targeting the banking industry as a source of funds to finance the new militarization and new Air Force. My relatives have been prominent in banking and now must flee or be trapped. I am unable to leave since the Army is obsessed with developing a super weapon and I and others are vital to that program. We are being watched constantly and with a young family I am especially vulnerable.

The Citizenship law has even issued a decree labeling Germans of a quarter Jewish parentage who are Christian as being Jewish.

October 5, 1935

Mussolini has made an unprovoked attack on Abyssinia. I cannot understand why he would attack an unarmed African nation. The liberal powers of the West have vacillated and not even imposed simple sanctions. Maybe that is his way of getting bad attention. It worries me that if this invasion is not being stopped, that it will lead Germany and Italy to try other invasions.

What would Mussolini possibly want with Abyssinia?

Mussolini seized power in Italy in 1922 so he may actually have been a model for Hitler in Germany. So far, no country has instituted sanctions against Hitler or Mussolini in spite of their numerous aggressions. Both appear to be testing America and Britain at a time that England's Navy could force good behavior on Italy. In short, there is no international force for deterrence that will stop Hitler and Mussolini.

December 8, 1935

My guidance research is directed by the General Staff. They simply want rockets to reach designated areas. I have explained this is a waste of time and money, and that we must pursue the much more sophisticated task of terminal guidance. Terminal guidance technology will direct the rocket to the target and it will also allow me to make subtle calibrations that will make most rockets miss the target.

Working with Wernher has helped me accept the Nazi intrusion on our research as he has a vision of rockets that will break the Earth's gravity and someday reach the moon and beyond. We all now believe that anything we can image can be done.

1936

January 8, 1936

My missile and guidance system research has taken me back to World War I when the U.S. actually built the first guided missiles. These were propeller-driven planes with pre-set controls. They actually had automatic pilots and vacuum devices to cause the planes to dive at their pre-set destinations. Of particular interest was the involvement of Elmer Sperry, who developed the gyroscope. Gyroscopes will be important in my guidance research. The U.S. navy developed the first command missile in 1924, and Britain expanded on this type of missile around 1935.

I realize that gyroscopes are based on physics and that does not change. However, the technology is evolving and that is where my lab work will make me a valuable asset to the Army's guided missile program. That will be the protection for my family and give me access to classified information.

January 10, 1936

Rocket guidance systems have been of great interest to me and are a complicated area that I understand. Wernher has allowed me to be his associate and assigned me guidance research and development. By design, I know that I can also tweak the systems so that a rocket will hit or miss its target, or "accidentally" malfunction. The technology is so complicated that missing a target can never be detected.

We are in early theoretical stages of refining inertial guidance (IG) methods of rocket control. The inertial navigator consists of gyroscopes that indicate direction and accelerometers that measure changes in speed and direction. The challenge is to use this information to guide a rocket on its course. This system will be suited to unmanned flight. Wernher has confided that the German high command wants us to develop a rocket that can carry heavy explosives and that in time of war cannot be jammed with false or confusing information. The principles of IG have been known since the early days of the 20th century when gyroscopes were first understood. My job is to master sophisticated refinements to the IG and install a working, accurate system in Wernher's surface-to-surface rockets, which he is calling V-1 and V-2, or Vergetungswaffe.

It seems that the gyroscope is very simple. Basically, it is a spinning wheel set between two circular frames, each orientated along a different axis. The framework can be tilted at many angles and the wheel will keep its position. I am supposed to perfect this for our rocket research, but the navy also wants to apply the finding to torpedoes and ship guidance. I must devise gyroscopes that work with instruments to keep our rockets from rolling and pitching. The rocket systems must remain stable and accurately define direction. These instruments must be so accurate that I plan to recruit fine watchmakers to help manufacturing precision. Because there is a very small tolerance for error, I can use manufacturing tolerances as a means to sabotage the landing target accuracy and thereby go undetected and lives are saved.

January 10, 1936 (Part 2)

The gyroscopes can be complicated and the rotors should rotate at a very high speed, being driven by self-contained motors. For rocket purposes, the gyroscope and its components must be highly accurate and I plan to produce them in a dust-free environment. My sense is that the rockets are to be produced for aggressive, un-manned warfare. Therefore, under wartime conditions it is madness to assume that accurate guidance systems can be installed in the V-2.

The gyroscope is complicated but understood and has the ability to point in the same direction, no matter how the support of the gyroscope moves about. It also is not affected by the earth's gravity or magnetic field. My plan is to install multiple gyroscopes that can control the rocket's lift and direction. This may take years of experimentation, but Wernher tells me this is a crash program and must be operational in just a few years for test flights. That confirms my suspicion that Germany is preparing for war.

Furthermore, I know that calibrating a guidance system for changes in wind direction, temperature variance, moisture, weight of payload, and related factors will affect the delivery accuracy. That means that if I oppose the purpose of the rocket program or events beyond my control occur, then the V-2 rocket will have little strategic value. I have no choice but to cooperate since the "Party" could hold my wife and son in "protective custody" to ensure that I will be an active associate to the project's senior team leaders.

February 11, 1936

The Gestapo has been placed above the law by the Nazis. This means anything goes and everyone must fear the Gestapo.

February 16, 1936

Germany is trying to show the World it has recovered and was chosen to host the Olympics in spite of Nazi policies. The Winter Olympics at Partenkirchenjust closed.

Across the Pacific, the Japanese Army has taken a page from the Italian and German dictators and seized power in Japan. While Japan is a "world away," it aggressively threatens all of Asia and the Pacific Rim.

March 4, 1936

Germany has been experimenting with "lighter than air" ships. The airship Hindenburg just completed its first flight. This airship is slow and vulnerable to damage, so I doubt that the military will have an interest.

March 8, 1936

Yesterday German troops occupied the Rhineland. Last year, when Hitler introduced military conscription in violation of the Versailles Treaty, he moved very rapidly to increase the size of the German Army. The Rhineland has strategic natural ores and heavy industrial plants. Both fit into Hitler's ambitions.

March 9, 1936

A historic milestone has occurred and not one country said a word of criticism. Today Hitler renounced the Treaty of Versailles. This is an obvious declaration to the world that Germany has aggressively pursued rearming and will revert to its militaristic roots.

March 29, 1936

An election has occurred here in Germany. Nazi propaganda claims 99% of Germans voted for Nazi candidates. The obvious outcome is for the party to do whatever it wishes.

May 5, 1936

Mussolini has been in control of Italy for more than a decade and has been friendly with Hitler. Italian troops have invaded Addis Ababa, Ethiopia. I cannot understand how invading a defenseless, poor African nation makes sense unless Mussolini wants to control nearby waterways?

May 24, 1936

Hitler is upset with Holland because Dutch Bishops forbid membership in the Nazi Party. Hitler is trying to spread Nazism to nearby countries. This appears to be an obvious move to create a supportive base for a future invasion by Germany.

June 6, 1936

German newspapers and radio are filled with the news that Leon Blum became the president of the Council of Ministers of France. This is, in effect, prime minister. It is a known fact that France has a long anti-Semitic history, and Blum is a vowed Jew. Jewish success in France draws anti-Semitic reactions. Chamber Deputy Xavier Vallent was quoted as stating that France is to be governed by a Talmudist. Blum has consistently stated that his Jewishness is a commitment to social justice. He is a public servant dedicated to progressive causes.

June 14, 1936

Hitler has opened a concentration camp at Oranienburg. He is increasing his arrest of "enemies" and needs a place to imprison them.

July4, 1936

When Italy invaded Ethiopia last month, the League of Nations imposed sanctions on Italy. Strangely enough, the League has lifted these sanctions.

July 18, 1936

Spanish General Francisco Franco has issued a manifesto declaring a Civil War. He is leading an Army uprising by right wing soldiers and it is rumored that Franco has an alliance with Hitler for aid and arms.

Spanish General Francisco Franco brought troops from Spanish Morocco to the mainland in a move to overthrow the Spanish Republic. It is well-known by Nazi officers that Hitler and Franco are in close touch and that Franco has received German weapons to test against other Spaniards. Fascist Italy is also backing Franco.

The Soviets have sent advisors and sold Spanish Republicans planes and tanks. However, the Western "Democracies" have withdrawn into neutrality. Thousands of volunteers from the U.S., Britain, and Europe have arrived to fight for the Republic and against fascism. It appears that the fascists are much more heavily armed and are testing German equipment. That can only mean Hitler is preparing his Army for battle. It also means that there will be many, many thousands who will die when facing heavy artillery and German bombers. It is easy to predict that the winner of this "Civil War" will dominate Spain for decades to come.

August 12, 1936

Our Rocket Lab has been using proving grounds not far from Berlin, but since our rockets are flying further and further, there is a danger for civilian populations. Von Braun has secretly gone to an island on the Baltic called Usedom. He has cleverly persuaded, by demonstration, the Army and Air Force to provide funds to acquire the western Usedom village of Peenemünde.

Extensive work is under way to change the island into a secret proving ground. This includes roads and communications.

The Air Force will use the western side for V-1 experiments and the Army will use the eastern side for V-2 research. Power and an airfield will be central.

Our V-2 rocket is quite complicated and requires thousands of precision parts. A large staff of scientists will be working on the V-2 at workshops, launching sites, and a wind tunnel. Since there will be thousands of people working on the island, I suspect that it will be "ripe" for espionage and leaks. Our budget has grown rapidly and it could take hundreds of millions of Marks to complete these projects.

August 20, 1936

Germany has hosted the Olympic Games as a way of showing its "rebirth" and power under the Nazis. Based on the evil dictatorship that has developed in just three years, hosting the Olympics was a farce.

The decision to award the 1936 Olympics to Germany came before Hitler's rise to power. Now, with Germany as a police state, the international community is upset. There have been boycotts of Jewish businesses and severe anti-Semitism, including the Nuremberg Laws of last year.

Efforts to boycott the Olympics were not very successful.

It is worth noting that Jesse Owens is one of 18 African Americans who represented the U.S. and they won 14 medals. Germany is an openly racist country and Hitler would not shake any of their hands.

Hitler banned German Jewish athletes, including women's high jump record holder Greta Bergmann. Jewish athletes from other countries won thirteen medals, nine of which were gold.

In the end, these Olympics solidified Hitler's position on the world stage. What will come next??

September 4, 1936

Franco's troops in Spain are capturing various towns.

September 10, 1936

The Nazi party held a "Rally of Honor" in Nuremberg. The speeches of Hitler, Goebbels, and Rosenberg have produced insane Jew-baiting lies. No one in Germany speaks of shame and there are no protests from abroad.

September 21, 1936

The Spanish fascist junta has named Franco the "Supreme Commander."

September 27, 1936

Franco's troops have conquered Toledo.

September 29, 1936

Germany has embarked on a massive infrastructure program under the direction of Albert Speer, Hitler's chief architect. Construction includes a highway system, the Berlin Chancellery, a stadium, and Hitler's Bavarian country house (Berghov). I suspect the highway system is planned for troop movement and wartime supply routes. The classical style used by Speer is said to support Hitler's authoritarian might and project strength, order, and unity. Added to this is the Nazi edict that modem art and architecture is degenerate.

October 4, 1936

The German Army is conscripting every able-bodied young man and some who are middle-aged. This has to be a clear warning to the population and any world leader who is observing this mass movement that the Nazis mean aggression in Europe.

I have been called for an Army interview, but as a child had a serious lung infection that left scars that show on x-rays and cause my breathing to sound labored (which it actually is not).

Also, my work in the rocket lab is considered so vital to national "defense" that I am exempted from military scrvicc.

October 20, 1936

Franco has set up his Spanish government in Barcelona and is calling for an alliance with Germany.

November 7, 1936

Franco has attacked Madrid and a battle is raging.

November 10, 1936

My distinguished ancestor, Felix Mendelssohn, was not raised as a Jew but attached importance to his Jewish heritage. So, it is no wonder that the Nazis have banned his music. Today, the memorial outside the Leipzig Gewandhaus was destroyed. Our family history is clear that Felix was baptized for pragmatic reasons and that he was very proud of being Jewish in his own mind. I share these feelings and am upset by the Nazis, but must keep my feelings confidential in order to earn the confidence of the rocket officials. That will allow me to execute my secret plan.

November 12, 1936

There is continuing to be a bloody civil war in Spain between the Leftist Republican Government and the insurgent Nationalists of Francisco Franco. It is an "open secret" that Hitler is helping Franco in return for Franco testing new German weapons and for testing German bombers. This could be Hitler's first act of his ambitions to conquer much of Europe. Fascist Italy is backing Franco and the Soviet Union has sent soldiers and sold the Republicans arms and planes.

November 15, 1936

Nazi Germany and Japan have signed a pact. The "Axis" is now in the Far East.

November 17, 1936

The German Air Force has built some new design fighter planes and bombers. They are being tested in Spain by bombing the loyalists in Madrid. This brutal assistance of Franco by the Nazis is a gross violation of international laws, but no nation has been in vocal opposition.

November 20, 1936

I have been designated as a critical person for the continuing development of the Army's secret ballistic missile weapon. Two men are assigned to watch me and make sure I am "loyal" to this program. We have set up our labs at Peenemünde on the Baltic Sea Coast. That means I will seldom be able to return to Berlin to see my wife and son. They are also under surveillance. This family separation preys on my mind and worry about Julia and our son's safety.

The navigation system that I theorized early in 1929 is still valid. Rockets can be calibrated to slightly miss a target. That calibration will allow me to satisfy the Army and reduce the rocket's destructive capability. Two gyroscopes and a lateral accelerometer guide the rocket's path and can be adjusted in flight. Signals can go to the rudders for flight control. However, it is up to others to design the rudders and make them of a material that will not be affected by the burning fuel. Further, when all these theoretical systems are created, I must integrate them into one system.

December 8, 1936–Hitler's Cretins

The rocket research group is science-focused and is happy to get financial support from the Nazis, even though many may simply be joining the Party as a way of staying out of trouble with the SS and Gestapo. However, Hitler has surrounded himself with top people who are dedicated, fanatical, violent, and as driven as is he. They are sociopaths, sadists, and ruthless murderers, and that is just a preliminary viewpoint.

Some of the top people include Vice Chancellor Hermann Göring, Deputy Fuehrer Rudolph Hess, and Propagandist Julius Streicher. They include perverts, dope fiends and liars. Hans Frank, Hitler's personal lawyer who framed the laws that are the basis for theft and murder, is known to wear women's clothing at times. Göring is a prima donna who wears gaudy jewelry and red nail polish. He has been described as a malignant narcissist.

Julius Streicher is a pathological Jew hater, convicted rapist, and depicts Jews in a very lurid, nasty way. If our country was even a little sane, Streicher would be locked in an asylum.

Instead, he is in a position of power, making life and death decisions about Jews.

Hess is said to be a hypochondriac, paranoid schizophrenic who some say acts like a mentally deficient child.

The top Nazis may be different types of cretins, but all are extremely fanatical, devoted to Hitler, have inflated egos, and lack conscience or decency. They are actively brainwashing the German public that Jews are trying to destroy Germany and therefore Jews must be destroyed (all the better to steal Jewish property). I believe there is no hope for Germany or for anyone who gets in Hitler's way. At this time no one has come forward to stop him or the Nazis, the U.S. is silent and Britain and France think that Hitler can be handled. May God help us.

1937

January 10, 1937

I have refined my formula for pinpoint guidance. With slight variations I can calibrate it to travel off course. This must be kept secret and if it is necessary to reveal the formula it can be altered enough to keep the variations a secret.

Variable components of the formula can be deleted to make the guidance useless. The course of the rocket will seem okay, but will just barely go off course. The variables include weight, propellant (quantity and mixture), temperature, atmosphere, distance, earth's curvature, moisture in the air, shape of the missile, launch site, destination topography, and air quality (clear vs smoky). If there are multiple shots, the subsequent ones must each be recalibrated.

January 17, 1937

An added assignment has been given to me to design the vertical stabilizer for our future rockets. These fins will be mounted on the rear of the missile and must reduce side slip and provide direction stability. I should be able to calculate the weight, shape, air speed, and trajectory, and arrive at the ideal weight and shape for testing.

March 10, 1937

Nazis are making life very difficult for Jewish professionals to the point where they cannot work, teach, practice their professions, or support families. Erich Mendelssohn is a distant cousin who has had a distinguished architectural career and has been totally affected by this blatant discrimination. This architect with a brilliant reputation has just moved to Jerusalem in British? Mandate Palestine. His plan was to escape the Nazis and to bring Jews and Arabs together through architecture. I can only predict that this vision is naive, since the Arabs deny that Jews should live in Palestine, even though Israelites (Jews) have lived there for thousands of years.

March 20, 1937

Pope Pius XI published an encyclical against Communism. Since this has been Hitler's theme, it appears that the Catholic Church is directly aligning with Nazi Germany.

April 26, 1937

The German Luftwaffe has been using the Spanish Civil War for testing planes and "target practice." They obliterated the Spanish town of Guernica, which was defenseless and suffered a great many civilian casualties.

April 28, 1937

Herman Göring has issued a bulletin gloating over the Luftwaffe's destruction of the historic Spanish Baroque town of Guernica. He claims to have planned this as a birthday present to Adolph Hitler, but it was obviously a rehearsal for future events. Göring used this brutal attack to test the Luftwaffe's ability to annihilate an entire city and crush the morale of its inhabitants. The attack was devised to maximize human casualties and deaths and involved three hours of air strikes that leveled the city.

As I think about Guernica, it was a small, defenseless city in a country far from Germany. Therefore, I can only imagine what Hitler has in mind for European countries that he covets in his uncontrollable, mad quest for power.

May 7, 1937

Germany has foolishly been experimenting with airships for long distance travel. Yesterday the airship Hindenburg exploded in flames and that ended the airship program.

May 30, 1937

The German Navy has joined the Spanish Civil War so they too can have live ammo target practice. Today German battleships bombarded a defenseless Almeria, Spain.

May 31, 1937

I have observed that there is a sinister genius behind the Nazi seduction of the German people whose name is Joseph Goebbels. He is highly educated and intelligent which is in contrast to my opinion of many Nazis. He has created numerous public events and a propaganda strategy that is all encompassing to completely brainwash the mass of the German people. The inside joke at Peenemünde is that he keeps his brain in his pants since he is such a womanizer. Perhaps this is because he is so insecure, emotionally needy, and narcissistic.

June 7, 1937

Stalin has been terrorizing Russia by murdering millions who might possibly oppose him. This has included most of the Soviet Central Committee, most of the delegates to the party congress, managers, scientists, etc. The NKVD secret police have arrested a million-and-a-half and have shot seven hundred thousand. This has included most of the Army's top officers, which has weakened the Soviet economy and decimated the Army. This. makes the Soviet Union an easy target for the growing threat from Germany and Japan. Stalin must be demented to weaken his own country in such a brutal fashion.

June 22, 1937

Yesterday the French government of Leon Blum fell. My guess is that the French could not accept a Jewish President. The French claim to be "liberal," but it is my opinion they may be as anti-Semitic as the Germans. After all, they have listened to the same slander emanating from churches for centuries.

July 1, 1937

Spanish bishops have come out in support of France, who in tum is supported by Nazi Germany. This reinforces my point that much anti-Semitism emanates from churches.

July 15, 1937

Yesterday Hitler announced the opening of Buchenwald concentration camp.

July 18, 1937

In Munich there is an art festival of Great German art that has been approved by the government. At the same time the Nazis are showing degenerate art that is no longer acceptable to be seen publicly.

This is obviously an attempt to mind control every aspect of German life, including public art. While this may create a population of controlled zombies, it will surely stifle creativeness and the ability to think about endeavors like our rocket research. I hope many will reject this mind control, even if they must do it privately.

July 19, 1937

What is puzzling is that Nazi art can only be defined by what Hitler likes at a certain moment. This is culture control that Hitler and Goebbels are using to infect the masses like a medieval plague.

November 1, 1937

Although Wernher is very young, he is clearly the Army's choice to lead our research and experiments. He is a believer in space travel, and that if we can imagine something like rockets, we can make them. It is even rumored that Wernher has had personal meetings with Hitler to discuss the rocket program and the progress of creating the massive complex in Peenemünde.

In the meantime, the Army maintains tight control over our lab and all of Peenemünde, under the command of General Walter Damberger.

I am increasingly being pushed to accelerate the guidance system research since other aspects of a future rocket are advancing at a fast pace. Walter Riedel has joined us from Heylandt Company and is the chief designer of the V-2 ballistic rocket.

November 6, 1937

An Army insider message has informed us yesterday that Hitler has advised his military leaders that he intends to go to war very soon.

November 8, 1937

The Nazis have opened an exhibit in Munich that is very unflattering and unfair to German Jews. I suspect that the decision to go to war includes war against the Jews.

November 11, 1937

The Luftwaffe is openly trying to gain favor with Hitler and has just tested a Messerschmitt ME 109Vl 3 and set a speed record.

November 17, 1937

Britain senses danger from Germany's bellicose nature and has been nervously appeasing Germany. Lord Halifax is visiting Germany right now to discuss the situation.

November 19, 1937

Although Britain and Germany are enemies, there has been a strange occurrence. The Duke of Windsor and his American wife, Wallace Simpson, have visited Germany often and appear to be Nazi sympathizers. The inside rumor at our lab is that the duke is actually passing intelligence to Germany. Perhaps the duke believes appeasement is preferable to war.

November 23, 1937

Hitler is clearly on a path to arm Germany, exterminate his internal enemies and confiscate Jewish property to finance his regime. He has named Stalin as a threat from the East and claimed that Communism is an enemy. However, it appears that Stalin is preoccupied with the task of killing his internal opponents and is relying on what is suspected as being a very brutal and extensive intelligence force. Our department's internal bulletin reports that Stalin has murdered Col. Konovaletz of the Ukraine for fear that he will lead a Ukraine independence movement.

Over the centuries, the Russians have been invaded from the West, so I assume Stalin looks upon the Ukraine as a buffer zone that he must control.

Our group is also aware that Hitler and Stalin have had diplomatic contact. These are strange bedfellows who must be planning an evil surprise for Europe.

December 12, 1937

Italy is an ally of Germany and has just withdrawn from the League of Nations. This is telegraphing their aggressive intentions.

December 14, 1937

The Nazis continue to exert a strong grip on Germany. On the one hand by coercion, violence, and installing fear in the population. Also, by flamboyant exhibitions of power and glory, such as massive rallies of troops, armaments, and airplanes. In the few years since coming to power it seems as if the entire country has experienced ominous mobilization.

When I think back about historical events in Europe that may have influenced Hitler, I think of Napoleon. He tried to enslave all of Europe with his unstable personal ambition and that is exactly what Hitler is doing. However, Hitler may not recognize that Napoleon overextended his resources and eventually that was his downfall and disgraceful defeat. Napoleon was ruthless, conquered Italy and Austria, invaded Egypt, lost the French Fleet in the Nile, went after the Turks and massacred thousands, creating what we call today a propaganda machine. He ruled France, suppressed free speech, and tried to enslave all of Europe. Ultimately, Napoleon invaded Russia in 1812 and left 400,000 dead Frenchmen. I wonder if the Nazis have any idea how great leaders learn from historical events.

1938

February 5, 1938

Yesterday Hitler seized control of the Army so that Nazis instead of professional military officers will be running it. It is now easy to predict they will plan aggressive use of force to further Nazi plans but not realize the military consequences.

February 13, 1938

The Austrian Chancellor has visited Hitler at Berchtesgaden. At the same time, we have learned German troops now under Nazi orders have entered Austria.

February 20, 1938

The news from Britain is that Hitler is moving so fast that Britain has been taken off guard. PM Chamberlain is a fool to think meeting Hitler publicly will bring peace. Now, UK Foreign Secretary Anthony Eden has resigned over this appeasement. The invasion of Austria is being openly discussed by German Army officers and that will be enough to prove Eden's point.

February 28, 1938

In an act of further appeasement, the UK and France have recognized Franco's Spanish (Nazi ally) government.

March 11, 1938

There is a new Chancellor in Austria, and German troops continue entering Austria.

March 14, 1938

SS Bulletin: The German Army has marched into Vienna and occupied Austria. Austria is now annexed by Germany.

Our family has known for years that Austria has had seething anti-Semitism below the surface. There is an affluent and successful Jewish community, but also a population that is not doing well. The Nazis have been greeted with enthusiasm and Jews are already being humiliated and beaten. Nazis are confiscating Jewish bank accounts and businesses, and assets "transferred" to Nazi Germany. Valuable artwork is being stolen by the Nazis. As I have noted elsewhere, Germany has targeted Jews so they can steal their assets. The Nazis are openly the world's biggest thieves.

What is starting to happen in Austria is the spread of the Nazis' 1935 Nuremberg laws in which Jews are classified by race, not religion. They have set the scene for trying to "annihilate the Jewish race in Europe." We have seen this as an excuse to steal Jewish property throughout Europe, including in Berlin's City Center. Jewish factories and department stores are now used by Nazi departments. Hitler has created a virus so evil that it may take centuries to reverse.

April 10, 1938

Austria is now officially a state of Germany. This happened in less than a month via a pseudo "election."

April 27, 1938

The stealing of Jewish wealth in Austria is now starting with a vengeance. Jews must register everything of value, which obviously makes it easier for the Nazis to steal.

May 4, 1938

The SS is bragging that a concentration camp is now open at Flossenbiirg.

May 4, 1938

The Vatican-Catholic Church has been very quiet about Hitler and not critical of Nazism. This lack of moral leadership is bad. The Vatican has also recognized Franco in Spain.

May 22, 1938

Because I have been under surveillance by the Army and SS, I have tried very hard to keep my wife, Julia, and son Felix from appearing in public and they have been very low key. I was informed by my SS "shadow" that my wife and son have been taken into protective custody and as long as I am diligently pursuing rocket guidance research, they will be alright.

My son just celebrated his 4th birthday, so this act of coercion is very cruel. They have promised that I will hear from them frequently. I am more convinced than ever that my plan must be continued. At one time I felt like a patriotic German. But the events of the past five years make me realize I will never trust or belong in Germany.

June 4, 1938

There is a new German law which legalizes the confiscation (robbery) of Jewish art. Some of the Jews of Europe have masterpieces which Nazis must want to sell and/or keep. In addition, Jews must fill out a detailed asset form. This makes it easier for the Nazis to steal.

June 10, 1938

Heinrich Himmler has published an article praising the quantum theorist Werner Heisenberg. Our lab knew that Heisenberg is not a strident Nazi, but my guess is that Himmler is supporting Heisenberg's research in order to further his work on the separation of uranium isotopes used to fuel nuclear reactions or weapons. I am certain that Heisenberg knows how an atom bomb works and only needs the facilities to produce one. There is, theoretically, great power within the atom's core and that it can be split and can cause a mighty chain reaction.

June 17, 1938

We learned today that Japan has declared war on China. Hitler sent his best wishes to Japan.

June 23, 1938

Germany has tried to showcase sports in order to tell the world how "great" Germans are. Max Schmeling has been promoted as a "superman" boxer. However, yesterday Joe Lewis knocked out Schmeling in the first round at Yankee Stadium.

July 10, 1938

A conference has been held at Evian to determine which country would take refugees; this means Jews who are being persecuted in Germany. Every nation made it clear they would not accept refugees. Many countries cited the U.S. and British immigration restrictions. To be fair, France already had 200,000 refugees and 3,000,000 aliens. Holland already had 2,500 Jewish refugees, and Denmark had already taken in German exiles. Even though the U.S. convened the conference and has vast areas of unsettled land, it will take a quota of only 23,000 refugees a year. I believe the failure of the Evian Conference to produce safe havens has given the Nazis a go ahead for mass persecution. Hitler is so obsessed with anti-Semitism that he may even invade France, Poland, and Holland in order to exterminate their Jewish populations. And after that, the Eastern European countries.

An exception is the Dominican Republic, which offered to take 100,000. The US shocked the other nations by stating a quota from Germany and Austria combined of 23,000, "who must guarantee they can support themselves." The British even reiterated restrictions on emigration to Palestine. When the Evian Conference concluded, all that was done was to form another committee on refugees.

July 14, 1938

Hitler's friend, Mussolini, has now published an anti-Jewish/African manifesto, taking a page from the Nuremburg Laws.

August 3, 1938

My work on vertical stabilizers has continued as part of the guidance research. These fins on the aft end of our V-2 rocket can reduce aerodynamic side slip and provide stability. I am proposing to install navigational radios in each stabilizer.

August 7, 1938

Our work has become much more intense and secretive as the Army presses us for a functional weapon that is so compact it may take years to perfect. Wernher has been instructed to communicate only by a cipher machine we call the Enigma. It sends encoded messages that are translated by the receiving machine. However, power is needed and that could be a drawback under battlefield conditions.

August 18, 1938

The Army's intelligence agency, the Abwehr, has been busy in England and the U.S. Abwehr believes the US could join England and France if and when Germany's aggression causes another World War. The US has developed a precision bombsight called the Norden bombsight.

One of Germany's sympathizers named Hermann Lang lives in Manhattan and works for the Sperry Company, which makes the Norden. Lang was successful in stealing the plans, which were brought to our lab for analysis. We decided that the Norden required a clear line of cloudless sight and therefore would not be of value. The Luftwaffe will not use the Norden. However, our spy network is extensive and taking advantage of the German-heritage citizens of the US.

August 28, 1938

Another concentration camp is now open at Mauthausen. This is a clear sign that Hitler intends to fill it with Austrian Jews and he is telegraphing there will be orders.

August 29, 1938

With Hitler's blatant preparations for war, the tensions are building between Britain and Germany. However, many people forget that British royalty has strong bloodlines ties to Germany. Queen Victoria was three-quarters German, and that was long before Bismarck really brought Germany together. Kaiser Wilhelm II led a belligerent Germany into the disaster of World War I; he was the son of Victoria's daughter Vicky.

September 1, 1938

Mussolini is trying to outdo Hitler's anti-Semitism and has cancelled all rights of Italian Jews. They have lived in Italy since the Romans destroyed the Second Temple in 70 AD and brought captive Jews to Rome. They have endured vicious persecution, including by the Catholic Church, and now must fear Hitler's associate, Mussolini.

September 13, 1938

Germany has always felt the Sudeten to be German and is demanding that Czechs vote on self? determination. With a heavy German population, Hitler is sure this vote will give him the authority to annex the Sudeten area.

September 17, 1938

British PM Chamberlain is well aware of Hitler's aggressive plans and came to see Hitler in Berchtesgaden near Munich. After the meeting, Chamberlain foolishly declared that he can negotiate with Hitler.

September 20, 1938

Hitler continues appeasing Chamberlain and at the same time is preparing to invade the Sudetenland. His excuse is his obligation to protect his ethnic cousins, and he knows he can get away with it.

September 21, 1938

Winston Churchill is the British opposition leader and former Secretary of the Navy. He strongly is condemning Hitler's plan to annex Czechoslovakia.

September 22, 1938

Prime Minister Chamberlain comes to Munich to again talk peace.

September 26, 1938

Soon after Munich, Hitler has issued an ultimatum to the Czechs.

September 29, 1938

In Munich, Britain and France accept the German annexation of Sudetenland.

September 30, 1938

Hitler continues his threat to "liberate" Czechoslovakia's Sudetenland, which he claims is rightfully German. The latest internal information coming to the Rocket Center is that he does not believe Russia, France, or England will try to stop an invasion by the German Army. He believes that the Munich conference with Neville Chamberlain of England and Edouard Dalaler of France has sold out the Czechs. Appeasement has won.

Winston Churchill of Britain clearly understood that the Western democracies needed an alliance with the Soviet Union. However, the hypothetical fear of Communism prevented this alliance from occurring. We also know that Stalin was murdering a high percentage of his top officers and diplomats, which weakens the Soviets' ability to react to Hitler's threat. Further intelligence reports from Britain say that the American ambassador, Joseph Kennedy, is advising Roosevelt that Britain and France will lose the war with Germany, and Kennedy appears to be a German sympathizer. It is now obvious that Hitler's plans outlined in Mein Kampf will be put into action.

October 1, 1938

Bulletins report on the recent Munich meeting of Germany, Italy, France, and England. Germany was "given" the Sudetenland. It will be taken from Czechoslovakia. Britain's Chamberlain is quoted as saying this will end Hitler's expansionism. It is obvious that Britain and France can see Hitler's armaments program and that appeasement will only fuel his ambitions. My guess is that Britain and France are totally unprepared for war and are praying for a miracle.

October 5, 1938

I am troubled by the thought that even though Germany is highly cultured (Goethe, Kant, Mozart, Beethoven, Mendelssohn) and has had great chemists and physicists, that a primitive gangster like Hitler can have absolute power.

October 7, 1938

Germany has declared the annexation of one-third of Czechoslovakia, Sudetenland. There is no one to stop Hitler and I fear that this rapid movement on Austria and Czechoslovakia will be like a drug, feeding Hitler's aggressive ambitions. In the meantime, Russia is silent and very fearful of Hitler's ambitions.

October 7, 1938

Germany is continuing to shut down Jewish citizen rights. Lawyers can no longer practice and passports are stamped with "J." Jewish doctors are stricken from the Medical Register.

October 10, 1938

Germany has completed the annexation of all of Czechoslovakia without any resistance by the outnumbered and out-armed Czech Army.

October 14, 1938

Our insiders learn that there is a secret SS Army meeting to further boldly plan the destruction of European Jews in conjunction with conquering all of Western and Eastern Europe. The plan is to create ghettos in every city, round up all Jews, and decide how to destroy them. I know that this will require a diversion of resources, but the Nazis are so obsessed with killing Jews that they will absorb these costs.

October 15, 1938

I try to be aware of the increasing change in German society. Anti-Semitism has a popular resonance in Nazi policies. Some Jews think that a country that produced Kant, Goethe, and Shiller will let the Nazi "phase" pass. Also, other assimilated Jews identify entirely as "German" are in denial of their Jewish background, believing this will protect them from the fate of the overtly religious Jewish citizens being persecuted now. It is obvious from the demented dedication of the Nazi leadership that Jews that stay in Germany may have delayed their escape for too long.

November 7, 1938

Herschel Gryszpan assassinated Ernst von Rath, a low-level German diplomate. Gryszpan is a very young Polish Jew who is upset by the way Jews are being badly treated. As far as I know, the assassination was personal and not associated with any organization.

November 8, 1938

The diplomat's assassination is used as an excuse for Nazis in Germany and Austria to attack Jews.

November 9, 1938

The Nazis have organized a large-scale act of anti-Jewish violence. Burning synagogues, smashing stores, killing Jews, looting shops. Every synagogue in Germany and Austria has been attacked. Germans are calling this Kristallnacht.

November 11, 1938

Jews are forced to wear the yellow Star of David and forced to pay for the damages done by the Nazis. This extortion and thievery is being listed by Göring as several hundred million marks.

November 11, 1938

In the last few days Nazi thugs have brutalized the German Jewish community with massive pogroms that have burned synagogues, ruined Jewish shops and businesses, killed hundreds of Jews and sent thousands to the dreaded concentration camps. The excuse given is the killing of a German diplomat in Paris by Herschel Gryszpan on November 7th• This relatively minor event is being used as an excuse to commence an all-out "war of persecution" on Jews. The SS has been preparing this brutal plan for years and merely wanted an excuse. It will only get worse.

German press is calling this mayhem Kristallnacht due to shop windows being broken and synagogue windows smashed and burned. Many "law abiding" Germans are looting Jewish shops. The press reports Jewish blood staining Berlin's sidewalks and streets.

Since the Evian conference the Nazis have been planning this massive event to accelerate their persecution of German Jews. In addition to every synagogue in Germany and Austria being vandalized, burned, or destroyed,

91 Jews were killed, 30,000 arrested and sent to concentration camps, and Jewish shops and homes were invaded and looted. I am sure the West will express outrage and denounce this “Kristallnacht” but do nothing. That is a further invitation for Hitler to do as he pleases, including looking beyond the borders of the Reich.

November 15, 1938

Jewish children are expelled from German schools.

November 15, 1938

German newspapers report that the American president, Franklin Roosevelt, has verbally condemned the recent killing of Jews, destruction of property and sending 30,000 Jews to concentration camps. However, beyond words, he has done nothing. Other world leaders have condemned the Nazi rampage and have labeled it Kristallnacht for all the breakage. But they have done nothing. The US Congress proposed legislation to allow 20,000 Jewish children into the US and Roosevelt opposed it. It seems clear that Hitler has taken the world inaction as an endorsement of his actions against Jews and others. This may be the beginning of the end for German Jews. Hitler now sees that he can murder Jews with impunity.

November 16, 1938

As I have written earlier, it now is clear that the Evian Conference, three months before “Kristallnacht”, set the scene since only one country in the whole world said they would take Jews. That was the Dominican Republic and, unfortunately, most German and Austrian Jews do not want to go to the Caribbean. Even the U.S. has strict quotas and President Roosevelt does not support Jewish emigration. It is no wonder the Nazis are becoming so bold. I have read that the U.S. State Department has placed insuperable obstacles before Jewish applicants.

November 20, 1938

Germany continues almost daily anti-Semitic acts like burning a synagogue and ordering stricter rules on Jews. The German public is both supportive of the Nazi laws and intimidated by the Nazi rules. Passivity by the citizens of Germany can only mean Hitler has a free hand to persecute Jews and others. It is as if an entire nation has lost its sense of what is right.

November 23, 1938

German newspapers have carried stories of Arabs in Palestine attacking Jewish communities. I think the Arabs are being financed by Germany and trained to kill Jews. There are groups of Jews who are forming private armies to fight the Arab attack. One of their leaders is named Jabotinsky, who has warned Jews that being good-hearted will interfere with their ability to fight.

November 26, 1938

After the Anschluss of Austria, many Jews are being sent to Dachau. That is in addition to the 26,000 German Jews sent to camps. Sometimes this is for a short time to intimidate Jews to leave Germany.

December 1, 1938

Our Mendelssohn family has been friends of the Rothschilds for generations. I have seen where untold value has been confiscated from the Rothschilds and other prominent Jewish families.

This is pure thievery by a Nazi regime that is committing the most enormous crimes in history to finance their fantasy of world dominance and racial cleansing. I suspect the art is being sold in France and Switzerland.

December 2, 1938

The SS bulletin today brags about burning the Leipzig synagogue and the Jewish department store, and then arresting the store owner for arson. Massive fines are being levied against Jews and curfew for Jews has been enacted. There is a new anti-Semitic law every day.

December 7, 1938

The justice system in Germany is now completely arbitrary. All means are legal if it serves Hitler. The Gestapo is known to interrogate people with vicious,

vicious torture; including drowning, electric shock, beatings and burning. Under the direction of Reinhard Heydrich, Germany is now a police state.

December 7, 1938

More laws are being passed. Jews cannot enter a park, visit a theater, concert hall, or a museum, must report assets, and turn in all jewelry.

December 8, 1938

Since our Rocket Research and Development Unit has the highest security clearance, our department head, Von Braun, possesses an Enigma Machine. Because he and I are so very close, he has entrusted me with access to the Enigma.

I understand the machine's letter substitution where each letter of an undeciphered message is substituted by another letter. The device is mechanically operated with an electric signal passed through wires and various mechanical parts. It "simply" changes one letter to another letter by way of complicated, connected rotors and contacts. The Enigma is ingeniously designed so entering the cipher text gives us the clear text.

My Polish contact advises me that in 1932 Poles had figured out an early German Army version of Enigma and that the cipher was changed infrequently. Now, in 1938, as the German war machine is on the verge of overt aggression, the cipher is changed daily. This has created millions of possible settings. The British have established a code breaking team at Bletchley Park under the direction of Alan Turing and others. It will be my objective to smuggle an Enigma machine to them as the way to unravel the German Army "key" so that Britain will be able to "listen" to German Army and air plans.

A weak link in the Enigma system is the need for electricity. I have smuggled messages to Britain that in future battles they must cut electrical supply as an early strategy.

December 9, 1938

Our short-wave reception of London news reveals there was a plot to kill Hitler at the Berhof which Himmler uncovered. This will surely lead to numerous executions.

December 11, 1938

The British Parliament has reacted to the Jewish humanitarian crisis in Germany and voted to receive 10,000 unaccompanied Jewish children. This is like a lifeline to German Jews who can at least save some of their children. The H.C. spy sources in the U.S. report that U.S. Senator Robert Wagner and Rep. Edith Rogers introduced a bill to admit 10,000 Jewish children in 1939 and 10,000 in 1940. It is not being supported by Roosevelt and will probably die in committee. A shameful lack of conscience that plays to American public opinion and gives encouragement to Nazi anti-Semitism.

December 15, 1938

Jews are desperate to flee Germany but the document requirements make that almost impossible. It is as if Hitler has them trapped for elimination. The published list of passport requirements after 1937 is very, very extensive. To add to this list, in order to emigrate to the U.S., a person must comply with another list that is intended to draw out the process indefinitely. Considering that the Nazis have stolen Jewish bank accounts, art and possessions, and thrown them out of work, there is slim chance of having funds to book passage.

December 18, 1938

German insurance firms are refusing to pay for the damages to the Jewish community during Kristallnacht. Instead, they are paying insurance proceeds to the Nazi Party and the Jewish community is being "fined" for rebuilding costs that could be hundreds of millions of marks.

This diary is my "witness" to the country gone berserk. Those who bum books and destroy others' lives will themselves be burned.

December 28, 1938

The Army has recruited many advanced chemists and physics professors to advise them about creating a nuclear weapon. One of the scientists they wanted was Lise Meitrie, but she had fled Berlin six months ago. However, her Berlin associate, Otto Hahn, remained in Germany and reported that a neutron striking the nucleus of a uranium atom could split that nucleus and release an enormous amount of energy. This meant the process can be used to create new weapons.

1939

February 28, 1939

I am deeply troubled by Hitler's recent Reichstag speech in which he blatantly foretold of Germany's plans to annihilate the Jewish race in Europe. It is impossible for me to speak out and my diary must be hidden for fear of being "turned in" to the Nazis.

When I think back about the progression of anti-Semitism, Jews were blamed for the disastrous Versailles Treaty, then blamed for inflation, then dismissed from civil service, then Jewish businesses were boycotted, then the Nuremberg Laws codified anti-Semitism, then Jewish property was stolen and often converted to perverse use, the Kristallnacht actually forced Jews to pay for damage caused by anti-Semitic attacks. On and on. What stuns me is that the ever? accelerating and often reported insanity was readily accepted by the German people, who are supposedly cultured and educated. It is possible that 1,000 years of hatred and jealousy promoted by German religious and political leaders with ulterior motives has become a permanent part of the German people. It is a virus that multiplies in a most offensive and dangerous way.

March 3, 1939

Hitler agreed to watch one of our lab's rocket demonstrations, also attended by the high Army command. It was a successful launch, but Hitler gave very little response. That was a disappointment to all of us who have spent years creating the rocket monster.

March 15, 1939

Germany has been quietly moving Army troops and SS into Czechoslovakia and has now declared it to be part of Germany. Britain and France did nothing and a longstanding pact with Russia for mutual assistance produced no results. Today Prague was occupied by German troops.

March 20, 1939

Hitler has made a major speech declaring that Germany must have Lebensraum that he was now gaining for the Third Reich. In other words, Germany must dominate all of Europe with land for Germany to colonize and expand.

March 31, 1939

Britain finally is awakening and has promised to assist Poland if Germany attacks.

May 15, 1939

The Berlin newspapers report that the British House of Commons has passed a White Paper proposing policies for Palestine. Since I have a great interest in current history, it is well known that the British Balfour Declaration of 1917 and subsequent League of Nations approvals had promised a Jewish homeland in Palestine. However, in order to placate Arab Muslim anti?semitism, Britain, under Neville Chamberlain, has produced the White Paper in an attempt to negate the Balfour Declaration. Opposition leader Churchill is opposed to the White Paper and I do not think it will go anywhere. However, it does give British support for restricting Jewish immigration, just when it is most needed to escape the Nazis. It is obvious that Hitler will see the White Paper as a win for Germany.

May 25, 1939

A high security memo relates that senior Army officers and Hitler have ambitions for eventually invading territories to the east such as Ukraine and Russia. Poland stands in the way and must therefore be "eradicated."

May 26, 1939

Foreign Ministry Report: The German implant in the U.S. White House offices reports a letter to President Roosevelt to aid refugee children who are in a desperate situation due to German Army invasions. The letter was forwarded to the State Department where Breckinridge Long, the blatant anti-Semite, instructed the following response:

"The U.S. government is unable, in the absence of specific legislation, to permit this immigration." The SS has stated that this is another green-light signal to the Nazis to persecute Jews as it wishes.

May 29, 1939

Refugees aboard the ship St. Louis have tried to land at various North American, East Coast ports, but pleas to disembark have been rejected. Roosevelt could have issued an executive order but did nothing. This is evidence to the Nazis that anti-Semitism in the U.S. is widespread and persistent and that the U.S. will not try to stop Nazi plans to exterminate Jews. The German spy services tell the high command that widespread U.S. anti-Semitism affects employment opportunism in every field. U.S. immigration law is a huge obstacle, just at a time when Jews need a haven. U.S. President Roosevelt could have intervened and rescued the St. Louis passengers. When he did nothing, it looked like an endorsement of Nazi Germany.

The U.S. State Department continues to place obstacles before desperate German Jews to make the path to immigrate impossible. The State Department's restrictive policies created indefinite delays so that even legal quotas are unfilled. The consensus at Peenemünde is that the U.S. will not try to stop Hitler's aggression, so there is no need to worry about the U.S. intervening.

May 30, 1939

Propaganda Chief Goebbels is spreading Hitler's "prophecy" that if Jews launch war they will perish. This absurd theme is after years of persecuting and deporting Jews and seizing their property. It is obviously a prelude to Hitler's war plans.

May 31, 1939

Hitler announced that a woman's concentration camp has been opened at Ravensbruck. One thousand women are being transferred from other camps.

June 5, 1939

Since the Nazis (very early on) took away citizenship from Jews, it has been open season to steal valuable art or force it to be sold for a pittance. Private Swiss buyers and Swiss museums appear to be the most frequent buyers of the paintings, even though they know the art is stolen.

June 8, 1939

Nazi architects have plans to destroy Jewish neighborhoods in Vienna and have listed 9,000 buildings to "Aryanize." In other words, to steal from Jews who have fled or been sent to camps. Nazi banners and symbols will now decorate all the fa9ade.

June 11, 1939

The SS has circulated memos boasting about their success in recruiting high level cooperation from some Americans. They particularly name a U.S. attorney named John Foster Dulles. As I have written before, Dulles is a senior partner in a major U.S. law firm (Sullivan and Cromwell) that has numerous German industrial and bank clients. Dulles' principal Nazi client is LG. Farben, which has a reputation of treating Jews badly. At the same time, the SS boasts of promoting Nazi organizations in the U.S., particularly in Boston, N.Y.C., and Milwaukee. They say that some Catholic Church leaders have also been supportive.

July 16, 1939

John Foster Dulles, the influential U.S. attorney from S&C, has been visiting Germany on a regular basis. Apparently, he is not disturbed by what he sees the Nazis doing, and is making speeches in the U.S. denouncing Churchill and Roosevelt. His law firm has offices in Germany and many German clients who are close associates of Hitler.

August 2, 1939

In 1938, British P.M. Neville Chamberlain met with Hitler and tried to appease him. Today, Chamberlain advised the British people that he has been badly mistaken and that very soon Englishmen will be going to fight and die.

August 14, 1939

Von Ribbentrop/Molotov

A communique has been received that Germany's Foreign Minister Joachim von Ribbentrop has contacted the Soviet Foreign Minister Molotov and they have arranged a treaty with two parts: One is to be economic and the other is to be non-aggression. What has not been mentioned is that in 1922 Soviet Russia and Germany quietly signed The Treaty of Rapallo. That allowed the WWI defeated Germany to secretly develop weapons and train men. In return, Germany helped Stalin modernize the Red Army. This became a "secret" war school.

August 19, 1939

The economic German/Russian pact commits the Soviet Union to supply food products and raw materials to Germany and Germany will supply finished products like machinery to the Soviets. Hitler will have the material to produce more weapons of war.

August 23, 1939

"England, France, and Russia had been in negotiations to stand together against Hitler. However, the negotiations had broken down. It appears that Stalin was simultaneously negotiating with Germany and quickly concluded the Molotov-Ribbentrop Pact. Indeed, the High Command's latest coded memo has revealed a secret non-aggression pact was reached between Nazi Germany and the Soviets. This pact divides Poland into spheres of control and influence along the Narew, Vistula, and San Rivers. The Soviets agree (foolishly, in my opinion) not to join a war in the West and, in return, Hitler has told the Soviets that they can take Estonia, Latvia and Lithuania. This means that Hitler and Stalin can each attack Poland and partition it.

Russia has always wanted extensive buffer zones to protect against invasions such as Napoleon's invasion of Russia. This secret pact, which Stalin denies even exits, now gives this desired buffer to the Soviets. It is also an ominous message to much of Europe since it divides East and West Europe between the Soviets and Nazis. This, of course, could open the door for Hitler to invade Poland because Germany wants Poland as a strategic military staging area. Now that there is a guarantee of non-retaliation by the Soviets if Germany invades Poland, there need not be any concern about yet another war front if France and England unite against such an invasion based on their guarantee to defend Poland following the destruction of Czechoslovakia in March. This means these two dictators can each attack Poland and partition it.

So, it seems fascism and communism agree to co-exist. Stalin must realize this is a fantasy and that the reality is that neither side can be trusted.

August 24, 1939

Just as locals in Austria aided the Nazis in 1938, Hitler expects local in Poland will be eager to exploit and persecute helpless Jews. Germans and Poles want to steal Jewish property, and the Germans can use Polish police to implement German racial policies. This is an ominous circumstance for Polish Jews.

August 26, 1939

Hitler has ranted on the secure coded communication network that his forces must be prepared to invade the Soviets to "cleanse the world of communists and Jews who live in the Soviet lands." The August 23, 1939 non-aggression pact with the Soviets was a time delay deception in order to allow Nazi armies to occupy additional Western European countries to "protect German flanks," and then proceed eastward when German armies are ready in a few years.

The classified memo to Nazi leaders states that Hitler would prefer permission from Poland to advance through Poland peacefully towards the Soviets, rather than to fight Poland and risk drawing in Western countries to challenge Hitler. He has offered the Poles some of the Ukraine if they allow him peaceful access.

September 1, 1939

Poland did not comply with Hitler's offer of peacefulness. Germany has invaded Poland. This seems like an obvious move for Hitler to use Poland as a staging ground to invade Russia.

Russia must know that Hitler hates Communists and will therefore never honor the Brest Litovsk Non-Aggression Treaty that divided Poland between Germany and Russia.

September 8. 1939

Hitler is now sure Stalin is committed and that France will stay behind the Maginot line.

September 17, 1939

The Soviets have invaded Eastern Poland to occupy their "sphere of influence" called for in the treaty with Germany.

1940

January 25, 1940

We have been copied with a decree establishing Jewish ghettos in Poland in cities like Lodz. Jews are now forbidden to travel on a Polish train. The objective is to seal off these ghettos and trap Jews.

January 31, 1940

The British Navy is very active in their battle against our U-boats and has sunk dozens of boats.

February 2, 1940

Russia is moving to control Eastern Europe and the Baltic States. A new Russian offensive against Finland is happening.

February 18, 1940

The German navy ship Altmark is stationed off Norway and has been boarded by the British navy.

February 20, 1940

We are receiving word that there are Jewish partisans in Poland who are resisting German occupation. One group existing in thc forcst under very hard conditions is led by Eta Wrobel.

They are setting mines on roads, cutting off supply lines and sabotaging rail lines to cause numerous derailments.

February 30, 1940

This has been a bad month for Germany's very large U-boat command. Forty-five have been lost.

March 8, 1940

The Nazis have succeeded in massive Jewish persecution, immigrations, and incarcerations. They have stolen Jewish possessions, banks, department stores, and assets to finance the war effort and their personal wealth. Hitler has just asked Alfred Rosenberg to secure new "ownerless Jewish possessions." This means looting tens of thousands of objects from Jewish collections in France.

March 13, 1940

Tiny Finland cannot hold out against Russia and has surrendered.

March 15, 1940

In a sign that German resources are getting scarce, Göring has seized church bells to use the metal to be smelted for war purposes.

March 15, 1940

The German force has raided the British Navy at Scape Flow.

April 7, 1940

Germany has been warned that the British and Russians have extensive spy networks that are attempting to learn more about German weapons development labs and to break our coding of messages. Germany in tum has penetrated British intelligence and with the prospects of American aid to Britain we now have "German-American" agents all over the East Coast of the U.S. Germany has attracted and paid off every type of person to spy for us.

A story that is circulating is that last November we tricked two members of British M16 to meet a dissident German general in Venlo, Holland. The SS kidnapped the Brits who cooperated fully and gave Germany information about their agents on the Continent.

April 9, 1940

Germany has been working to develop nuclear weapons. Heavy water is important to this research and there is a heavy water plant at Vemork,

Norway. It was designed by the Norwegian scientist Leif Tronstad. The German physicist Wemer Heisenberg uses heavy water in his work and it has been hard to obtain. So, Hitler has invaded Norway and Germany will occupy Vemork and will control the supply of heavy water. German troops were not abusive or combative, unlike other German invasions.

April 8, 1940
The German Navy has sunk the British aircraft carrier Glorius.

April 9, 1940
Britain retaliates by sinking the Cruiser Blucher, with great loss of life.

April 14, 1940
The British Navy continues to sink numerous German warships.

April 15, 1940
Britain has landed troops in Norway.

April 27, 1940
Himmler has issued a decree establishing a new, massive concentration camp at Auschwitz.

May 10, 1940
Army Bulletin: German troops invade Holland, Belgium, and France.

Today in England, Winston Churchill succeeded Neville Chamberlain as Prime Minister. We will see if he can resist Hitler. As a test, Hitler has sent bombers to harass British civilians.

May 12, 1940
Army Bulletin: German Army moving rapidly in France.

May 12, 1940
The British Army and a large French force are moving quickly into Belgium.

May 14, 1940
Luftwaffe reports heavy bombing of Rotterdam, massive deaths, and rapid surrender of the Netherlands.

May 14, 1940
The Wehrmacht pushed through the Ardennes where the French Army is weakest and literally burst through French lines.

May 15, 1940
Army Bulletin: More advances in France. Belgium is the next target.

May 15, 1940
To avoid being encircled by the Wehrmacht, the British Army is falling back quickly.

May 16, 1940
The Wehrmacht has reached the channel and cut off the British, the Belgians, and the French 7th Army from the bulk of France's forces further south. Evacuation is the only option for Britain.

May 20, 1940
The British Army is trapped on the beaches of North East France. More specifically, this is Dunkirk. Hitler has accepted Hermann Göring's assurances that the Luftwaffe will annihilate the British like sitting ducks. Therefore, the German Amy has disengaged and is allowing the British evacuation. Also, France has forty-three divisions further south and that is taking the attention of the high command. Hitler is publicly stating that he will inflict very heavy casualties on France. It may be that he is haunted still by the Versailles Treaty, which caused considerable German hardships.

May 22, 1940
Hitler has called for all Jews to be expelled from Europe. Belgium surrenders.

May 23, 1940

Luftwaffe Reports: British Spitfires are now challenging German raids. Dogfights are happening. The Spitfire English fighter planes have exceptional maneuverability and fire power, and seem to be flown by well-trained pilots.

May 25, 1940

Army Bulletin: More advances in France, Belgium, and Norway.

May 31, 1940

Churchill and Petain of France meet in desperation and Petain is willing to make peace with Germany.

June 1, 1940

German spies in Britain have reported that the new Prime Minister, Winston Churchill, had a show down with his cabinet members who favored seeking a deal with Nazi Germany. At this time, Hitler's Army is easily moving towards Paris and British expeditionary forces in Europe are being evacuated at Dunkirk. German generals want to go after the British and trap them, thereby depriving Britain the ability to resist capitulating. However, Hitler seems preoccupied with the easy French victories and has not given the order to go to Dunkirk and eliminate the surrounded British forces.

June 2, 1940

Luftwaffe reports: British troops continue to be sitting ducks on Dunkirk's beach and are being bombed. The British evacuation continues via an armada of small boats crossing the channel. Luftwaffe has been sinking British Navy ships.

June 3, 1940

Luftwaffe has bombed Paris.

June 4, 1940

Army Bulletin: German troops enter Paris.

June 6 & 7, 1940
Reports of mass execution of Poles in the city of Poznan.

June 7, 1940
French and British troops evacuate other areas. Hitler appears unstoppable. Norway is close to surrender.

June 10, 1940
Norway just surrendered to Germany.

June 10, 1940
Churchill has made a monumental mistake by sending more troops back to France.

June 11, 1940
Army Bulletin. This seems to be a joke: News that Germany is rolling fast. Italy declares war against already defeated France, Belgium, and Britain.

June 14, 1940
Himmler's press release promotes Auschwitz as his accomplishment for new concentration camps.

June 14, 1940
German troops enter Paris. French resistance has collapsed in about a month. Horrifying. Surrender is imminent.

June 15, 1940
Churchill reversed his plan and brought back to England the British, Polish, and other allied troops, including a large number of French. Now England had to leave weapons and equipment behind, just as happened at Dunkirk. This effectively disarmed Britain, so Hitler must believe nothing will stop Germany's advances, especially on the Eastern front.

June 16, 1940

German U-boats have been active in sinking unarmed merchant ships.

While Hitler is busy in Western Europe, Russia is occupying portions of Eastern Europe, such as Estonia and Lithuania.

June 17, 1940

Army Bulletin. Göring has issued a command to confiscate horses, cattle, and crops in those countries that Germany occupies and to round up Jews for deporting to concentration camps.

June 17-19, 1940

France has surrendered to Germany. Prior to this surrender, Churchill of England did everything possible to persuade France to stay in the war rather than sign an armistice. However, the German armies moved with lightning speed to overwhelm the French and push British troops to the sea. Churchill has now proclaimed England's determination to fight till the last. It is known that France had built a very substantial fortification known as the Maginot Line. Germany simply skipped the fortifications.

Marshall Petain becomes the French Prime Minister. He is a total Nazi collaborator, so German control of France is sealed.

June 17-19, 1940

Germany is victorious over France and Marshall Petain has formed the Vichy Government, whose aim is to cooperate with Germany and to get "revenge on the Jews who had led Socialist reforms under Leon Blum and the Popular Front Political Movement."

June 19, 1940

Radio broadcast last night from England by Churchill urged Britain to resist Germany during the Battle of Britain. This battle for the skies over Britain will determine Britain's chance to survive massive Luftwaffe air raids.

June 22, 1940

France signs an armistice with Hitler.

June 22, 1940

France is disarming. Germany now has control of the sizable French navy to help challenge British sea power.

In the various European countries recently invaded by Hitler, Hermann Göring continues to give order to seize farm animals, cars, ships, buses, and anything of value that can be confiscated for the German war effort. This is an unprecedented plundering of Europe.

June 22, 1940

The Vichy French government has arrested Leon Blum and put him on trial "for causing the defeat of France." The truth is that he is Jewish and his arrest by Marshall Petain is to win points with the Nazis.

June 23, 1940

The Netherlands fall to the Nazis.

June 24, 1940

High Command Bulletin: Our Nazi sources tell us that at the U.S. State Department an assistant Secretary of State, Breckenridge Long, is in charge of immigration. His policy is to delay indefinitely the granting of visas so as to nearly eliminate the admission of Jews to the US. This is tantamount to a death sentence for these trapped people, so it seems like BL must be a blatant anti-Semite who makes the Nazis job easier and "more productive." One must conclude Jews are not wanted in the U.S. and therefore will be the Nazis for the taking. Germany knows that Britain has slammed the door shut in Palestine to appease Arabs whose oil Britain needs for their war effort. Germany's plan to invade Africa and seize oil resources is part of its strategy to supply German armies and deprive Britain of this resource.

June 25, 1940

Germany has taken over 40,000 British troops as prisoners. Two-hundred thousand other British troops escaped to Britain.

June 25, 1940

Hitler made a publicized visit to Paris to visit Napoleon's Tomb. I wonder if he realizes that Napoleon's ego eventually led to his downfall after the death of hundreds of thousands of French soldiers.

June 27, 1940

While Hitler was invading much of Western Europe, the Soviets have been occupying much of Eastern Europe. This is now a giant chess game. Is it possible Stalin does not understand he will be next?

June 28, 1940

The Vichy government that has been formed in France with Marshall Petain as its head can be expected to do the dirty work of the Nazis and relieve German manpower for further European conquest.

June 29, 1940

High Command Bulletin: German troops have occupied a good portion of France. Some French are expected to resist the occupation and many others are expected to collaborate. The French military proved to be a joke and collapsed. France may be an ally of Britain but the collaborators and deep-seated, anti-Semites will be an asset to Germany regardless of "Free-French" claims of patriotism.

June 30, 1940

The German Navy reports very heavy loss of U-boats this month.

June 30, 1940

The German Army reveals plans to invade Britain by using the Channel Islands (Jersey and Guernsey) for staging the invasions.

July 2, 1940

The German High Command plans to invade the British Isles. This will involve thirteen divisions to be transported by ship and protected from air attacks by Göring's Luftwaffe. Göring has commanded sorties over the Channel and is trying to engage British fighter planes.

July 3, 1940

The Soviets and Nazis now occupy a divided Poland. Both the Soviets and Nazis are sending hundreds of thousands of Poles to slave labor camps, murdering Polish Army captives, and destroying Poland. Since so many Jews live in Poland, it is clear that the Nazi-Soviet pact is a danger to these Jews.

July 3, 1940

German troops have swept through Europe with little resistance. Army bulletins again claim that Hitler's appetite for conquest is heightened and he has set his sights on England. This will include extensive aerial bombardment to soften England's defenses and the will to resist invasion.

July 3, 1940

Yesterday Hitler ordered the invasion of England. I disagree with the plan to invade England for many reasons. England has a formidable navy which could heavily destroy German transport ships required for an invasion and subsequent supply lines. The British Air Force has quietly built a large quantity of Spitfire fighter planes, which if deployed in concentrated squadrons, can defend England from air attacks. Hitler is also denying intelligence reports that Britain has a well-trained guerilla force stationed in the South and that could impede an invasion by sea.

Unlike the cowardly and collaborating French, the British would fiercely defend and fight. Hitler's' ambitions in the Middle East, Western and Eastern Europe, the Soviet Union, and now England, will be an eventual disaster of stretching resources and manpower way too thin. The High Command must surely know this obvious miscalculation but are too intimidated and frightened to give Hitler and his command staff an honest assessment.

July 4, 1940

The navy has ordered German U-boats to increase the sinking of unarmed merchant ships in the Atlantic. This is clearly to open the path for an invasion of Britain, preceded by aerial bombings to inflict civilian deaths and weaken Britain's will to fight, especially where Britain has withdrawn troops from the continent.

July 5, 1940

Navy Bulletin: The French Navy was to be turned over to the German Navy. Earlier today, the British Navy sunk the French fleet off the coast of Algeria, which will prevent Germany from using this French fleet.

July 7, 1940

German agents have infiltrated the U.S. State Department and have reported that in late June they received an explosive memo from Assistant Secretary Breckinridge Long. Long comes from a "blue blood," wealthy, East Coast family and has been well schooled in anti-Semitism. He is a personal friend of Roosevelt and he is well suited to carry out the administration's' policy of suppressing immigration. The memo to all U.S. consulates worldwide is to "postpone and postpone and postpone granting the pieces of paper to refugees." Previously in the 1930s, Roosevelt had kept the German quota to a fraction that is permitted by law, and now Long was continuing the same hostility to German Jews. The Long memo is a death sentence to thousands of European Jews and gives Hitler the message that he can accelerate this persecution of Jews without interference. Our German agents are most elated and consider that the U.S. government is collaborating with Nazi policies to exterminate trapped Jews.

July 8, 1940

Army bulletin: The Luftwaffe has been ordered to bomb Britain and to attempt to destroy Britain's Air Force.

July 10, 1940

The Battle of Britain has commenced. The Luftwaffe bulletin states airfields and factories will be targeted.

In retaliation, and to Germany's great surprise, the RAF has bombed Germany. The Battle of Britain is now fully underway, which includes aerial dog fights and the attacking of British shipping in the channel.

July 18, 1940

Himmler has advised all upper-level officers to be on the alert for the British secret organization called Special Operations Executive (SOE). He says that

SOE has infiltrated every country that Germany occupies to work with underground movements to sabotage German instillations and spy on Germany. We are especially vulnerable to Peenemünde due to a very large civilian workforce.

July 19, 1940

By radio broadcast we hear Hitler order Britain to surrender. I believe that British feelings are so strong that such an order will only add to the British will to resist.

July 20, 1940

Wherever Germany has occupied countries they are arresting prominent citizens and sending them to concentration camps.

July 24, 1940

Last night the Luftwaffe commenced all night bombings of London. We were told this might break the will of English civilians.

July 28, 1940

German U-boats have sunk thirty-eight merchant ships this month. These ships are carrying food and supplies to Britain, so this loss is a real threat to British survival.

August 1, 1940

Britain, led by Winston Churchill, is trying to stand up to Nazi Germany. It seems to me that Britain is ill prepared and ill equipped at this time to fight on the Continent, and that the U.S. has not been of great or generous help.

August 2, 1940

With Germany now in command in France, General De Gaulle has been sentenced to death even though he is now safe in England.

August 3, 1940

Italy is now trying to show it is an Axis power and is going after African countries like Somalia and Ethiopia. A joke; attacking African countries with dismal armies. At the same time the Soviets are forcing Baltic nations into the Soviet "orbit."

August 5, 1940

Resistance movements in France have created an underground force to aid what they hope would someday be an allied invasion. This seems remote and German forces are in complete control.

The Communists seem to be cooperating since Germany and Russia have a pact at this time. I suppose they want to be tolerated by the Germans.

Foreign Jewish immigrants to France may become an important part of the Resistance. Many of them had been eager to fight Hitler and had joined the Foreign Legion in 1939. However, in 1940, Vichy France demobilized Jewish veterans and gave them forced labor or internment.

Zionists have organized to start relief work. I predict they will be an active part of the Resistance as Germans and French collaborators make life precarious for Jews.

August 8, 1940

A new lab has opened at Peenemünde that is devoted to research on remote controlled aircraft, such as a glide bomber that can be used to attack warships. This lab is directed by Herbert Wagner, who is also an expert on jet engines.

August 9, 1940

Germany has a four-fold plane advantage and has commenced bombing Southern England.

August 11, 1940

Luftwaffe is raiding British harbors and cities as Herman Göring's "Battle of Britain" rages on. Every night the Luftwaffe is losing dozens and dozens of aircraft. I do not think this air war on Britain is sustainable.

August 15, 1940

British fighter planes are challenging the Luftwaffe, which is boldly staging daylight raids.

August 15, 1940

Aerial dogfights over Britain are taking a huge toll on German planes. The Luftwaffe did not realize the quality and quantity of the British Spitfire fighter planes.

August 16, 1940

The German Army is now occupying Polish towns that had been seized by the Soviets. They have immediately enlisted local populations to "cleanse" their communities of Jews by collaboration with the Germans, to humiliate and degrade Jews and then to initiate pogroms. This same methodology is being used by Germany in Latvia where an auxiliary police force named Arajs Commandos has already killed two-thirds of Latvia's Jews. As the German Army advances in Soviet territory, various Soviet nationalities have rushed to aid the Nazi campaign of murder, with an appetite for Jewish property.

August 17, 1940

The German Navy is blockading Britain to choke off supplies and materials.

August 20, 1940

The SS has learned that Russian spies are advising Stalin that Hitler plans to attack the Soviets and that Stalin refuses to believe this.

August 23, 1940

Luftwaffe continues bombing central London in an attempt to terrorize British civilians.

August 26, 1940

In a surprise move, Britain has just bombed Berlin. Hitler is furious and has moved to an underground bunker complex.

August 31, 1940

Navy Secret Bulletin: Admitting to the loss of over fifty U-boats this month. The huge German U-boat fleet is being hunted by the British navy using advanced depth charges.

September 4, 1940

The US is at last waking up and has given fifty destroyers to Britain. These will surely be used to hunt German U-boats.

September 15, 1940

Luftwaffe has had intense raids on most major British cities; a nightly occurrence to force a surrender. However, Germany is losing dozens of bombers every night. Göring is purposely targeting Buckingham Palace and civilian shelters in an attempt to inflict loss of life.

September 15, 1940

Luftwaffe has not gained a victory over British fighter pilots so Göring is again trying massive bombings of London. British pilots have been joined by Poles, Czechs, Dutch, French, Canadians, and Norwegians. In spite of Germany's propaganda and control of the media, this news of the prolonged Battled of Britain is getting through by radio to countries occupied by Germany.

September 17, 1940

Germany is continuing to steal Jewish possessions in Germany and every country that is occupied.

September 18, 1940

Luftwaffe is going after British arms factories but the loss of planes is so heavy that the "Battle of Britain" will surely be lost.

September 18, 1940

(The Army and Morocco). Earlier this summer Germany overran France in a matter of days and made a deal with French Marshal Petain to collaborate with the Nazis so Petain could control a portion of France and also French Morocco. Hitler and the high command need Middle East oil and the supply lines from France to North Africa are very direct. The German Army under the command of General Rommel made rapid advances in Morocco and Egypt, and were headed toward the real oil reserves of Iraq, Syria, and

Persia. Hitler is also obsessed with killing Jews, of which there are large ancient Jewish communities in Libya, Egypt, Palestine, Iraq, Syria, and Persia. So, this insane leader will now go for oil and killing Jews in the Middle East.

In my opinion, Hitler did not consider how thin German resources and supply lines are being spread. Just as German armies are moving rapidly in Eastern and Western Europe, Hitler has opened a new front in Africa and the Middle East. I believe this is not sustainable.

September 27, 1940

Germany, Italy, and Japan have signed a pact. This Axis alliance combines three armies that are focused on global control and mutual aid. Neither party can control the other party's ambitions.

September 30, 1940

Germany continues to lose a large quantity of planes and U-boats. It seems to me that the pilots and sailors are being sent on suicide missions. Britain is far outnumbered in the air and under the sea, but is putting up a brilliant defense.

October 4, 1940

Germany's bombing of Britain continues, but with a reduced Air Force that continues to endure heavy losses.

October 7, 1940

German spies in England have learned of a British plot to provoke Japan into attacking the U.S., so that the U.S. will enter WWII and save Britain from being invaded by Germany. This will involve untrue "leaks" to provoke Japan.

October 7, 1940

Hitler's conquest of Europe continues with German troops entering Romania. Germany wants Romanian oil and knows there are many Nazi sympathizers in the extreme right in Romania. The Romanian Orthodox

Church has consistently presented Jews as "Christ killers" and demonized them. Therefore, the Church set the scene for Hitler and made this invasion a very easy exercise. Romania has even passed laws that restricted the rights of Jews.

October 8, 1940

Army Bulletin: German troops occupy Romania with the help of a fascist Romanian government. Their oil will now supply the German Army.

October 12, 1940

Britain is winning the air battle and its navy is sinking many of our U-boats. Therefore, Hitler has put the invasion of Britain on hold. German air raids are still inflicting heavy loss of British civilian lives.

October 15, 1940

Hollywood movies have been popular in Germany. However, Charlie Chaplin has made a film making fun of Hitler. Hitler is very upset and vows to "eliminate" Chaplin (who is Jewish).

October 17, 1940

We are told that Hitler has a plan to murder all the Jews of Poland. His first edict is to establish a ghetto in Warsaw and force all Jews in Poland into that ghetto along with German Jews he plans to transport to Poland.

October 20, 1940

The Luftwaffe has sustained tremendous losses and our High Command Bulletin estimated half of the German Air Force is gone. This will alter Germany's overall invasion strategies to employ massive land campaigns that move very quickly since they will not now have adequate au cover.

October 26, 1940

The U.S. has unveiled a fighter plane called the P51 Mustang. Hitler must be aware that it is only a matter of time before the U.S. is drawn in to WWII and that will be big trouble for Germany.

October 30, 1940

As our German conquest of Europe and Africa moves with great speed, I have continued to think about European history and the lessons learned and not learned. Napoleon wanted to reign over all of Europe, including Russia. He left Russia in defeat and eventually in June 1815, Napoleon lost at Waterloo to combined allied armies, which included British and Prussian armies.

The very obvious lesson is over extension of supply routes, vast distances, brutal winters, and motivated opposing allied armies who ended Napoleon's brutal reign. I wonder if Hitler has thought about this.

October 31, 1940

The Battle of Britain between the RAF and Luftwaffe is ending in defeat for the German Air Force. That gives our rocket program more reasons to forge ahead. This means that Hitler will give greater importance to Peenemünde and the V-1 and V-2 program. Dornberger and others are going often to Berlin to lobby for materials and workers. Britain's strength on the sea will preclude an invasion of Britain. Since Hitler's appetite for conquest is insatiable, I believe he will tum to the "East."

November 1, 1940

Since Julia and Felix were placed in protective custody, I have only been allowed to communicate by written notes which are monitored by the SS. It has been two years since we have had personal contact and I worry that they are in good health and that Julia and her parents are being left alone by the SS.

November 2, 1940

German spies who are embedded in British Intelligence, report that Britain has received a warning about German radio-controlled rockets being tested at Peenemünde in the Baltic. In other words, German security has been penetrated and compromised by someone who is an Allied spy. However, our men now report that British Intelligence does not believe the report and thinks it to be a German propaganda ploy. I am relieved since our design and testing can continue undisturbed. The more I can accomplish the greater will be Julia and Felix's chances of survival.

November 4, 1940

Franklin Roosevelt has been re-elected President of the United States. It remains to be seen if he will continue the USA isolationist policy. If history is a guide, it is possible the U.S. will again belatedly come into the war and save Britain and much of Europe from Nazi domination.

Roosevelt is known to be an ally of Britain and wants the U.S. to help Britain win the war against Germany. He has also been antagonistic towards Japan and has stopped their purchase of U.S. commodities.

November 8, 1940

The V-1 and V-2 programs rely on a great number of workers. Since this is a secret place, only German workers should be used. However, labor is in demand by many projects, so many foreign workers are being brought to Peenemünde. This is a huge security mistake that I have complained about to no avail.

November 10, 1940

The U.S. State Department has issued an offer to European Jews to come to the U.S. Virgin Islands provided they meet certain requirements. However, the assistant Secretary of State, Breckenridge Long, a virulent anti-Semite, has blocked this offer. Germany knows he is a Hitler admirer, which gives our SS encouragement to doubt resistance from the United States. Long claims he will have Roosevelt's support.

November 12, 1940

Britain is fighting Germany alone and is badly outnumbered, however, the RAF is bombing German cities. The Royal Navy has engaged the Italian fleet and sunken half of it.

November 14, 1940

Luftwaffe reports destroying the British city of Coventry.

November 16, 1940

The RAF has retaliated for Coventry by bombing Hamburg.

November 19, 1940

Luftwaffe continues attempts to level British cities. What Göring is causing is a will for revenge by the British that could level German cities.

November 23, 1940

Hitler announces a coup. Hungary, Romani, and Slovakia have joined the "Axis." In other words, he may have threatened "join or be destroyed." However, all three countries have numerous Nazi sympathizers.

November 26, 1940

Jews are desperate to escape Hitler. The British have restricted immigration to Palestine, so hundreds attempt to illegally enter Palestine since there is a 3000-year-old Jewish presence there. Yesterday an illegal immigrant ship sunk in Haifa harbor, killing hundreds.

November 26, 1940

Himmler's memo: The Ghetto in Warsaw, which was created earlier this year, is now being walled off to prevent Jews from escaping.

November 30, 1940

Navy report: Dozens of U-boats continue to be lost each month. British destroyers with depth charges are extracting a very heavy toll on the German Navy.

December 4, 1940

German spies in high places in the U.S. continue to report that Jewish scientists who fled Nazi persecution are working in the U.S. on nuclear fusion.

Germany has Werner Heisenberg, the nuclear bomb pioneer, who had been very close to Jewish colleagues. But, he has family ties to Himmler's grandmother and therefore is allowed to continue his work.

We were told that Werner Heisenberg advised Speer it would take two years just to build a cyclotron, so Speer dropped the plans for an atom bomb.

December 7, 1940

The resistance movement has circulated posters ridiculing Nazis. They seem harmless, but their artists are being taken to Gestapo, H.Q., and are not corning out.

December 8, 1940

It is my opinion that Germany made a big mistake by invading Africa, especially simultaneously with the invasion of much of Western Europe and moving troops into position in Eastern Europe. However, German forces are dominating North Africa and seeking to go to Cairo and Tel Aviv. The British armies in North Africa are fighting back and staging counter-offensives, including the area around Benghazi, Libya. The British have effectively used hit and run guerilla tactics to precede battles.

December 10, 1940

Jews fleeing Europe are trying to enter Palestine and the British are deporting them. It is ironic that Britain is fighting Germany, but Britain cannot allow the people Germany is persecuting to find a safe haven in Palestine.

December 20, 1940

High command officers visiting our rocket labs say that Hitler is planning for a war against Russia. I think this was obvious when Molotov and Von Ribbentrop signed an agreement to divide Poland. We know Hitler despises Communism.

December 29, 1940

Luftwaffe has resorted to dropping 100,000 incendiary bombs on London and setting London on fire. This takes a heavy toll on civilians but does not seem to have military value. I continue to worry that the Allies also have incendiary bombs.

1941

January 1, 1941

Walter Dornberger, a top leader at Peenemünde, has done everything possible to lobby Berlin for support for our rocket program. He has conferred with influential people and visited factories, which have limited raw materials and labor. Most highly skilled people that are needed in Peenemünde are in armed services. We have tried to recruit workers from other countries but with little success.

Young people have been sent forcefully from Poland to work in factories and are treated like slaves. I am told that a further source of labor is planned: Manpower from concentration camps. We know about Dachau, Oranienburg, Sachsenhausen, Flossenbiirg, Mauthausen, and Ravensbruck. Now, there is a new, larger one called Auschwitz.

Another competitor for materials and works is Himmler's SS "enterprises." To our amazement, the SS is creating or confiscating industries so Himmler can profit and expand the SS into a giant organization and Army with independence to do as they please. We are told he plans to have millions of forced laborers working at SS factories on or near the camps.

Peenemünde is a secret, high security "village" working on weapons experiments. Yet, due to rivalry and stupidity we must use whatever workers we can get, including other nationalities, prisoners, and even political prisoners. My worry is that using foreign workers in Peenemünde is a serious error for Germany, but one that will benefit my intention to "alter" flight path navigation.

January 2, 1941

Hitler has ordered increased bombing of Britain, including landmarks such as cathedrals.

January 4, 1941

Even though the U.S. is not officially at war, the U.S. Government has announced a program to build fleets of transport ships to bring supplies to Britain.

January 7, 1941

Even though the Wehrmacht thoroughly beat Britain on the continent, we learn that Britain is fighting well in North Africa and elsewhere in Africa.

January 14, 1941

SS Bulletin: The SS is bragging about exterminating thousands of Jews in Bucharest, Romania.

January 21, 1941

SS: Instituting anti-Jewish measures in Bulgaria.

January 25, 1941

Xavier Vallat has formed the Vichy French government's first commission for "the Jewish problem." Historically, French Jews had played a role in the French Republic after 1875, but anti-Semitism was rampant. The Dreyfus Affair in 1894 involved Captain Alfred Dreyfus being falsely accused of being a German spy. France was engulfed for a decade quarreling over this injustice.

In the 1930s, France became the destination of choice for Jews fleeing Nazi violence and now they are faced with a Vichy government anxious to please the Nazis by heavily persecuting French Jews.

January 31, 1941

The British Navy continues to sink dozens of German subs just this month.

February 5, 1941

Navy Bulletin: The German Navy has created U-boat formations to prey on supply lines vital to Britain. It is known that 70% of Britain's food and 90% of its oil must come by sea by way of very slow and often unprotected merchant ships that are like "sitting ducks." This means the U? boats can sink thousands of vessels and kill tens of thousands of seamen. However, if the allies add warships to protect the merchant ships and are able to anticipate the U-boat formations, then there is the risk that this will become a destructive naval campaign.

February 11, 1941

Italy had occupied many areas of Africa. We think Mussolini wanted to show his Army's power. However, we now hear that the British Army is destroying Italian armies throughout Africa.

February 13, 1941

SS Bulletin: Nazis are now attacking Jews in Holland and deporting Jews from Amsterdam and transporting them to concentration camps.

February 15, 1941

SS Report: The Dutch Communist Party organized a general strike to protest anti-Jewish measures by Nazi troops. It was quickly put down and key leaders executed.

February 22, 1941

Wehrmacht attacks in Libya.

February 23, 1941

I have relied on German industries for some of the materials used in rocket production, especially my instruments. My contacts at LG. Farben tell me they will build a factory at the Auschwitz Concentration Camp and use prisoners as free, slave laborers. This is sure to please Himmler.

February 25, 1941

We continue to lose many U-boats in the battle for control of the Atlantic.

March 3, 1941

There is no end to how thin the German Army is being spread. Now we have invaded Bulgaria.

March 15, 1941

Nazis tighten restrictions on Jews in Holland.

March 24, 1941

Wehrmacht Report: German troops under the command of Erwin Rommel are occupying Libya.

March 27, 1941

Hitler now directs an assault on Yugoslavia.

April 1, 1941

Germany has cultivated and bribed Muslim leaders in the Middle East so that most are pro German. Just today in Iraq a pro-German leader gained power.

April 4, 1941

Nazi spies in Britain are at the highest levels. Today, we learn that Churchill is warning Stalin of a German invasion. Stalin refused to listen, which will make it easy for Germany.

April 7, 1941

Wehrmacht continues to gain in Libya. I see this as further spreading of our resources and troops.

April 14, 1941

The Foreign Ministry reports that Japan and Soviets have signed a neutrality pact. This is not a good event for Nazi Germany since it will free the Soviet troops now in the Far East and deploy them on our Eastern Front. Stalin is said to be elated that Japan will tum its attention to Southeast Asia and the United States.

We confidentially have been alerted that Hitler plans to attack Russia, having had time to group troops and supplies in Eastern Poland. The Japan-Soviet pact will surely accelerate the attack timing in order to precede Russian troop movements from the Far East to the Soviet West and Ukraine.

Another reaction of the Ministry is that if the Soviets convince the United States to supply war materials to the Soviets, that Japan will have redeployed its navy from the Vladivostok approaches and make it safe for U.S. ships to reach Soviet ports.

I see this pact as a diplomatic victory for Stalin and very bad for Germany's ambitions.

April 2, 1941

The Nazi spy in the British MI6 tells us that British Intelligence has broken the German codes and is sending reports to Stalin that Germany will attack Russia. The Nazi spy in Moscow tells us that Stalin has rejected these intelligence reports; Germany knows it is preparing to invade. To further strengthen Germany's position, Stalin is foolishly shooting scores of his top intelligence officers and dropping contact with many foreign informants who were giving him accurate intelligence.

May 2, 1941–The Middle East

Germany has succeeded in winning the sympathy of many Arab/Muslim states to take a pro-Nazi stance. In Iraq, there has been an orgy of murder, rape, mutilation and looting of Jews, six? hundred of whom were killed. The Palestinian Grand Mufti of Jerusalem is in Berlin working with the Nazis and is active in promoting the killing of European Jews. The radical Muslim Brotherhood is being funded by Germany.

May 3, 1941

Hitler announced Martin Bormann will replace Rudolph Hess as Hitler's deputy. Germany continues air raids on Britain. I think this is a waste since the air raids have only created more resolve by Britain.

May 7, 1941

Churchill has received a 90% vote by the House of Commons. He has a strong military background and will be a formidable but weakened opponent of Nazi Germany.

May 10, 1941

I have sent information about our secret spy codes to the British and believe they are now able to decipher our messages.

May 14, 1941

Hitler announced Martin Bormann will be head of the Nazi Chancellery in Germany.

May 15, 1941

The SS bulletin states that with French help, thousands of Jews are being rounded up in Paris.

May 28, 1941

Navy Bulletin: The German battleship Bismarck attempted to race for safety in occupied France. The Royal British Navy pursued the Bismarck and sank it with great loss of life and loss of strategical naval power.

June 4, 1941 -Times of London

Churchill's speech to the House of Commons:

> "We shall fight on the beaches, in the fields and the streets, in the hills–we shall never surrender."

June 5, 1941

I often reflect on the Mendelssohn family history. My name is clearly Jewish as a descendent of the noted philosopher Moses Mendelssohn. Yet, the Nazis have not bothered me. That must be because I am a vital link in designing rocket guidance systems and possibly because Wernher is very protective of his lab colleagues. I secretly believe that guidance can be solved rapidly but need to drag the solution out for years to keep my life and family protected and to be in a position to "delay" the Nazi deployment of what may be a weapon with great and robot-like destructive powers. Its destructive power will depend on the condensed explosive power that can be packed in the rocket's warhead.

The Mendelssohn family started converting in the early 1800s with the family of Abraham (Moses' son) becoming Lutheran. The irony is that some Lutherans in Germany were and are anti-Semitic and that the Nazis look to Jewish roots for their persecution mandates. Felix Mendelssohn, the great composer, started his career at an early age, and was fortunate that his banker father, Abraham, was so successful that he could support Felix's career, provide the best education, and expose his work to the "rich and famous." Ironically, I was born almost exactly a century after Felix.

June 8, 1941

Germany continues to issue "laws" to restrict Jewish rights to exist and raids Jewish populations throughout Europe.

June 19, 1941

The Turks backed Germany in WWI and now Turkey has signed a treaty with Nazi Germany.

June 21, 1941

Even though Germany is not "at war" with the U.S., the U-boat 203 did attempt to sink the U.S. Battleship Texas and failed.

June 22, 1941

The Germans and Soviets have kept their non-aggression pact for about two years. It has been obvious that Germany has used Poland as a staging area to invade Soviet territory even though a second front is not advisable. I assume that Hitler is over-confident and so obsessed with Communism and Jews that he has rejected the advice of his general command. This is known since the coded messages to our rocket control have carried cryptic complaints from the general staff. Today Germany made a surprise attack and invaded the Soviet Union. Hitler has stated that he must wipe Leningrad from the face of the Earth.

Furthermore, Stalin has purged/murdered so many of Russia's top leaders that Hitler is sure that Russia is not able to resist the invasion by Germany. It is spelled out in Hitler's Mein Kompf. As of now, Germany has caught the Soviet command by complete surprise and the Russians are retreating rapidly.

It is also possible that Hitler is informed that the U.S. has strong voices that speak against going to war. However, with Britain standing alone, the invasion of the Soviet Union could force U.S. leaders to more actively help Britain and Russia.

June 22, 1941–High Command and Party Communiques

Operation Barbarossa is launched: The invasion of Russia is underway. Now the Einsatzgruppen can be unleased to round up Jews in every city and every village and kill them en-masse.

June 22, 1941

Army Command Bulletin: Along a 1,500 kilometer front, 130 German divisions invaded Soviet Territory today. The Red Army has pushed back hundreds of kilometers and over a million prisoners taken. German intelligence was aware that Stalin disregarded warnings of Hitler's plans and Russia was unprepared for the German invasion. I believe this may relieve a lot of pressure by Germany on Britain, which immediately offered assistance to the Soviets. Since it is Britain that needs the assistance of the U.S., this offer seems meaningless and politically motivated.

June 23, 1941

Gestapo Bulletin: In Warsaw the Nazis have rounded up 500,000 Jew and packed them into a ghetto that is a few miles square. There will be fifteen people to a room and they will be cut off with no communication to the outside. Through starvation and disease, they will die and those that do not die, the Nazis will kill.

June 23, 1941

Army Bulletin: Yesterday Germany invaded Soviet territory.

We have been briefed on Germany's betrayal of the agreement with Russia and the massing of troops, armaments and supplies for a swift campaign to overwhelm Russian resistance and drive towards the Russian cities of Leningrad and Moscow. Anyone with even a slight knowledge of Eastern European weather and distances would have questioned the wisdom or perhaps insanity of his action. Hitler calls this invasion of Russia "Operation Barbarossa."

I must keep my thoughts to myself or will risk being questioned as not being loyal to Hitler and could be accused of breaking the loyalty oath (we were forced to take). Some of my thoughts are:

Germany has limited manpower and this push East will weaken our ability to hold on in Africa and to pursue German ambitions in Western Europe. Russia and Stalin have shown little regard for human life and therefore can be expected to throw millions of soldiers against German armies once Russia recovers from the shock of the German invasion.

The distances are so vast that if Germany is able to drive to Leningrad and Moscow, the lines of supply will be stretched very thin and the quantity of supplies will be enormous even if Germany "rapes" Russia for food and supplies. This will take material away from other fronts. Also, it will mean that soldiers will be very far from home and therefore not have the connections or proximity to family they need for morale. The majority of supplies will come by train and trains are very vulnerable to sabotage. If Russia organizes large bands of Partisans, they simply need to remove a small section of rail and there will be a derailment.

Russian winters are well known for extreme cold and snow. Anyone who has tried to operate machinery in extreme cold knows that the equipment might fail and the operator might freeze to death. Germany surely must know that trucks and tanks and mobile artillery could be useless if there is a severe winter.

History may not repeat itself but is a good guide for what might happen. Over the centuries Russia has been invaded and the invaders have always been driven out by weather and Russian resistance. It is true that Russia was badly beaten by Japan less than 35 years ago, but a dysfunctional Czar was in control and it was a very different location and circumstances.

Ignoring history and the odds of failure may prove to be a disaster for Germany. Hitler is obsessed with destroying Communism and it may destroy him.

June 23, 1941

Army Bulletin: After Germany's invasion of Russia, it is interesting to see Churchill reach out to help Stalin, even though Stalin is a diabolical tyrant who has stayed in power by murdering millions. Maybe Stalin and Hitler can be compared. Churchill and Stalin are now trying to woo the U.S. to enter the War. History repeats, since the U.S. came to the aid of Britain and France in 1917.

June 24, 1941

Our spies in Moscow report that Stalin is so shocked at the German attack that he has withdrawn to the Kremlin. He had expected his alliance with Germany to last long enough to bring his military up to modem standards and fighting trim. He had ignored repeated warnings from his own agents.

The SS reports killing the entire Jewish populations of many Eastern European cities. In most cases, they are aided by local anti-Semites and are encouraging non-Jewish civilians to kill Jews.

June 24, 1941

Hitler's invasion of Russia may be a monumental miscalculation that does not recognize recent history. During World War I when German submarines tried to rule the Atlantic supply lines it forced American and British Navies to work together to break the sub blockade and created an alliance that eventually defeated Germany on the battlefield. America developed massive manufacturing facilities to produce weapons of war and conscripted millions of soldiers.

Now in 1941, Germany is ignoring the close relationship that Churchill of Britain and Roosevelt of America have developed. Although America is not officially in the War in Europe, it has been lending ships, armaments and supplies to Britain. Although neither Churchill or Roosevelt likes Communist Russia and Stalin, this new front of aggression by Hitler could convince isolationist America that it can no longer stay out of this war that Hitler is spreading like wildfire. The consequences of Germany overreaching through all of Europe could foretell very bad things for America as well. Britain took a beating in Europe on the ground, is fighting back in the air and sea, and is desperate for an all-out U.S. military commitment. Germany's latest action could convince Roosevelt to start the conversion of American factories into unbeatable war production machines and then wait for an event that will force Congress to take action and declare war.

Another factor that Hitler has ignored is diplomacy. German Intelligence Service and the SS assumed that Joseph Kennedy, the U.S. Ambassador to Britain was pro-Nazi and that would not accommodate cooperation with Britain. Germany missed the fact that Roosevelt has openly criticized his State Department as being a useless disaster and has sent a personal representative to privately meet with Churchill. It is rumored that Kennedy will be replaced. The American, Harry Hopkins, is prominently mentioned in the British press (which is read by German Intelligence agents). Hopkins is Roosevelt's "right hand trusted aide" and also has a close relationship with Churchill. Germany is not paying attention and obsessed with killing Jews and Soviets.

June 24, 1941

Hitler's speech to the German people about the invasion of the USSR:

1. He hates Communism.
2. "When Germany beats Russia, Germany will control so much territory and be so strong that Britain and USA will have a go along with Germany."

I am unclear about Hitler's reasoning and unsure he can succeed with this vast plan.

June 24, 1941

Hitler has made it clear to the German people that the attack on the Soviet Union will be a war against the Slavs and Jews, which he claims will solve Germany's problems. This illogical obsession is still called Operation Barbarossa. Poland is noted for anti-Semitism and openly had said in the late 1930s it wanted to get rid of its Jewish population. So, the Polish population in general is aiding Hitler's program.

June 25, 1941

Hitler and his advisors should also have considered that Stalin has murdered many millions of Russians and Ukrainians in order to hold on to his power. I have no doubt that he will sacrifice many more millions to stop the Germans. Stalin's concentration camps in Siberia are models for Hitler's camps.

If this invasion brings the U.S. into this war, then Germany is doomed. Hitler must know that the U.S. has huge industrial capacity that can be mobilized for use and to supply the Russians. I suspect that Hitler thinks this will not happen. What may influence his thinking is business such as the Rockefellers sell oil to Germany; Farben owns a lot of Aramco; John Foster Dulles has many German clients, and the Chase Bank does business with Germany's Schroder Bank. What these fanatical Nazi Party leaders have forgotten is that the U.S. came into World War I to stop Germany and could easily do the same for WWII.

June 28, 1941

SS Bulletin: The SS has been very vocal about murdering all Jews and being determined to eradicate all Jewish art and culture. The Wehrmacht has just captured Vilna, the cultural capital of Eastern European Jewry. The Army has started rounding up Jews to force them into a ghetto.

Alfred Rosenberg, the leading ideologist of the 3rd Reich, has announced confiscation of books and artifacts for his institute for study of the Jewish question. To accomplish this, he plans to force Jewish scholars to help. He will focus on Vilna.

Martin Weiss is in charge of herding thousands of Jews to their death. He has announced that the abandoned Russian fuel pits in Pona will make a perfect and isolated place for his mass murder plans.

July 1, 1941

The collapse of the Soviet Union seems imminent. This means Hitler will soon commence huge scale massacres.

July 1, 1941

Ukrainians in German uniforms are now occupying Eastern Poland. These are fanatics who have fled the Soviet Union in order to aid Nazi Germany.

Reports from just one small town, Lvov, say that the Ukrainians are killing thousands of Jews in cold blood massacres.

July 2, 1941

Our reports are full of Nazis/SS following the Army and committing mass murder in towns and villages. In Lvov, the SS bragged of killing 7,000 just yesterday.

Another report says that some of the Partisans who are fighting German soldiers are also participating in the killing of Jews.

July 3, 1941

Bulletin from Reinhard Heydrich: Germans must cleanse Jews and Communists in an intense way and produce pogroms by the local people. In Poland the Catholic Church has preached intense anti-Semitism for years, so getting Polish citizens' participation is easy.

July 7, 1941

More reports of Nazis executing Jews. This time 5,000 in Kovno, Lithuania. Hitler has given orders to exterminate Europe's Jews and his faithful followers in Latvia, Poland, the Baltic States, and the Ukraine are rushing to follow his orders.

July 10, 1941–Jedwabne

My boyhood friend Gerhard Schneider is an officer in the German Army, and was assigned to advance units in Poland when Hitler invaded in September 1939. We have maintained constant contact and he provides me with classified bulletins and I keep him advised of the progress we are making with rocketry here at Peenemünde.

Bulletin from SS: The Polish town of Jedwabne has been under Soviet control until Germany attacked the Soviet Union on Jun 23, 1941 and the Red Army withdrew. Germany was still setting up its occupation regime and gave Poles a few days to cleanse the city of Jews. The Poles drove hundreds of Jews from their homes and then into a large barn near the town center. The mob then set fire to the barn and murdered the Jews of Jedwabne.

July 14, 1941

Bulletin: Jews in Lithuania are being forced into camps and then murdered there. There is no end to the insanity. In addition to murder, the Synagogues and the Torahs are being burned. So far, we have not heard from the rest of the world who must know what is happening in every occupied city. The SS is perpetrating mass murder with intensity and no one is stopping them.

July 20, 1941

Romania joined the Nazi Axis and has had a large fascist Army. There are reports that Romanian troops in Bessarabia and Bukovina are mass murdering Jews by the thousands. The report states that many Romanian civilians are participating in this murder spree. There are over 500,000 Jews in Romania and all are targeted.

July 21, 1941

Wehrmacht Report: The onslaught of the Soviet Union continues and today the German Army has entered the Ukraine.

July 23, 1941

German Navy Bulletin: U-boats have sunk dozens of Allied ships this month. I can sense that this is a high-risk game since many of those are U.S. ships trying to bring supplies to a starving Britain. It is like taunting Roosevelt, whose patience must be running thin. If America enters the war, it will be lost since the U.S. has such massive productive capacity and raw materials.

July 24, 1941

Catholic Bishop Galen is openly supporting the Nazi invasion of the "Jewish Bolshevik" Soviet Union and has refused aid to Jews who are being increasingly persecuted. This is clearly moral failure by the Catholic Church.

July 27, 1941

Wehrmacht Report: The Romanian Army is working closely with Einsatzgruppe D. to massacre Ukrainian Jews. In Odessa, 26,000 Jews have been killed. The Wehrmacht and the Organization of Ukrainian Nationalists have incited a Lviv pogrom in which 9,000 Jews were killed by the native population. Our lab workers have received photos taken by men of Einsatzgruppen showing the killings. These photos are also being sent to families in Germany. So, Germans on the Homefront are aware of the massacres.

August 9, 1941

Wehrmacht: Yesterday the German Army surrounded twenty Russian divisions and they have all surrendered. The Russians cannot imagine how brutally they will be treated.

August 10, 1941

Churchill has come to the U.S. for talks with FDR. I know this will spell trouble for Germany. Churchill is able to convince FDR of the seriousness of the situation in Europe.

August 12, 1941

In France, Marshall Petain, who leads the Vichy government, has pledged full support of the Nazis.

August 13, 1941

Wehrmacht: The Red Army is in full retreat and being pursued by the Wehrmacht.

August 20, 1941

The latest bulletin from the high command brags about the success of carrying out Hitler's policies in Poland regarding rounding up Jews for transit to the death camps. The Army has organized the Polish population to tum in and murder Jews, especially whenever Jews have asked them for help. Thousands of Poles are volunteering to help. The Army has publicized that anyone helping a Jew escape will be killed by the Nazis. This "hunting" mechanism is made up of informers, police and firemen. The giant web has made it almost impossible for anyone to escape. Sometimes villagers have surrounded an entire village to hunt for Jews and win "prizes offered by the Army for captured Jews, along with taking away the possessions they steal from Jews who are literally tom from their homes. Then the hunters steal the homes and businesses of the people they have betrayed.

I am horrified by this subhuman behavior of the German people and can say nothing or my position in the rocket lab will be threatened. As the German Army moves further east, I fear that this mechanism will be employed many times over. Some German officers are even talking about a scorched earth policy for the Ukraine and Russia.

August 23, 1941

German armies reached the outskirts of Leningrad. This is an exceptional military event. It appears that the Soviet Union could be on the verge of collapse. Army strategy is to create a siege of Leningrad and hope for Russia to surrender. I know this is a losing game because our supply lines are a long distance away.

August 28, 1941

SS Report: The Czech resistance perpetrated a plot to assassinate Reinhard Heydrich. He is a mastermind in the program to kill all Jews in Europe. In reprisals, the Nazis have killed 15,000 Czechs and destroyed many small towns.

September 3, 1941

Auschwitz reports using Zyklon-B gas on Russian prisoners.

September 6, 1941

An order is issued that all Jews in Germany and occupied countries must wear a yellow star of David. In Vilna Poland, Jews are confined to the ghetto. The SS brags that the entire Jewish community of Lida, Lithuania has been exterminated. The SS says they will duplicate this in every Lithuanian community.

September 12, 1941

Memo from Nazi Party agents in USA.

“Hitler’s investment in Nazi activities in the U.S. for many years has been successful. In addition to German Bunds in major U.S. cities, the Nazis have financed anti-Semitic propaganda and promoted isolationism. We know that if the U.S. gets into the war, its vast resources will save Britain and the Soviet Union. Nazi propaganda is promoting the concept that the war is already won by Germany, so why bother to get involved?

“The Nazis best known advocate in the U.S. is Charles Lindbergh, who made a major radio speech last night in Des Moines, Iowa. Lindbergh blamed the Jews for the war in Europe in an attempt to deter the U.S. from entering the war. Roosevelt is furious at Lindbergh and it appears that the U.S. press will strongly support Roosevelt. The Nazi Party has paid vast sums to Lindbergh by transferring money from Schroeder Bank, NY branch, to Lindbergh’s private accounts at Chase Manhattan and United Swiss Bank.

“Nazi propaganda and espionage agents have also been working with certain members of the U.S. Congress who are anti-Semites and isolationists. If this is revealed, we believe those Congressmen will not be re-elected. Some German funds have gone to the America First Committee, which has provided Lindbergh with a platform.

“End of report”

September 10, 1941

A published report from the front in Lithuania: “After the occupation of Kovno, the SS has armed and unleashed Lithuanian civilian collaborators to invade Jewish homes and murder men, women, and children. This mass extermination of Jews includes making them dig their own graves and shooting them in large groups. This is happening in broad daylight in front of thousands of witnesses. In some cases, the Jews are being tortured before being murdered.” “This operation has involved sheer barbarity, torture, rape, looting, and destruction.”

September 17, 1941

Wehrmacht: German tank corps have surrounded Kiev Ukraine and expect to conquer Kiev within a few days. Simultaneously the SS has announced plans to kill the Jews of Kiev.

September 18, 1941

Nazi persecution knows no bounds. Many members of my family had been Christians for generations, so the Nuremberg anti-Semitic laws did not impact them a lot. However, the Wach branch was victimized by the Nazis and Lili Mendelssohn Wach was sent to Theresienstadt.

Many family members were stripped of university posts and deprived of honors and livelihood. This naturally has forced some to emigrate. For example, Albrecht Mendelssohn Bartholdy, a leading authority on international jurisprudence, was dismissed as a professor and in 1933, went to England to lecture at Oxford, and to the U.S. to lecture at Harvard. Other descendants of Lili Mendelssohn Wach were distinguished scholars who also emigrated.

The family history is a bit confusing since many cousins married cousins and they often repeated first names from prior generations. Luckily most family members had left Germany when the Nazis came to power and they now reside in England, Switzerland, and the U.S. Almost all had distinguished careers in their fields of music, banking, acting, and business. My father, Robert, had control of the Mendelssohn bank so I was raised in a grand fashion and was able to pursue the scientific studies which have made me indispensable to the Nazis and which have saved my life, and that of my wife and child.

Von Braun has assured me that my skills in rocket guidance are so critical to the Nazis that I need not worry about being harassed or persecute by them.

September 19, 1941

My older sister Elenora was born in 1900 and became an accomplished actress. She left Germany early when Hitler came to power and became a Broadway actress in the U.S. I was much younger and in the midst of my studies, so elected to stay on after being recruited by Von Braun.

The famous Mendelssohn bank was liquidated in 1938 and the only thing that survived is Felix's music; and that too has been banned by the Nazis.

September 22, 1941

Reports from the Eastern Front are of unspeakable brutality, with entire villages being slaughtered by German troops. This is a Russo-German struggle of massive proportions. The German leadership has gone mad and does not realize that if the tide should tum this brutality will beget revenge. The SS has issued many reports that Jews in some villages were herded into a basement, the doors locked and car exhaust pumped in to kill them.

September 30, 1941

SS Bulletin: The SS is bragging about killing 8,400 Jews in one day at Babi Yar Ravine in Kiev. The bulletin even highlights burying thousands alive. I cannot understand how German soldiers who are ordinary people can follow orders to inflict pain and suffering on others.

October 1, 1941

Hitler has captured Kiev and encircled Leningrad and is now extending mass deportations to all of European Jewry, with the concentration camps in the east as their destination.

October 1, 1941

Announcement: A concentration camp is being built at Birkenau.

October 10, 1941

Our lab leadership has been briefed by the Army that a scientific group in England had done advanced research on a nuclear bomb. A German scientist who now lives in England, Frederick Lindemann, is in charge of the nuclear research. He is aided by Jewish scientists who have fled Nazi Germany, including Otto Frisch. As recently as 1938, nuclear fission had been noted. The British have taken their nuclear findings to the U.S. and have succeeded in jump-starting a U.S. program at a remote desert town in New Mexico.

October 10, 1941

Foreign Ministry Internal Paper. Our V-2 project and the V-1 rocket program will need vast amounts of petroleum-based fuels for testing and we hope eventual flights. This is in competition with the Army and Air Force fuel consumption, since they also have vast fuel requirements. We have had access to an internal foreign ministry document that outlines how cleverly Nazi Germany has acquired oil, both natural and synthetic.

The documentation commences in the 1930s. John Foster Dulles of the U.S. law firm Sullivan and Cromwell represented German companies such a LG. Farben. Dulles and S&C also had major U.S. oil companies as clients. He had Farben buy major shares of Texaco, Standard of California and Standard of New Jersey. Moreover, Dulles and his brother Allen connected the Rockefellers of Chase Manhattan Bank and Standard Oil with the German Schroeder Bank. The Rockefellers controlled Standard of New Jersey oil company. The diabolical concept is based on huge fortunes and huge legal fees and gives the German clients access to oil production and allows them to copy the U.S. process secrets for synthetic fuels.

U.S. capital was "loaned" to German companies, many of whom prospered while the U.S. was in a deep depression. Much of the capital that was badly needed in the U.S. came from S&C clients. All of this was happening as Germany was confiscating Jewish companies, banks and private wealth. The records show that the Dulles brothers were making contributions to the Nazi party. They also represented Swiss banks that were used for secret transfer of funds. As rewards, Farben had JFD on its board and Allen sat on the Schroeder Bank board. Money laundering was easy.

Texaco Oil has long-standing connections with Franco of Spain. Texaco and the Rockefeller oil companies formed Caltex oil, which controls the Saudi Oil company, Aramco. The Saudis hate Jews and are happy to sell oil to us and deliver it by way of Spain and Italy. That way the Rockefellers can secretly do business with our Nazi party: LG. Farben owned major interests in Standard Oil and the Dulles law firm received massive fees even though Germany has been on an aggressive campaign of terror in Europe and North Africa. If the U.S. enters the war against Germany, our foreign ministry believes that the Dulles' treasonous activities may be exposed and must cease. However, the Saudi oil will not continue flowing to Germany and the Ministry believes that Germany will seize the oil fields of Romania. Thereby Germany will have unlimited supplies well into the future. What the Saudis do not realize is that if Germany is successful in North Africa, then the Nazis will also occupy Saudi Arabia and steal the Saudi oil rather than pay for it with stolen gold.

October 12, 1941
SS Bulletin: In Czechoslovakia, Germany has established a ghetto at Theresienstadt. It will assemble huge numbers of Jews for transport to death camps.

October 15, 1941
Killing of Jews is accelerating throughout Eastern Europe and German Jews are being transported to camps. Killing by the thousands is "old news."

October 17, 1941
Wehrmacht: German and Romanian troops have captured the Soviet city of Odessa.

October 19, 1941
A U-boat has torpedoed a U.S. destroyer. The U.S. is not in the war, so I sense this is a move that Germany will regret.

October 20, 1941
Wehrmacht: Advancing and occupying troops are massacring Jews throughout the USSR. Odessa, Crow, Rovno, Riga, Vilna.

October 22, 1941
Heinrich Himmler has publicized his drawings for the Auschwitz Concentration Camp including expansion for Birkenau. The plans have been co-authored by Hans Kammler of the SS Building Department and Auschwitz commander Rudolph Hess. They are boasting that this will be the largest extermination center of European Jewry.

October 23, 1941
SS: The Romanian Nazis have brutalized tens of thousands of Odessa's Jews, including burning thousands alive. This animal behavior has nothing to do with our war effort. Madness.

October 28, 1941

SS: "We have massacred 34,000 Jews in Kiev."

October 30, 1941

The Wehrmacht has pushed East into Russia with 185 Divisions and holds territory that is 500 miles deep and 100 miles wide. Germany now controls Poland, Estonia, Latvia, Lithuania, and much of Ukraine. In this vast area millions of Jews have been caught and face extermination as "the enemy." The SS is leading the killing aided by Ukraine fascists and other anti-Semitic groups from each country. I again must question why the diversion of Army resources to kill innocents.

October 30, 1941

Report from Kovno, Lithuania. A Lithuanian police battalion has exterminated about 10,000 Kovno Jews. The German plan is to move these collaborators to help them murder Jews in places such as Belarus, Russia.

November 2, 1941

Wehrmacht: Occupy Rothe on the road to Russia.

November 4, 1941

Luftwaffe Report: Germany continues to pound London with nightly bombings, yet the British seem to be more and more resolute in their defiance of Hitler. Germany's chance for successful invasion of Britain seems slim. We read of Churchill's leadership in explaining why resistance to Nazism is a key to Britain's very existence; even though Hitler's armies have swept through Europe. His eloquent speeches are rallying the British people to be courageous.

November 7, 1941

Britain is retaliating against German air attacks by bombing of Berlin.

November 10, 1941

Report from the Soviet front: German Army Tanks Corps have reached the outskirts of Moscow. German bombers have pounded Moscow day and night and the city is in flames. Two years earlier Stalin had made a pact with Hitler that gave Hitler political and moral support and huge amounts of raw materials. Stalin thought this would prolong a western war, which in fact ended quickly and Hitler turned his attention towards Moscow.

For the first time there is an organized defense, including civilians. Masses of Russians are fleeing fast from Moscow in panic. A similar situation exists near Leningrad, where the German Army has taken town after town.

In my opinion, Hitler has made very serious military mistakes by attacking a huge country and psychological mistakes by ruthlessly exploiting and terrorizing the Russians. Himmler of the SS only sees this as a source of slave labor and was content to starve the Soviet population. This suffering and death will cause resistance by the Russian Army and civilians. The German lines of supply by rail are very long and vulnerable to being sabotaged by resistance partisans.

November 12, 1941

The Army has broadcast its Muslim strategy. The Balkan Muslims were encouraged to participate in violence against Jews. Heinrich Himmler is a vocal advocate of the use of Islam in this war. His calls for Jewish extermination motivated Arab nationalists in the Middle East to accelerate their anti-Semitism. The Grand Mufti of Jerusalem, Amin Al-Husseini has moved to Berlin to collaborate with Nazi propagandists.

Al-Husseini is founder of the Muslim Brotherhood and has incited Muslims to riot and kill Jews by the hundreds. Therefore, he is a perfect ally with Hitler for the destruction of the Jews.

November 17, 1941

Financing the German war is immensely expensive, so what seems obvious is Hitler's minions have perfected methods to rob their enemies. Started in Germany by confiscating Jewish property business and banks, now Hitler is spreading this robbery to all of Europe and to the Soviet Union.

November 22, 1941

Navy: The British Cruiser Devonshire has sunk Germany's Cruiser Atlantis. The British Navy is an impediment for the invasion of Britain.

November 25, 1941

Hitler has issued a decree that the Jews of the Netherlands are stateless. This ploy is to trap Jews from having a passport to leave.

November 28, 1941

Wehrmacht: USSR has begun a winter offensive and it is advisable for German troops to fall back and regroup.

November 30, 1941

Navy: Germany continues to lose numerous U-boats and it is getting more difficult to assemble front end U-boat crews.

December 8, 1941

Berlin dispatch: Yesterday Japan attacked the U.S. Naval Fleet at Pearl Harbor Hawaii, inflicting heavy loss of ships and lives. The U.S. has declared war on Japan. Germany immediately declared war on the U.S. Since the U.S. has been helping Britain and preparing for war for more than a year, these declarations of war are not a surprise.

The U.S. Navy was totally surprised at Pearl Harbor. There was a lack of naval intelligence, no spies in Japan to witness an armada departing and no U.S. naval spotter ships in the Pacific.

Worse than that, the Pearl Harbor commander had grouped all the ships together as sitting duck targets.

I have often emphasized that history can be an indicator of human and/ or national thinking. The U.S. Navy admirals should have remembered that in 1903 during the Russian-Japanese war, the Japanese had been preparing a strong Navy for years and immediately went for the Russian fleet, destroyed it, and then controlled them and won the war. They have employed the same naval build up and early destruction of the U.S. Navy as a World War II strategy. In 1903-1905 Russia had very long lines of supply and could not recover the loss of its navy. The Japanese have miscalculated since the U.S. aircraft carriers are mainly at sea and the U.S. has enormous production capacity to supply a war machine.

The effect of all of this on the Rocket Center will be night and day pressure to produce accurately guided missiles to deliver explosives to the battlefield and across the English Channel.

December 8, 1941

The U.S. declares war on Japan. This means the U.S. will be at war with Germany.

December 11, 1941

Hitler declared war on the United States.

December 11, 1941

Germany has declared war on the U.S. I know that the mighty production facilities of the U.S. and potential for large armies will spell trouble for Germany. Germany has fronts on East and West Germany, USSR, Africa, and now must fight the U.S. This is not sustainable. It seems that Hitler has saved an unquestionably beleaguered Britain by invading Russia and declaring war on the U.S.; two arrogant and dumb decisions.

December 11, 1941

Command Bulletin: At Rocket Research we are ordered to use the Enigma code, even though our spies in Britain told us that Britain is making a secret effort to break the code. Even if they are successful the code has so many variations that it will be impossible for Britain to have full access to our plans or to diminish Germany's great military strength. What is not being reported in the official bulletins are the rumors that our U-boat movements are being detected and our losses are mounting. This could mean that Britain has broken our code. If my involvement in smuggling code patters to the British is ever discovered, it will mean instant execution. It is the least that I can do to help stop this runaway monster.

December 11, 1941

Insiders of the Party have told our lab that the leader of the Mid-East Muslims, the Mufti of Jerusalem, spent a great deal of time with Hitler last month. The Mufti is Hajj Amin al-Husseini. Supposedly they discussed the Mufti's commitment to eliminate Jews, met with Heinrich Himmler, and urged Hitler to make mass murder an official policy of Germany. Hitler revealed that a conference at Wannsee is planned for early 1942 to do exactly that. Why German generals would divert men and material to persecuting a defenseless people is beyond comprehension.

But I suppose as "good German soldiers" they will carry out Hitler's demands. I also heard that the Mufti has pledged to raise three Muslim divisions in the Balkans to fight alongside the Germans. This means drawing Bosnia and Albania into the German sphere of influence.

December 11, 1941

We have been working on the V-2 rocket and its liquid fuel rocket engines at the Army Research Center in Peenemünde and possess the technology to move forward. It has taken years to reach this stage and has been very expensive. Original tests were not stable but now we can produce the engine, supersonic aerodynamics, gyroscopic guidance and control rudders. I have purposely delayed guidance solutions for years but can no longer do so and avoid suspicion. Hitler has complained that this is simply a very long-range artillery shell and an absurd cost.

Confidentially, I think he is right but it is fine with me if the Wehrmacht wants to experiment and sap resources that might have been put to more effective use.

December 11, 1941

Orders from Berlin. Wehrmacht HQ: Hitler has ordered a halt on the assault on Moscow. There is a concern for severe cold weather conditions. Also, the High Command is meeting to assess the serious effect of the U.S. entering the war and potential U.S. supplies and military equipment to save Russia. It is determined that a Russian counterattack is of little concern due to the heavy casualties Germany has inflicted on them.

Personal: The German High Command is, off the record, very concerned that Germany has lost the war due to the diversion of troops and resources, i.e., Hitler's obsession to kill Jews and Russian Communists. He committed vast divisions of men to make a "quick killing." This has not gone as swiftly as expected and is tying up untold troops, weaponry and supplies. Yes, he has slaughtered millions along the way, but in relation to Germany's manpower and resources, the Eastern Front invasion was unwise. German lines of supply are very stretched and supply trains are being derailed by Partisan sabotage.

December 12, 1941

Hitler Bulletin to German Forces in France: Search house to house to find Jews in hiding.

December 15, 1941

Report from the Eastern Front: Hitler has failed to achieve the pivotal objective of seizing Moscow before severe Russian winter sets in. German generals have catastrophically underrated Russian resistance. They have also overrated the German economy's ability to sustain a long campaign in the vast territory of the Soviet Union. The Russians have had a flood of reserves to replace the dead and wounded and have shown skill in counter attacking. As a student of history, I can only think of other armies in the past years that have been devastated by Russian winters and vast distances traveled for supplies and support. German leadership is intoxicated with their own sense of invincibility and leading Germany to a rapid disaster.

December 19, 1941

Wehrmacht: Hitler is upset by Russian counter attacks and losses in Africa and has taken command of the Wehrmacht.

December 20, 1941

Wehrmacht: Russian counter-offensives resulted in numerous local engagements that were stopped by Wehrmacht counterattacks. The SS is still 35 miles from Moscow, but the Russian Army has intensified pressure and panic is starting to occur on our front lines and even by some commanders.

December 23, 1941

Wehrmacht: Hitler has assumed control over the Eastern Command and has issued a halt order to stand fast at "all costs." He has ordered large supplies of the addictive stimulant drug Pervirtin to be distributed to the troops so that they can fight without sleep and adequate food.

General Walter Model is tasked with stabilizing the front and inflicting major losses on the enemy.

December 23, 1941

SS Bulletin: Reports of an SS massacre in Vilna and bragging about 32,000 dead. Those body count entries in my diary are done with the intent that one day they will be read and remembered as a witness against the Nazis and a message to future generations.

December 24, 1941

Lithuania plays an important role in European Jewish history. From the 14th through the mid- 20th centuries, Lithuania was a hub of Jewish life. During the Middle Ages many Christians blamed Jews for the Bubonic Plague and killed their Jewish neighbors. Survivors fled east and thrived. By the mid-1700s Lithuania had the world's largest Jewish community with Vilna at its center. Jews dominated the economy, which provoked Catholic Lithuanian ultra-nationalists with a call to break from the supposed stronghold of the Jewish minority. In 1939 when Hitler and Stalin divided Eastern Europe, Stalin absorbed Lithuania and Jews suffered under Soviet occupation, including thousands deported to Siberia. Ironically, the Lithuanians blamed Jews for the Soviet occupation.

In June 1941, Hitler attacked the Soviet Union, took the Baltics in a few weeks, and the Christian majority welcomed the Germans as liberators. Subsequently, thousands of Jews were being murdered with the zealous collaboration of local Lithuanians, many of whom serve as volunteer triggermen. I ask "Why?" Why are local armed Christians collaborating with the Nazis to kill unarmed Jews? Why are Lithuanians shooting Jews? Why are they forming vigilante killing squads as volunteer executioners?

1942

January 4, 1942

SS Bulletin to Werner: "United States has declared war against Germany following the Japanese attack on Pearl Harbor, December 7, 1941. Our German foreign service has long established moles and sympathizers in the U.S. State Department and in what they will call the newly formed O.S.S., the Office of Strategic Services. O.S.S. is an intelligence, spying and propaganda agency. Therefore, we believe that the U.S. will first be preoccupied with Japan. We will not stop our conquest of Europe and with the U.S. officials either anti-Semitic or complacent, we will have little opposition to our Nazi war on the Jew."

"For example, there are two prominent U.S. attorneys who have had numerous German industrialist clients and negotiated major German-U.S. industrial transactions. These are the Dulles brothers, John Foster and Allen. John is influential in Washington D. C. at the highest State Department levels and Allen is high up in the O.S.S. Both have kept and protected their German clients.

"In the State Department we have Breckenridge Long, a known anti-Semite. We can count on him to block Jewish refugees seeking asylum in the U.S. With nowhere to go they are easy prey for our extermination plans. We are told there are others who are outright fascists." "Our mole in the U.S. State Department tells us about numerous other important U.S. officials who will give lip service to humanitarian needs, but block a real effort to help. All one has to do is know that Jews are excluded from certain professions in the U.S. and from certain hotels, clubs, and organizations to realize that our radical purity plans will go unopposed."

While I am always grateful that Werner has given me access to the confidential bulletins, I seriously disagree that the U.S. preoccupation with Japan will prevent a focus on Europe. The U.S. has vast resources and manufacturing capacity and expertise, so that the U.S. will soon be producing war equipment at an unheard of rate. For example, a resupply of Russia from protected Alaskan Waters will give the Soviets an opportunity to push Germany out of Eastern Europe.

January 6, 1942

Adolf Eichmann's bureau has issued bulletins from time to time describing his monstrous "final solution of the Jewish problem." These bulletins are boasting of mass killings of innocent people. Working with Eichmann is General Reinhard Heydrich.

One of these bulletins received recently by our lab and distributed tells about Kovno, Lithuania. The German Army initially occupied Kovno in June 1941 and immediately began killing Jews and (with the help of Lithuanians) created a ghetto where they hoarded thousands of Jews into very limited space. The Wehrmacht bulldozers created fifteen huge pits and then proceeded to transport over time many thousands of Jews to these pits and murder them. The bulletin mentions that Christian Lithuanians helped the Army and the Gestapo.

I fail to understand how killing innocents and diverting troops and equipment can help the German war effort which is now fighting in Western Europe, Eastern Europe, and Russia. Supply lines are already stretched and yet Eichmann must rush his program of mass murder.

January 8, 1942

Naval Report-Adm.: Karl Donitz has amassed an extensive fleet of underwater vessels-U? boats. He claims he can sink American supply ships faster than they can be built. His theory is to sink ships carrying food and arms from the U.S. so as to starve Britain into submission.

Donitz's report refers to the German Navy's earlier success sinking the HMS Royal Oak stationed at Scotland's' Scapa Flow naval base.

What Donitz does not say is that there have been considerable U-boat losses and Germany may not be able to divert resources to rebuild the U-boat fleet. It seems apparent to me that a lack of trained U-boat personnel will eventually prove Donitz to be recklessly over optimistic.

January 10, 1942
The Wehrmacht and SS report German tanks and supplies have reached North Africa for a campaign there. I cannot understand how we have the resources for a Russian front, an Eastern front, a Western front, and occupation. It is obvious that Hitler's ambitions exceed German resources, even as we steal our way across Europe. However, General Rommel in Africa is brilliant and may make some very rapid advances.

January 14, 1942
Since we are now at war with the U.S., our many U-boats are going after U.S. East Coast shipping.

January 16, 1942
SS reports they have trapped 160,000 Jewish people in the Lodz Ghetto. They plan to murder them at Chelmno and Auschwitz.

January 18, 1942
Hitler has issued a manifest that will aid our rocket research and manufacturing. "Scientists have a special purpose within the racial community to make weapons and better guns to improve the strength of the races. All the better to dominate the weak."

January 21, 1942
Yesterday at Wannsee, a conference was held where General Heydrich announced the "final solution" (of the Jewish problem). Hitler is "intoxicated" by his quick victories over the USSR and now talks of a "final solution" (of the "Jewish problem"). Heydrich talks of "resettlement," which we all know means murder in death camps, such as Auschwitz and Treblinka.

Implementation is scheduled to start in the spring. This will require the participation of countless Germans in all walks of life, and the citizens of many countries. It is a certainty that Russian and British spies using German born agents have infiltrated the SS. If they were not at Wannsee they will surely soon learn of this extermination plan and the Allies must try to stop this mass murder.

January 22, 1942

Germany's top rocket scientists have been assigned to Peenemünde to help the V-2 to become functional. Ernst Steinhoft is a co-director of Guidance and Control here at the Rocket Research Center. We work closely together and, so far, he has not realized the intentional error I have programmed into the V-2. Ernst is also instrumental in designing launch platforms. Ernst and I have had technical assistance from Hermann Steuding and Helmut Hozler.

January 23, 1942

Germany is aware that the Soviet Union has penetrated Germany's Abwehr military intelligence service. This concerns me since the V-2 work must remain secret. However, German use of captured Russian labor makes Russian spying much easier. Hitler isn't worried about the British M16, since they seem very inept.

January 26, 1942

German spies in Britain report U.S. troops are arriving.

January 29, 1942

German troops in North Africa have taken Benghazi, Libya.

January 31, 1942

The U.S. and Canada are pursuing our U-boats and sixty-two have been sunk this month.

February 2, 1942

Wehrmacht: Plans to invade England have been cancelled.

February 3, 1942

War Production Report: Albert Speer is known as Hitler's closest companion and has just been put in charge of war production. Tanks, planes, and even our V-2 program. He has come to Peenemünde to check on our V-2 progress and told us he plans to use slave labor from the concentration camps to operate his factories 24-hours a day.

February 5, 1942

Wehrmacht: A retreat from Moscow is imminent. Temperatures are dropping to minus 30 Celsius, our equipment is frozen and the Russians are coming in waves. Orders have been given to destroy everything in the path of retreat to deny our pursuers shelter.

February 8, 1942

Wehrmacht report from Russia: This past winter has been defense since Russians have fought back fiercely and Russia has designed and produced a massive tank. Despite heavy losses, the Wehrmacht has held and is now ready for a new offensive to the south and east in an effort to seize Russian oil fields. Reaching the Caspian Sea could block Lend-Lease shipments from the U.S.

February 9, 1942

Heinrich Himmler has insisted that all scientists at research units that are dependent on Army funding be indoctrinated with the history and his master plans for concentration camps. We have no choice but to voice support for this inhumane and twisted system of mass persecution.

We know that early on (1933-34) Himmler used the Dachau camp to intimidate opponents and to consolidate Nazi power. Communists and Socialists were sent to Dachau since they might challenge Hitler. Himmler advocated using camps to "improve the German race," so people he labeled as unfit for society were interned in camps. The expanded camp system now includes Sachsenhausen, Buchenwald, Flossenbiirg, Mauthausen, Ravensbruck and many others that are spread throughout Europe.

The Nazis have drastically altered the lives of German Jews. First by intimidation to get them to leave Germany. As I have maintained in other diary entries, I think this was a way for Hitler to steal the hard-earned assets of German Jews in order to finance his mad scheme of world domination. Following the invasion of Poland in September 1939, the camps were expanded to eventually include the very large Polish Jewish population and hundreds of thousands of non? Jewish Poles. Jews were forced into ghettos so that their wealth could be stolen and they could be controlled in one place for "efficient" transport to the camps. Camp inmates have been murdered, worked to death, and kept in appalling conditions.

Soon after the invasion of Poland, Auschwitz was constructed to carry out Himmler's warped plans and certainly as a tool to intimidate the Polish citizens. Last year when Hitler stupidly invaded the Soviet Union in July of 1941, he instituted a policy of rounding up and killing every Jew in Soviet territory; or sending them to Auschwitz for extermination. As of this diary entry, we know that German troops have made extensive advances into Soviet territory and are sending huge numbers of captured Soviet troops to Auschwitz for certain death. Also, since there have been so many Soviet prisoners, we have learned that mass starvation has been practiced by the German Army.

Himmler is in a position of power and has gone mad. He controls the police, influences the Army's allocation of troops and resources, controls the camps and sets racial policies. He has unleashed a war of extermination. If the tide of war turns, then Germany will be in deep trouble, possibly even destroyed, as the persecuted will surely come after the persecutors and destroy Germany.

February 20, 1942

The SS has assigned a person to "guard" me since I am supposed to be irreplaceable for the V-2 program. Actually, I believe that he shadows me so that I do not defect and so that there is someone who reports in writing to von Braun and Himmler's office on my every move and every conversation.

I have gotten to know this person very well and he speaks perfect, academic German. In fact, I became very suspicious of him. There has been an occasional slip by me, mentioning my distaste for many of the Nazi policies and my extreme anger at the "party" for taking my wife and child into what they call protective custody. Using my wife and child as leverage keeps me working night and day on various guidance programs out of fear for what they will do to my family. I will not write my guard's name here and just call him X. He sensed my anger and knew that he could speak confidentially with me.

For one of my experiments, I was missing a precisely machined part that is designed and made at what had been the Ferrari factory near Milan, Italy. It required a train trip to Milan, accompanied by X so I can instruct the machinist making the part. During that trip, X revealed that he is actually a British agent of German descent from Ml6 who has worked his way into the SS Guard in order to get my help with certain scientific matters and to try to get the secret codes that the German military uses in the Enigma coding machine. I was targeted as a prospect due to my knowledge and precisely because the Nazis had taken my family into protective custody.

When we arrived in Milan, X left the train station to make contact with his "associates" and I went to our hotel. Soon thereafter he arrived at the hotel with an old walrus skin German suit case. He explained that in order to communicate with Ml 6 headquarters I was to take the suitcase back to Peenemünde and that inside was a Special Forces, Type MKl 1 radio that was to be concealed under the clothes in my suitcase. It could transmit around 800 km so that I can discuss codes with London. This transmitter is designed so that it can even be hidden under water. Should this radio be found, it would be certain death for me and my family. However, it presents the opportunity to make a major contribution to the effort to stop Hitler from his mass murders and maybe save Germany from total bombing destruction. X and I discussed that within a year von Braun expects the V-2 to be operational and to start raiding London. I told X that with my miscalculations on guidance gyroscopes and rudder designs, that I will try to delay that massive launching until 1944; at which time, it would be too late to help the German efforts. X explained that the MI6 plan was to discreetly radio British target coordinates that will be close to prime targets, but removed from heavy population centers. This could render the entire V-2 programs worthless, even though some innocent lives would be lost.

Britain has a massive research effort at Benchley trying to break the German codes and to understand the Enigma machine. I will very discreetly feed them the information they need to break this code and to understand the complexity of the code machine. It must be gradual and in "innocent" wording so that if someone somehow listens to even a few transmitted words, he or she will not be suspicious.

February 27, 1942

We have had bulletins that French citizens are participating in the round up of French Jews in collaboration with Nazis to transport to camps and for slave labor in Germany.

March 3, 1942

Our General Dombenger has briefed us that he now has an ally in Albert Speer, the new Minister of Munitions and War Production. Speer is convinced that Rockets production will win the war. However, Hitler is occupied with the war in Russia and commanding his armies. Speer has stated that the German economy cannot sustain a prolonged war, so he must produce weapons needed right now and not experimental rockets.

March 7, 1942

SS Abwehr: Abwehr has captured an underground radio operator in The Hague. The plan is to force him to transmit back to London with false information. This will encourage the British to parachute agents who can be seized on landing and then interrogated. This has the potential of a big win over the British Ml 6.

March 12, 1942

SS deportation trains are leaving Paris to bring French Jews to Auschwitz camp.

March 19, 1942

One of our experimental rockets has exploded!

March 20, 1942

The British air raid on Lubeck has caused Hitler to seek revenge and he now wants us to immediately produce 3,000 V-2 rockets a month "or else."

March 20, 1942

Von Braun and Dornberger have feverishly tried to fire a V-2, but it exploded. Hitler now wants 5,000 a month to be built since he is furious about British air raids.

March 20, 1942

SS: Thousands of Polish Jews from various cities are being transported to camps such as Belzec. The mass murder by the Einsatzgruppen has not gone fast enough and Hitler will now use gas chambers.

March 22, 1942

The concentration camps have become hellish and have followed a pattern of unspeakable atrocities. Hitler uses the excuse of "social cleansing" of Germany. The reality is that the camps are an integral component for stealing Jewish wealth. The Jewish population is unarmed and easy picking for the heavily armed Nazi regime. Hitler has made a relentless assault on Jews' economic position, forcing them out of business and professional life. I have often thought about camps started when Hitler came to power, where they are today and what they became when Germany went to war. The victims of the camps, in addition to Jews, were Communists, criminals, homosexuals and perhaps anyone who decided to criticize the Nazis.

As I have written before, the first camp was a factory outside Dachau, near Munich. During 1933 Hitler came to power and created makeshift camps all over Germany to incarcerate political opponents who were beaten and tortured and murdered. Hitler then used the camps for alcoholics, vagrants, and "social deviants." By 1939 there were six such camps: Ravensbruck, Sachsenhausen, Dachau, Flossenbirg, Buchenwald, and Mauthausen. As war progressed, they became brutal centers of forced labor in conjunction with industrial sub camps.

These spread all over Germany and Austria. The conditions in the camps are so bad that prisoners are exterminated through labor. Auschwitz provides a labor force and is an extermination factory where hundreds of thousands of Jews are being murdered as they are brought from all over Europe. In camps where inmates are not murdered the conditions are so horrible that survival rates are very low. I have personally witnessed some of the camps.

April 4, 1942

Personal: My Resistance sources advise me that there is a remote, mountainous area called Vivarais-Lignon that has opened its doors to fleeing Jews. The residents of this region have a many centuries long history of sheltering strangers. It is tragic that the rest of Europe does not follow this humanitarian tradition to protect the victims of persecution.

However, in Vichy France things have gotten much worse for Jews. Vichy anti-Semitism goes back to the Church teaching that the Jews killed Christ. A myth created in the early days of Christendom to persuade the people to become Christian and hate Jews. There are also French fears of Jews taking their jobs and the hatred French nationalists had for Leon Blum, the first Jewish Prime Minister.

Vichy anti-Semitic laws and total co-operation with the Nazis added to the Vichy discrimination and to the theft of Jewish property and businesses. I am told Vichy France is determined to round up its 80,000 Jews and do the "dirty work" for the Germans.

April 5, 1942

The secrecy of the Rocket program is at risk due to so many foreign workers on the island of Usedom; many of whom may be reporting what they see and hear to British spies.

April 7, 1942

Navy report: The Japanese front. Germany's Japanese ally has been occupying the Philippines, Thailand, Singapore, the Dutch East Indies, Wake Island, the Gilberts, and Guam; and has been inflicting many losses on the U.S. The Japanese Navy has set sights on Northern Australia.

April 9, 1942

Personal thoughts: Germany is an educated and cultured nation but is pursuing a barbarous and genocidal war. Why?? Most Nazis and neo-Nazis support Hitler even when it is clear that we are over extended on many fronts (West Europe, East Europe, North Africa, plus resources for our V-1 and V-2 rocket program). There is no way we can match the production of the U.S. and British armies. With Russia being supplied by the U.S. with arms, tanks, and food, it is only a matter of time before Stalin will counter attack in force on all Eastern fronts. We have descended into blind barbarism.

April 11, 1942

The Fieseler aircraft factory in Kassel has built the fuselage of a "bomb." On it was mounted a jet engine based on extensive research, supervised by engineer Robert Lusser.

April 19, 1942

Radio Berlin: Yesterday the U.S. bombed Tokyo in a surprise raid of B25 bombers that had been launched from a carrier ship. I believe this may panic Japan since it is only four months after Japan's attack on Pearl Harbor. It also is a signal that Hitler may have made a mistake to declare war on the U.S.

April 23, 1942

The SS brags that outside of Uman, Ukraine they have murdered 1,000 Jewish children.

May 4, 1942

Luftwaffe: Continued bombing of Britain, with little success in breaking Britain's resolve.

May 8, 1942

Wehrmacht: An offense has been opened in the Crimea; yet another front. Along with the offensive, thousands of Jews are being rounded up.

May 9, 1942

Navy Bulletin news reports: There was a major naval battle in the Pacific for the past five days that engaged U.S. and Australia against Japan in the Coral Sea. The Japanese planned an invasion of New Guinea but were intercepted by a U.S. Carrier Task Force that used planes as spotters for heavy guns. Both sides suffered heavy losses, but Japan disengaged and recalled their New Guinea invasion.

Naval reports claim that this battle of Coral Sea could be a turning point for our Japanese ally that points to the U.S. having broken Japan's naval code and ambushed a formidable Japanese fleet. The U.S. has decisively stopped Japan's offensive just a few months after the Pearl Harbor attack.

May 11, 1942

Albert Speer, Hitler's architect, is an early member of the Nazi Party and has grandiose plans for major structures. He has evicted Jews from their properties to free real estate for his projects.

To satisfy his need for large amounts of stone, he has sent Jews to quarries to work until they drop. When confronted about this cruelty, Speer said "Jews made bricks while in Egyptian captivity."

May 13, 1942

Naval Report: Nazi U-boats are being sent across the Atlantic in large numbers to attack U.S. shipping up and down the East Coast of the U.S. Hundreds of U.S. ships are being sunk. The U.S. is foolishly allowing the lighting of cities at night, which gives our subs backlighting for targets.

May 14, 1942

Report from the Eastern Front, Wehrmacht: Quick German victories backed by the Luftwaffe and artillery have taken Sebastopol on the Black Sea. The plan is to continue east and take Stalingrad. That can stop U.S. materials from entering Russia from Iran, the Caspian Sea, and seize more oil fields.

May 15, 1942

H.C. Bulletin: Nazi planners have come to the conclusion that Americans and the British are indifferent to the fate of Jews. There has been evidence of this since the 1930s and German concentration camps have increased in number and brutality. The H.C. believes it can do as they please.

May 16, 1942
Wehrmacht: A siege of Leningrad has been in progress for some time and many thousands of Russians are dying of starvation.

May 18, 1942
Cairo to Wehrmacht: The German consulate in Cairo reports that the British Army has numerous deficiencies in supply and strategy and that General Rommel can beat them. I believe this will give Hitler a misguided motive of continuing to send resources to the Middle East, just as they are critically needed on the Eastern Front. This miscalculation may weaken the Wehrmacht on both fronts, especially as the U.S. now starts supplying Russia and plans to send troops to North Africa.

May 20, 1942
Reports from the Eastern Front tell about Germans systematically going from one Polish town to another following the order to get rid of all Jews. "Judenrat" German soldiers are involved and they have widely used Ukrainian policemen to round up and guard, and murder the Jews of Poland. The Polish population is aiding this roundup of Jews, then opportunistically looting empty Jewish houses and business, further learning that some of the Polish Jews are being sent to Germany as slave laborers so that German civilians can live a "normal life. It is obvious to me that if Germany can bomb other countries, it will only be a matter of time before Allied bombers will retaliate. Then, "normal" will become "hell" for German cities.

May 28, 1942
Wehrmacht–Hitler Bulletin: In retaliation for the ambush of a high German officer, Reinhard Heydrich, Hitler has ordered 10,000 Czechs to be murdered.

May 31, 1942
Luftwaffe is continuing to bomb England.

June 2, 1942

Our internal confidential memos tell us that the flying bombs have many faults and are not totally functional. Faults include changing flight direction and falling back to Earth. I know that the reason is the information I have supplied the Air Force, based on calculations that sabotage the flight pattern. Eventually and after a long testing, they will realize that exterior instruments need new calibration.

June 4, 1942

SS: General Heydrich dies of wounds sustained in the Prague ambush. Mass retaliation is certain.

June 8, 1942

Report from Bunds in U.S: The U.S. Navy inflicted heavy losses on Japan in yesterday's Battle of Midway.

June 8, 1942

Wehrmacht bulletin and news report: I am stunned by the news that the Battle of Midway between Japanese and U.S. Navies has occurred in the Pacific Ocean. It has been raging for five days, with a stunning and decisive blow to Japan just six months after Japan attacked Pearl Harbor. Japan had planned to use a massive naval Army to eliminate the U.S. as a power that could keep Japan from dominating all of the Pacific. Instead, the U.S., under Admiral Chester Nimitz, defeated the attacking Imperial Japanese Navy. This will dismay the German command who has assumed Japan would keep the U.S. off balance.

I had leaked the joint German-Japanese code to the Allied spies about a year ago in the hope it could make a difference in harming the impending Japan-German Axis. Judging from the reports it appears the U.S. knew the timing and location of the planned attack and was able to ambush the Japanese Fleet, sinking four large carriers and a Heavy Cruiser. I know that the U.S. has massive industrial potential and hope they will focus on defeating the Nazis by bolstering England and Russia and participating in freeing Europe. This battle may have broken Japanese Pacific defense and, if that is the case, Japan will be very wise to sue for peace right now.

June 9, 1942
SS reports killing all inhabitants of Lidice in retaliation for Heydrich's killing in Prague.

June 9, 1942
BBC Broadcast: Wladyslaw Sikorski, Poland's Prime Minister, exiled in London. Revealed that that 700,000 Jews had been systematically murdered in Nazi concentration camps, in ghettos, and in gas chambers. This is no longer a secret, so I wonder what the world leaders will do and say.

June 10, 1942
Foreign Ministry Memo: Since 1933 Germany has had agents working in all major U.S. cities. The objective has been to foment anti-Semitics to permeate American society. This has been a success since hospitals, universities, clubs, law firms, etc. have long discriminated against Jews. However, with the U.S. now in WWII, the ministry is concerned to see the extraordinary role New York Jews are playing in the war effort. So far, 800,000 New York Jews have enlisted and thousands more are working in the War Industries, including the Brooklyn Navy Yard producing battleships. Hitler issued a statement saying he is pleased FDR has only admitted a trickle of Jewish refugees.

June 13, 1942
Today we launched a V-2 at Peenemünde that reached 1.3km. A major step forward in producing this major weapon system.

June 17, 1942
The SS has organized a vast bureaucracy to industrialize the extermination of Jews in death camps. This massive undertaking is being aided by leaders and populations throughout Nazi controlled Europe.

June 18, 1942

Wehrmacht Report: Our steamroller offense has crossed Eastern Ukraine and pushed Russian armies back beyond the Donets River. Russia is clearly outnumbered and has inferior equipment in this particular location.

June 20, 1942

SS Bulletin: An SS spy embedded in the Washington DC White House staff has reported the U.S. formation of the OSS, the Office of Strategic Service. The U.S. is very late getting into spying and the SS vows to track it as close as they do the British MIG. Of concern is that the OSS will use Germans to penetrate the SS.

June 23, 1942

Our spies in Britain report that the British Army in Palestine will form a Jewish Brigade to be attached to the British Army.

June 24, 1942

German spies on the West Coast of the U.S. report convoys headed for Archangel to deliver supplies and arms to Russia. This is bad news for Germany since it will enable Russia to counter attack on the Eastern Front. It is surprising that in just six months the U.S. can be spreading massive amounts of war materials.

June 25, 1942

Navy Report: Our once large U-boat fleet is losing major numbers sunk by Allied warships. This month we lost 144 U-boats. At this rate our U-boat attacks will be very limited.

June 25, 1942

Internal Memo–Wehrmacht: Our best scientists have been assigned to a project to develop nuclear weapons. Werner Heisenberg has been selected to head this program. We have occupied Norway since April 1940 as a direct way to use the heavy water facility at Vemork, along the Norwegian Coast.

Our spy embedded in the British war cabinet reports that Vemork is now a high-priority target so the Wehrmacht has increased security and protection.

June 26, 1942

SS: The plan to industrialize the extermination of Jews is proceeding. Death camps are being constructed and this massive undertaking has the full co-operation of Germany's bureaucrats and technocrats, assisted by populations throughout Europe.

June 26, 1942

SS Report from Himmler: Einsatzgruppen death squads have spread through the Soviet Union performing mass murders of Jewish populations. Their operations have lasted for days in each town, with the full logistical support of the Wehrmacht. In addition, the group has incited anti? Jewish programs to encourage the cooperation of civilians. The death squads have also operated in the Baltic States of Lithuania, Latvia, and Belarus.

Himmler is adamant that the SS killing methods are too costly, inefficient and too stressful on his men. Therefore, Himmler is working on a method to gas remaining Jews, just as he had announced at the January 20, 1942 Wannsee conference.

June 27, 1942

My friend, Gerhard Schneider, who is with the German Army in the Ukraine, reports to me that he has witnessed the Army rounding up the entire Jewish population of villages, leading them to trenches and shooting them in mass. Sometimes he says that if a mother is holding a baby, the baby is shot, then the mother. This is happening in every city and every village. The civilian population are forced to watch, so it is certain to intimidate them, but that also produces witnesses for this hideous mass killing war crime. Hitler is so obsessed with murdering Jews that he is diverting important military resources from the front lines. The surge into portions of the Eastern Front is going well for now. However, only a fool would believe that Germany can extend supply lines so very far for extended periods. The General must obey Hitler's hate of Russians and keep going. Everyone knows that Russian winter can be brutal and that will be a real test of the Army's staying power.

I also believe that Germany has taken too much of Western Europe too fast. The diversion of men and material to the Eastern Front before consolidating gaps in the West may prove to be a deciding factor in the outcome of WWII.

June 29, 1942

The Nazis are starving slaves, especially in the POW camps. The Nazi military failures and frustration and the Red Army's Counterattack defending Moscow have created a "tipping point." However, the Nazis are focused on killing Jews rather than solving their own serious problems.

The Nazis are using poison gas at Belzec, Chelmno and Mogilev. Hitler is deporting German Jews to Eastern concentration camps. October 21st of 1941 saw Hitler stop all Jewish immigration. This year he has told high officials he will "get rid of the destructive Jews."

July 1, 1942

Nazi and SS Bulletin: "We have just opened a camp at Treblinka dedicated to killing Jews." Wehrmacht: German troops have captured Sebastopol and are advancing deeper into Russian.

July 4, 1942

U.S. has begun flying out of England and is now bombing German cities. This could demoralize German civilians.

July 5, 1942

Wehrmacht report from the East: We have crossed the Don River and have cut Russia's railroad between Stalingrad and the Donetsk, thereby, severing supplies to Russian armies.

July 10, 1942

Heinrich Himmler: "All Jewish women are to be sterilized."

July 13, 1942

Himmler: “Germany will accelerate the killing of Jews in Poland and in the Ukraine; and commence shipping Jews from some camps to be terminated at Auschwitz. This plan includes all French Jews with the help of other French citizens.

July 17, 1942

Our Associates at the V-1 site have a successful jet engine test.

July 18, 1942

The Nazi spy in the U.S. State Department reports it is official State policy to prevent news of the mass slaying of Jews from reaching American Jewish leadership. In particular, the Jews of Lithuania are being murdered by the SS. American Jews tried to transfer large sums to save Romanian Jews and the State Department delayed and killed the transaction. This deliberate acquiescence to Jewish murder gives Hitler the confidence to continue this unbelievable war against the Jews.

July 19, 1942

French anti-Semitism and collaborations with the Nazis appear to have no limits. French police have arrested massive numbers of French Jewish citizens and confined them to Velodrome d’Hiver. I can only guess that their fate is to be dispatched to Nazi extermination camps.

July 20, 1942

Codes: I have continued to leak codes to the British spies that work at Peenemünde. They are Germans who fled Hitler, went to England, and then were infiltrated back to Germany. The code works the enigma machine which has been smuggled to Britain. Wehrmacht uses this three-rotor ciphering machine and has no idea that the Allies know Wehrmacht secrets.

July 21, 1942

Foreign Ministry: The foreign Ministry is gloating over its success in creating Nazi sympathy in South America. Emphasis is on Brazil, Argentina, and Chile. This has produced funds and a climate that welcomes Germans and provides fuel for German submarines, as well as food and supplies. Some Germans are transferring stolen fortunes into South American Banks.

July 22, 1942

Navy Bulletin: Two-hundred and eighty-one American ships have been sunk or damaged by German U-boats operating off the east coast of the U.S.

July 22, 1942

Gestapo SS: There are 300,000 Jews in the Warsaw Ghetto that are being moved to the Treblinka extermination camp. The objective is mass murder.

July 23, 1942

Hitler has ordered the Wehrmacht to occupy Stalingrad and the Caucuses. I believe this is spreading German resources too thin.

July 25, 1942

Wehrmacht has advanced in Russia and now occupies Rostov. Russian resistance is minimal. This may be a trap to extend our supply lines so finely that a counter-offensive could break through. SS has stayed with Wehrmacht and is killing all Jews as the Army advances. So far 35,000 have been killed just in Minsk.

July 28, 1942

Wehrmacht- Netherlands: Wehrmacht has enforced the doctrine of collective responsibility. This involves relentless punitive measures against an entire population. A Dutch Archbishop has complained about Gestapo's deportation of Dutch-Jews to Auschwitz. The Wehrmacht then sent all Dutch-Jewish converts to Catholicism to Auschwitz and executed 2,000 hostages.

July 28, 1942

SS: The plan to capture all Polish Jews has moved into the countryside. Peasants and villagers are playing an instrumental role in rounding up and denouncing Jews. They often take an initiative without even being encouraged by the SS. Local Poles have been very active about betraying Jews to the SS.

July 28, 1942

Army Bulletin: Jewish resistance is being organized in the Warsaw Ghetto and the Wehrmacht is determined to destroy the resistance movement.

July 31, 1942

Navy: Continued massive U-boat losses; ninety just this month.

August 1, 1942

Navy Bulletin: Britain's survival is very dependent on supplies by convoys from the U.S. The Krigers-Marine B-Dienst intel group has often broken British Naval codes. The submarine Wolfpack slows the Atlantic Convoy operations.

August 3, 1942

The SS bulletin received today related how the Jews in the Warsaw Ghetto have been tricked into being rounded up and taken to trains. Those that refuse to cooperate are treated brutally. The trains are going directly to the death factory called Treblinka. They go from the train right to the gas chambers.

The Warsaw Ghetto has been the home of hundreds of thousands of Jews who are living in filthy, crowded, disease-ridden apartment blocks. The SS is telling them they will receive a loaf of bread if they come to be "relocated." My reaction to the SS boasting of these killings is that Germany is setting a horrific example of mass murder.

August 8, 1942

Germany's plan has been to plunder the occupied countries in order to finance the war effort and enrich its leader. However, Hermann Göring reports that most Soviet cities are void of things to plunder.

August 9, 1942

Wehrmacht from Leningrad: Today was to have been the day Leningrad was supposed to surrender. We have bombarded it constantly and prevented food from getting into Leningrad. Our spies tell us the streets are littered with dead and starving bodies. Instead of surrender, the Russians have set up loudspeakers and started broadcasting Shostakovich's 7th Symphony as a sign of defiance and will to resist surrender. This means a prolonged siege and great difficulty in defeating the Russians.

August 11, 1942

Wehrmacht: At Stalingrad, Russia has made a counter-offensive attempt, with great loss of life for both sides.

August 12, 1942

Navy: AU-boat has torpedoed and sunk the British aircraft carrier Eagle.

August 12, 1942

More Army advance in Russia.

August 20, 1942

Army: Getting close to Stalingrad which will start with hundreds of planes to bomb the Russian city.

August 20, 1942

I have made secret progress on an inertial navigation system that will guide our rockets. There will be advanced motion sensors (accelerometers) and rotation sensors (gyroscopes) to calculate the position, orientation and speed of the V-2. All of this must be integrated with a computer and that will take time to create. My system should be able to detect a change in its geographic position and rotation, and also be immune from allied jamming.

Right now, the V-2 system has two gyroscopes and accelerator, and a very simple computer.

August 22, 1942

Nazi informants in the U.S. reveal that telegrams are being sent from Romanian Jews to the U.S. State Department. There is a proposal to save 20,000 Romanian Jews. Assistant Secretary of State, Breckinridge Long, has ordered state employees to destroy the telegrams and to not believe the first-hand report of what is happening to Jews in Europe. This means the U.S. government is acquiescing to the murder of Jews in Europe. Major U.S. newspapers are delegating these killings to back pages. Bottom line, Germany interprets this non-action as approval and continues mass killings.

August 22, 1942

H.C.: Nazi spies inform Hitler that German industrialist, Eduard Schulte, has informed Jewish Congressmen and that NSC has informed State about the mass murder we are perpetrating. The State Department is trying to silence W.J.C. Schulte, and now that Hitler knows that he is revealing our secret extermination programs, he will "take care" of Schulte. The U.S. Treasury Department, under the leadership of Secretary Henry Morgenthau, who is Jewish, is at odds with State and has made a strong effort to publicize the mass murders. The State Department and Breckinridge Long have intentionally lied to Congress and have altered information. The Nazis could not ask for better colleagues.

August 22, 1942

Gestapo Memo: The Night and Fog Decree–Suspected anti-Nazis will vanish into the night. (This ever-present threat robs Germans of any freedom. In addition, the Gestapo is burning books that they think might incite opposition activity.)

August 22, 1942

Berlin news release: Hitler is furious that the Wehrmacht has not yet destroyed Leningrad. A siege bombardment and starvation have not budged the Russians. To make matters worse, as I noted earlier this month, the Russian composer, Demetra Shostakovich, has written a symphony that is so powerful that it has become the Russian symbol of survival. The

Russians are proud and broadcasting it with loudspeakers, and it is affecting German troops.

August 23, 1942

Guidance research: Werner has given me great leeway in researching rocket guidance systems. In addition to conventional gyroscope guidance, I am looking at gravity waves that could be produced by objects beyond our universe. If I can measure and calibrate these waves, then maybe I can produce a new method for navigation and modify the conventional gyroscope.

August 28, 1942

It is now clear that Germany's appetite for conquest has overreached, and with the tide potentially turning, Germany may have limited resources to tum back powerful enemies such as the U.S. and the Soviet Union. While we are presently fighting in Russia, there is the prospect of winter fighting and very over-extended supply lines. We are told that Germany has millions of prisoners in camps and is running out of ways to feed and control them. Hitler and his inner circle are starting to label all prisoners as saboteurs and talking about "eliminating" them.

Auschwitz commandant, Rudolph Hess, has circulated a memo to us telling where he has experimented with mass killing by the use of cyanide gas. With his German pride in efficiency, he claims the cost is just pennies per person killed.

I cannot understand why sane people would obsess about using precious resources to kill Jews rather than to try to prevent losing the war and in the process destroying Germany as we know it today. We know that the food situation in Germany is not good for civilians and that Goebbels is blaming the "Bolshevik" Jews. This is an old Nazi standby as an excuse for brutal behavior. It is hard to imagine how the Nazis will justify their behavior and even harder to imagine why Germans will knowingly support their misguided actions.

September 2, 1942

Wehrmacht: German troops have entered the outskirts of Stalingrad.

September 4, 1942

Report from the Ukraine: Ukrainians have helped Nazis kill Jews at Babi Yar, in Kiev, in Crimea, in Galicia, and in Romania. Ukrainians have been brutal to Jews, openly robbing, torturing and killing them.

September 5, 1942

Luftwaffe: British and American bombers have struck L Havre, with the Luftwaffe engaging them in battle. This port is vital to the German war effort.

September 8, 1942

The high command has bragged that an agreement has been made with the Pope. The German Army will form a Ukrainian Catholic division to fight against Russia. Germany has agreed to leave Ukrainian Catholics as "undisturbed" as possible by the German Army. In return, the Pope has agreed to not publicly criticize Nazi Germany even though he is well aware of the atrocities Germany has committed against Jews and others. I suspect this agreement also includes a promise by the Pope to not excommunicate Catholic Nazis, including Hitler.

September 9, 1942

Wehrmacht has issued a strict policy in the Eastern Front: Captured Jewish Russian soldiers are to be sent to extermination camps. Any Jewish American prisoners, should they invade Europe, are to be sent to slave labor camps and worked to death.

September 9, 1942

SS is continuing to transport huge numbers of Jews from France to Nazi Germany. Germany has received news from the London operative. The Times reports "Ruthless Roundup of French Jews by Vichy French Police." "A train with 4,000 children left Lyon without papers to Germany."

I worry about my son, but Dornberger assures me he will be okay. However, he is not sure of the whereabouts of my wife. It is possible that because her father is Jewish that she cannot be saved. Dornberger' s assurances are meant to keep me working on the rockets.

September 11, 1942

Luftwaffe is no longer able to stop Allied bombers from reaching Germany. Yesterday the RAF dropped many thousands of bombs on Dusseldorf. I believe this loss of command of the skies will contribute to a loss of this war.

September 14, 1942

Wehrmacht: German troops are pressing ahead in the attack on Stalingrad.

September 18, 1942

SS: The Nazi Minister of Justice, Otto Theirack, has ruled the prisoners can be "exterminated by labor."

September 19, 1942

As recorded in an earlier entry, I have been required by the SS to visit various concentration camps. It is as if they want to actually brag about brutality practices on Jews and others. At Auschwitz, it is particularly troubling to be shown how medical experiments practiced by Joseph Mengele are meant to harm rather than heal. Mengele and other German doctors are torturers and assassins.

They are performing grotesque experiments on certain prisoners. Mengele seems especially fascinated by twins and subjects them to monstrous surgeries and deliberate infections.

September 24, 1942

Wehrmacht: Russia has started a counter-offensive at Stalingrad. The Wehrmacht plan is to make a heavy assault on Stalingrad. This includes bringing the Luftwaffe to bomb Stalingrad into oblivion.

September 28, 1942

The German Navy reports the loss of 98 U-boats this month. I believe that these can no longer be replaced and that the remaining U-boat crews are inexperienced.

September 29, 1942

SS Bulletin: A confidential SS bulletin brags about creating Theresienstadt Concentration Camp forty miles north of Prague. It is being used as a gathering place for Jews from Eastern Europe for deportation to death camps. The village was once able to hold a few thousand people and is now packed with 58,000 at a time. The SS just says they are using Theresienstadt to fool the world by bringing the Red Cross to see conditions that are "dressed up" just for the outsiders' visit.

September 29, 1942

SS Publication: An Einsatzgruppen has been organized to kill the 500,000 Jews living in Palestine and 50,000 Egyptian Jews. The plan includes the Grand Mufti of Jerusalem engaging in anti-Semitic, radio propaganda, along with inciting local residents to perform murder. At this time, General Rommel is in Africa and can supply help in the killing.

September 25, 1942

Wehrmacht: Tanks and air power has been shifted from the Russian front to the Southern Front. This predictably will make it easier for Russia to counterattack since we are now outnumbered. With winter approaching, the lack of supplies and armor may expose German troops to perilous battle conditions. Hitler and our generals must realize that Wehrmacht is feeling spread too thin.

September 25, 1942

SS report on Theresienstadt: This walled garrison town created by the Hapsburg Empire has been used to gather Jews from various locations in Europe and then they will be sent to death camps.

It is being staged so that the International Red Cross can be fooled into thinking it is a humane home for Jews. The reality is that the town was meant to house about 2,000 people which Germany has now packed with 58,000. This creates misery and disease, as planned by the SS.

September 26, 1942

Wehrmacht, North Africa Bulletin: The British have cracked German codes since German supply convoys to North Africa are being frequently attacked and sunk, and it appears the British Army commanded by Bernard Montgomery has ambushed the Wehrmacht attacks at Alam el Halfa. My colleagues are unaware that I have transmitted Wehrmacht codes to Ultra, the English code-breaking unit.

September 27, 1942

Reports from the Eastern Front: Wehrmacht has focused on the Soviet Ukraine and Soviet Belarus. The Army has advanced to Moscow and Stalingrad, but a large percent of Russia has not been attacked. The Russians are using parts of the Ukraine and Belarus as buffer zones to absorb the Wehrmacht campaign.

October 1, 1942

Gestapo Lyon France: The Vichy regime's Gestapo have executed Professor Victor Basch and taken his vast library. These books are to be added to the millions of books already taken from Jews. Basch was a renowned, Jewish, literary scholar who was once a prominent lecturer at Sorbonne.

October 1, 1942

Foreign Ministry: Germany continues to fund right-wing groups in the U.S. in an attempt to sway public opinion. A good example is the Irish Christian Front and its leader, the radio preacher, Charles Coughlin. He refers to himself as Father Coughlin and he regularly maligns Jews. He has encouraged Irish Catholics to stalk and assault Jews in urban U.S. communities. The Front has gone as far as plotting to assassinate Jewish members of the U.S. Congress.

October 3, 1942

Personal observation: As I have mentioned in a prior entry, we successfully launched a V-2 rocket. Wernher von Braun, Werner Dornberger, and Walter Rudt were instrumental in the rocket's design. The V-2 rocket was launched to a height of 85 km. This proves the ability of the launch and altitude that will permit distance has to be targeted. I must still "perfect" the guidance systems. Werner Dornberger and I cheered a flawless flight of this pioneer ballistic missile.

October 5, 1942

As I have noted in September, the SS continues a diabolical program that forces all scientists to visit concentration camps. Some of their theory may be pride in being murderers and some of the reason is to intimidate us as to what can happen to us and our families if we do not cooperate and design the missile.

I was taken to the Treblinka Camp to observe train loads of Jews arriving from Theresienstadt and other gathering locations. The men and women were separated. Women and children undressed, their hair was cut and they were forced to march on a path to their death in gas chambers. I could hear their screams, which finally died away and then complete silence. I assume the men are being used as slave labor for the war effort. Humanity is dead in Germany, and I am more convinced more than ever that slowly creating undetected flaws in the rocket guidance systems is a must for me.

October 6, 1942

SS continues programs to massacre Russian Jews in German-occupied Russia.

October 7, 1942

Wehrmacht: Russians in Stalingrad are fighting back with heavier Wehrmacht casualties.

October 7, 1942

Wehrmacht Bulletin: Spies at Bletchley Park in England advised Germany that the code breakers have cracked the Enigma codes. Even though we are instructed to change codes frequently, we have seen evidence of this in North Africa where Rommel's moves seemed to be known in advance and by the vast number of German supply ships being sunk by Allied subs that seem to know the ships' routes.

At Peenemünde, Germany fears that code-breaking will reveal our rocket research location and lead to an attack. The German Enigma code machine has three moving rotors and fifteen button potential readings, yet it is known that the British have broken the code.

October 7, 1942

The rocket program has had other scientific disciplines sent to us. The head of aeromedical research for the Luftwaffe, Hubertus Strughold, has worked to spend time in our labs. He is studying the effects of high altitude and high-speed flying using our technical data. There is a rumor that prisoners at Dachau have been subjected to medical experiments which may be monitored by Strughold. These involve oxygen deprivation and extreme cold temperatures.

October 10, 1942

Wehrmacht Report- Soviet Union: Germany is tracking six Soviet armies moving north of Stalingrad. This could be a trick to stop the Wehrmacht from sending reinforcements to Stalingrad if there is a Russian counteroffensive.

October 12, 1942

Wehrmacht: Russia is mounting a serious counter-attack at Stalingrad.

October 15, 1942

Wehrmacht: Russian defenses were embedded in a tractor factory. Wehrmacht has lost three thousand troops taking the factory. Can Germany sustain such heavy losses?

October 20, 1942

We have perfected the V-2 rocket to the extent that it was timely to try to reach the boundary of space. Once that was achieved, our speed and trajectory can be hard to stop. Yesterday we had a vehicle that reached 100 km from Earth.

October 28, 1942

Wehrmacht–North African Bulletin: General Rommel has been locked in battle with Allied Forces for the last five days at El Alamein. He issued a plea for reinforcement but has been denied since the Wehrmacht is already spread thin on the Eastern Front.

October 29, 1942

SS: In Pinsk, Russia, the SS reports killing thousands of Jews. Bulletin from the Wehrmacht pleading for reinforcements while the SS is using valuable resources to murder innocent Soviets. It is sheer madness that may lead to serious defeats.

October 31, 1942

Navy Report: The German Navy continues to inflict heavy damage to transports carrying men and equipment across the Atlantic from the U.S. However, this month alone we lost ninety-four U-boats and that kind of heavy loss is impossible to replace.

October 31, 1942

One of my colleagues is Korach Dannenberg, who had a major role in designing the V-2 rocket. However, he is an ardent member of the Nazi party, so I must be very cautious. He also knows how to make our ethyl alcohol into Schnapps.

November 2, 1942

SS Statistics Report: From August to October this year, 1.2 million Jews were slain in death camps. The lethal killing camps of Belzec, Sobibor, Treblinka, and Auschwitz are "processing" 15,000 people a day. This has involved 450 train loads from 393 separate Polish towns. This three-month space will slow as we run out of victims.

November 8, 1942

German newspapers have published a report released by Harry S. Truman, a U.S. Senator from the state of Missouri. This report relates that a prominent U.S. attorney named John Foster Dulles had made pro-Nazi arrangements that are considered treasonous to the U.S. However, Dulles and his law firm are so powerful that Truman is having resistance from others in the Senate to prosecute this friend of Germany and the other prominent Americans who worked with and for Dulles.

The following are some allegations: In 1936, Dulles arranged for the Schroder Bank of New York to act as a front for German industries, for Nazis to launder money from Germany into the U.S., and for funds from German Bunds to flow to the Nazi war effort. Dulles also tied the Chase Bank to the Schroder. Since Chase Bank is controlled by the Rockefeller family, this means that the Rockefellers are aiding the Nazis and hurting the Allies. It is well known that many of the German industries were stolen from the Jewish families and that much of the Nazi wealth has been plundered from Jews and others in the largest robbery in history.

Truman further states that the Rockefellers control Standard Oil of New Jersey. Dulles has arranged for Standard Oil to supply critical oil supplies to the Nazi war effort by way of Spain. Since Spain is controlled by the Fascist regime, the transit arrangements are easy. Germany cleverly has allied with the occupied Italy so the flow of oil to the Western and Eastern, and North African fronts is simple.

It is a fact that the U.S. is placing a higher priority on fighting Germany in Europe than the Japanese in the Pacific. The British and the Russians are desperate for reinforcements to stop the German advances in Russia and prevent the invasion of Britain. The U.S. and Canadian navies are trying to stop German U-boat attacks on Atlantic shipping, with some success. Therefore, Germany is intent on stopping the flow of U.S. food and material from the vast farms and industries to the U.S. West Coast via the Panama Canal to the Atlantic. Germany has an extensive U-boat fleet and has moved a considerable number to the Pacific side of the Panama Canal to try to sink West Coast transport ships that are not as heavily guarded.

That is because the U.S. Pacific fleet sustained considerable damage last December 7th at Pearl Harbor and in the Battles of Midway and the Coral Sea. The Truman report states that the Rockefeller Standard Oil is refueling the U-boats off the coast of Central and South America. Again, a treasonous act by the Rockefellers.

My own opinion is that some of the prominent Wehrmacht officers perceived that Hitler is mad and has over-extended the Wehrmacht beyond repair. Therefore, I think they are scouting possible relocation to South and Central America if and when Germany should lose the war.

November 9, 1942

Confidential note from a German friend who also despises the Nazis: "There is a non-occupied zone of South-Central France where some French men are hiding Jews from Nazis and collaborators. Special mention is made of Le Chambon and surrounding parishes. Being saved are thousands of orphans whose parents had been sent to the death camps."

November 10, 1942

Report from the Eastern Front is that in spite of numerous tank assaults that have pulverized Stalingrad, the Russians continue to fight back from a city choked with devastated buildings. German spies in the Russian government say that Stalin has issued orders to fight to the death.

November 11, 1942

Personal Note: As war and persecution rages on, I have seen much of Europe abandon their commitment to morality as it justifies and encourages the persecution that Germany is indulging in. Fear? Self-preservation? A thousand years of Christian anti-Semitist preaching? The irrational Jewish persecution?

November 12, 1942

"The handwriting is on the wall." It is obvious to me that Hitler is way overextended and drunk with his early successes. The U.S. has vast resources and productive capacity which is now being accelerated. This means that by 1943 and 1944, Germany may be outgunned. Already, Allied combat planes outnumber us three to one. Our Tiger and Panther tanks are superb, but the Allies may soon have so many tanks that ours will be of little use. The U.S. produces vast quantities of fuel and Germany must get fuel from Romania and the Middle East where the Allies may be able to destroy our transports. LG. Farben is attempting to produce synthetic fuel, but has not had success. Without fuel, our planes and tanks will be useless sitting ducks.

November 14, 1942

Naval Bulletin: U-boats are sinking Allied ships more quickly than they can be replaced. The British are starting to coordinate air power with their destroyer protection and that could take a toll on the U-boats.

November 16, 1942

U-boats have intercepted U.S. supply ships. However, German spies in Britain report that the Allies are designing planes, radar, and special mortars to destroy U-boats. The Allies are reported as being close to breaking our codes, which will then expose the U-boats to being attacked.

November 18, 1942

Reports from the Eastern Front: German occupation of Eastern countries has brought suffering and mass death. The people inhabiting the Soviet Union have now turned to resistance and partisan organizations. This is now diverting Hitler's attention and our rocket production has taken a backseat to the production of conventional arms.

November 19, 1942

Report from the Eastern Front–Army Group Center: The German Army has lost enormous numbers of troops. The Army had built loyalty on small units with each soldier identifying with their comrades. It is obvious that all that must change to a "factory" approach, with troop replacement as interchangeable components. It is predictable that this is bad for the German Army.

The Army is turning into an instrument of mass murder. Jews, local civilians, and Soviet prisoners of war are falling victim to this mentality of genocide. This diversion from the military's effective focus will have a negative effect on the Wehrmacht and ultimately Germany's future. Thousands of villages are being destroyed and hundreds of thousands of civilians murdered. In addition, young women are being sent to work as slaves in Reich armament factories.

November 20, 1942

Hitler's orders: All of a sudden Hitler has changed course and is demanding that Dornberger produce 3,000 V-2 rockets per month. We believe he is upset that German cities are being bombed. His goal is not possible. We do not have nearly the liquid oxygen to fuel half the number of rockets Hitler has demanded.

November 20, 1942

Poland–SS: The SS has been given the task of killing Jews who live in occupied Poland. Polish non-Jews have proactively informed on Jews and handed them over to the SS. It is the SS's estimate that the Jewish survival rates will be minor, all due to Polish citizen aid.

November 20, 1942

Wehrmacht: Russia has launched a counter-offensive.

November 22, 1942

Wehrmacht: Rommel in Africa has been battling Allied Forces for weeks. Hitler has ordered Rommel to fight to the last man.

November 22, 1942

Wehrmacht: The Russians have surrounded our 4th and 6th Army at Stalingrad. The Wehrmacht Romanian Corps surrendered. A million Russians have breached German lines as freezing weather has made Wehrmacht equipment unusable.

November 22, 1942

SS: The rapid invasion of the Soviet Union has resulted in millions of Soviet prisoners of war. The SS has openly stated that Germany has executed and starved to death over two million Soviet POWs.

November 23, 1942

News of the extermination of Jews never makes the front pages in the U.S. This news is buried in the back pages of the New York Times and Washington Post. Both papers have Jewish ownership, so it is all the more disturbing. This is another message to Germany to not care about world opinion since there is none.

November 23, 1942

SS Bulletin: The SS suspects the villagers in unoccupied France are hiding Jewish children and smuggling some to Switzerland, even though Switzerland is not sympathetic to Jews. Some of the adults have been arrested by the SS and beaten to death without revealing the information needed by the SS.

November 24, 1942

SS Papers: "Facilities such as Treblinka, Auschwitz, and Birkenau have been constructed for the single purpose of mass murder." "In Auschwitz alone we will kill one million Jews." "As slave labor is needed for war production, inmates will be worked to death and exterminated through labor."

November 24, 1942

Reports arrived with details of German atrocities on the Eastern front in the expansion of the concentration camps. I question how a highly educated and cultured nation can pursue a murderous and barbarous war. Why do most German's support Hitler?

November 25, 1942

German policy of murdering deformed infants and the mentally ill is hardly protested by prominent religious leaders.

November 25, 1942

It is becoming evident that Nazi officials are living very "high on the hog" while the average German must endure rationing and hardships.

November 27, 1942

SS: Even though troops are needed at the battles of Stalingrad in Moscow, the SS has remained in many Ukrainian cities in order to pursue entire Jewish populations by mass killings. The bodies are dumped in mass graves, Jewish cemeteries destroyed, and property stolen. Many of the captured Russian soldiers are old or very young, all are being starved to death. The SS is also mass murdering Russian prisoners.

December 2, 1942

My earlier diary entries have chronicled that German advanced weapons programs in the late 1930s and later attempted to create a nuclear bomb. German-Jewish physicists and other scientists who fled Nazi persecution went to the United States. These brilliant scientists included Albert Einstein who was successful in persuading U.S. President Roosevelt to fund a crash U.S. program using the German-Jewish physicists to create a nuclear reaction. They were joined by Enrico Fermi, an Italian Nobel physicist who had fled Mussolini's fascism.

The German nuclear program was delayed by the lack of the Jewish scientists and the mistake of stealing and relying on the Norwegian heavy water plant, which could subsequently be bombed out of existence by the Allies. As the V-1 and V-2 program that is advancing in Germany becomes overextended, Hitler's attention is diverted to the nuclear program. The trap of the Russian winter is of great concern to Wehrmacht leaders.

A Jewish physicist's family is still in Nazi captivity in Germany and the Nazis have extorted from him inside information to which we are privy. He reports that a few days ago at the University of Chicago, they had been successful in triggering the first of its kind; man-made nuclear chain reaction. This will lead to atomic weapons capable of a destructive force that can eliminate an entire city. It is ironic that the very scientists whose families are persecuted by Hitler may prevent the Nazis from creating a weapon so horrible that it can end this war for Germany and would change history for generations to come.

The German nuclear program has been led by Werner Heisenberg. We hear rumors that he has told Albert Speer and Hitler that the job to produce a bomb is just too big for Germany in wartime. He says the program is going nowhere. We do know that the Gestapo is constantly checking on him since he had taught Einstein's theories, which the Gestapo called "Jewish physics."

December 5, 1942

Wehrmacht: Rommel's Army defeated at El Alamein in North Africa. This is a blow to Germany since it puts an entire Army corps out of the war effort.

December 6, 1942

The German Air Force has tried to set major English towns on fire with tens of thousands of incendiary bombs. This blitz has been going on for a few years. The Germans embezzled British War Cabinet reports that Britain is planning to strike back and intends to destroy dozens of German cities.

The especially equipped British bombers are to blow off rooftops, then drop incendiaries, and then more bombs on the rescuers and firemen. Violence begets violence.

An added problem is the soon-to-be added big bombers, which means German cities will be obliterated. It seems obvious that Germany has made a senseless war on the world and the price will be paid by every major German City.

The Luftwaffe has been shifting to the Eastern Front so that there may be little resistance to the Allied bombers over Germany. Germany's civilians by the hundreds of thousands will pay for Hitler's madness.

December 8, 1942

The great German physicist, Albert Einstein, became a U.S. citizen in 1940. In 1940 he appealed to the U.S. State Department to allow Jewish refugees from Hitler to enter the U.S. The State Department refused and said they were "protecting against subversive elements." This argument was absurd, since why would Jews spy for a Germany that was killing them?

It is now the end of 1942 and almost half of Europe's Jews have been murdered by Germany. The U.S. State Department still refuses to help, which has been a direct sign to Hitler to do whatever he wishes.

December 9, 1942

Dateline, Majdanek Camp, SS Bulletin: Female SS guards have been indoctrinated with Nazi policies and have become violent overseers with radical behavior.

December 10, 1942

German agents in the Soviet Union, U.S., and UK report that these governments are well aware of the German concentration camps and their plans to exterminate Jews and Soviet prisoners.

This must come from witnesses' testimony smuggled from the camps and certainly from partisan resistance groups. It is very upsetting that none of the countries are doing anything to stop these atrocities and we hear no public pronouncements. The obvious result is to let the Nazis believe they can do whatever they wish. It is a mortal crime by those who commit murder and those who do nothing to stop it, or even denounce it. M.M.

December 14, 1942

Wehrmacht: The Battle of Stalingrad is continuing. Reports of massive numbers of Soviet troops cutting through Wehrmacht lines. Freezing cold weather has made German tanks and guns inoperative and losses are mounting.

December 22, 1942

We have again received Hitler's signed order to mass produce the V-2 weapons.

December 23, 1942

Hitler's orders: British air raids are destroying German factories and towns and Hitler is furious. He has again signed the order to mass produce rockets.

I know Hitler made a big order to attack the Soviets while he was going after Britain. It gave Britain time to build a bomber fleet to attack Germany. In addition, Britain knows about Peenemünde and has pictures of our V-2 rocket.

December 23, 1942

A win for our research group. Hitler has been upset by losses in North Africa and Russia so that he will emphasize rocket warfare.

December 24, 1942

Our co-workers on the other side of Peenemünde have successfully flown a V-1 "buzz bomb."

December 25, 1942

Wehrmacht: The U.S. has supplied Russia with arms and supplies in Russia and this is changing the tide of battle at Stalingrad.

December 26, 1942

I still have not had direct contact with my wife and son. The SS keeps assuring me that if l produce the guidance systems for V-2 rockets, then they will be kept safe. My son is eight years old and I do not know what he looks like. Having promises from the SS is not reassuring, but I have no choice but to continue my work.

December 26, 1942

I have always believed that Catholic literature for the past thousand years has promoted anti-semitism. The Pope today is Pius XII and it seems that he is failing to speak out against the fact that Jews are being slaughtered. Some people call him Hitler's Pope by not reminding Catholics of their ethical responsibilities. There are others who clearly defend the Pope.

December 27, 1942

Hitler's Orders: In 1941 Hitler had ordered the SS to exterminate all Jews. This is happening in death camps such as Treblinka and Auschwitz–Birkenau.

December 27, 1942

SS Bulletin: The SS claims to have created thousands of Jewish Ghettos, plus killing centers and forced labor camps where prisoners produce war material. They are in Poland, Belarus, Lithuania, Latvia, and Ukraine. The SS boasts about detaining hundreds of thousands in the Warsaw Ghetto. Because so many camps exist in Germany and German soldiers write home, it is obvious that the German citizens are well aware of the SS activities.

December 28, 1942

SS Bulletin–Bratislava Ukraine: The SS reports throwing live Jewish children over a cliff into a freezing river where the weight of their small bodies breaks the thin layer of winter ice.

December 29, 1942

SS Internal Report: German infiltrators in the U.S. White House have reported that U.S. President Roosevelt has full knowledge of Hitler's intent to kill all of European Jews and has obstructed attempts to rescue them. He spoke to his staff about distrusting the reports. Even though the American public is overwhelmingly in favor of letting an unlimited number of Jews into the U.S., Roosevelt is working to make sure this does not happen.

This is not surprising to me since during the 1930s, including Kristallnacht, Roosevelt never brought up the oppression of Jews by Hitler. He obviously thought that would have increased pressure for Jewish immigration into the U.S. Another key indicator to the SS is in July 1938 at the Evian conference the U.S. never offered to take even one person.

The conclusion by the SS is that they can and will do whatever they wish to the Jews of Europe and they will not be stopped by Roosevelt.

1943

January 4, 1943

Army intelligence. "German armies are thrusting deep into the western part of the Soviet Union." Germany also is fighting in North Africa. It is obvious to me that supplying armies at the gates of Leningrad and Stalingrad and controlling much of Europe, Germany has overshot its capacity by trying to also fight a war in North Africa. In the meantime, Russia is urging the Allies to open a front in Europe in order to take pressure off of Russia.

January 10, 1943

Wehrmacht: In a surprise move, the Soviets have begun an offensive in Stalingrad and in the Caucasus.

January 10, 1943

We have been alerted that our lab is targeted by a secret British outfit known as MD-1. They are known for creating an explosive known as a limpet mine, one of which could wreck an entire building. MD-1 is said to have other explosives and to operate in a stealth manner behind German lines. Our guard patrols are doubled and night surveillance is on guard against MD-1 parachutists.

January 12, 1943

Wehrmacht-North Africa: The Army has been most annoyed by the British Command Group, Special Force that has surprised and sabotaged numerous Wehrmacht bases. This includes numerous airfields. They will parachute in and strike undetected through vast stretches of desert.

The Italian Army is also based in North Africa and has been dealt some major blows by the rogue unit that has attacked with skill and flair.

January 15, 1943
Spy reports: In French Morocco, Churchill, Roosevelt, and De Gaulle are meeting in Casablanca to discuss strategy. The German informant says the three already believe Germany will be defeated and they will insist on unconditional surrender.

January 19, 1943
Bulletin from SS: Spies embedded in Allied joint command report that the Allies decided to invade Sicily. Wehrmacht will be waiting.

January 22, 1943
Wehrmacht: Allies invade Sicily. Wehrmacht stops them at the beach.

January 23, 1943
Wehrmacht–North African campaign: Britain landing troops in Tripoli.

January 24, 1943
Wehrmacht: The battle for Stalingrad is raging. Hitler has gone berserk and orders the Wehrmacht to fight to the death. Confidentially, experienced officers say this is unwise, risky, and very hard to supply in freezing weather.

January 24, 1943
Wehrmacht analysis: It now seems clear that Stalin's plan was to give up vast amounts of territory in an effort to keep Russian armies intact. Space, time, and winter weather are Russia's allies, along with millions of aid from the U.S. The German Army has been led deep into Russia.

January 24, 1943
SS boasts of increasing the incineration of captives at Auschwitz-Birkenau.

January 27, 1943
Luftwaffe: In spite of our strong air defense, the U.S. has accomplished a mass bombing of Germany. This is a first and the civilians are panicked.

January 30, 1943

Navy report: The Navy has lost thirty-nine U-boats just this month. That means that my effort to smuggle Enigma codes may have worked, along with Allied anti-sub warfare.

January 31, 1943

Wehrmacht–"Doomsday" Bulletin, Stalingrad: General Friedrich Von Paul has surrendered his troops at Stalingrad. This could be the beginning of the end. The Wehrmacht has treated Russian prisoners brutally and I will not be surprised if the Russians retaliate. Hitler withdrew Luftwaffe coverage to protect Germany. So, the Army had no air cover and frozen equipment and arms.

Personal: The German Army was starved in position and could only mount a weak defense.

There are piles of dead soldiers everywhere. This is a lesson for the German people but falls on Hitler's deaf ears.

February 2, 1943

Wehrmacht Communique: Complete surrender of twenty divisions to Russia. The Battle of Stalingrad has ended. (This massive loss will be a turning point. Germany must now retreat from Russia while holding against an expected invasion in Europe, and while German cities become vulnerable to Allied bombing.)

February 6, 1943

Wehrmacht: North Africa Corps in full withdrawal.

February 8, 1943

SS: Leon Blum has been taken from his Vichy French prison to Nazi Germany. (The rumor here at the rocket center is that Blum is at Buchenwald, but still alive.)

February 9, 1943

Bulletin received: Jews in Paris are continuing to be rounded up to be sent to the death camps. France already sent Jews to the Draney transit camp outside of Paris. They were taken to Montluc prison, then Draney, and then on to death at Auschwitz in Poland. I believe they will die because they are Jews, and for that reason alone. The Nazis' demented anti-Semitism joined by French anti-Semitism, has condemned them to death.

It is painful to realize that the centuries-long religious anti-Semitism of the Inquisition and the nationalist anti-Semitism of the Dreyfus Affair have been joined by the worst of them all, racial anti-Semitism of the Nazis. Truly a manifestation of barbarism by a nation.

February 9, 1943

Wehrmacht: Retreat continues and Russia recaptures Kursk. However, Hitler is furious and has issued an order to regroup and is sending extensive forces to stop Russia.

February 10, 1943

Von Braun Memo: The battles at Stalingrad and Leningrad had not gone well for Germany. Hitler is much more supportive of the V-2 program. Therefore, he has allowed us to recall 4,000 rocketeer PhDs who have been in combat. They will work at Peenemünde on an accelerated program. Werner Osenberg has helped locate these scientists.

February 10, 1943

Wehrmacht- North Africa: The British 8th Army is sweeping away Wehrmacht resistance. Too many fronts and too many supply challenges. Hitler orders counter attacks.

February 12, 1943

Foreign Service Bulletin–Confidential: The U.S. Dulles Brothers have been successful in stopping Britain from exposing U.S. oil firms that are selling oil to Germany. The Dulles' threatened to cut off supplies to Britain if they persisted in exposing Nazi ties to their clients. It has helped for I.G. Farben to be paying enormous "legal fees" to the Dulles law firm, Sullivan and Cromwell.

Personal: A further irony is that the British Imperial Chemical Company

(ICI) has ties to I.G. Farben, and British banks are "moving" money confiscated by our SS.

February 13, 1943

Personal: My older brother, Kurt, fled Germany and immigrated to England almost ten years ago. I have had no contact from him since then. As a leading scientist in low-temperature survival, his expertise may have helped Russians to survive the siege of Leningrad, Moscow, and Stalingrad, when the Wehrmacht lost hundreds of thousands who were frozen to death.

I may never know what happened to Kurt and also continue to worry about whether or not my wife and child are still alive in Nazi custody.

February 14, 1943

Wehrmacht: Retreat continues. Rostov lost. Kharkov will be the next target for Russian forces.

February 16, 1943

Army Bulletin: America is concentrating air power on bombing Germany and is believed to be weak in protecting the Atlantic convoys. This means that food, oil, and armaments needed by Britain, the Russians, in North Africa, England, and elsewhere, are not getting through.

Therefore, the damage to the English economy is great. The U-boats continue to maul Allied convoys and are sinking many dozens of vessels every month. In return, Allied navies are sinking large numbers of U-boats. The massive production of boats in the U.S. could outweigh the number of U-boats.

February 21, 1943

Germany has made great strides towards creating a nuclear bomb that could change the war instantly. However, many of our best physicists fled Germany due to Nazi anti-Semitism and are now helping the U.S. with a similar project. This means the German project is moving slowly towards its destructive goal. Hitler is maintaining an industrial plant at Vemork,

Norway in order to produce the heavy water (deuterium oxide) that Germany needs to actually complete an atom bomb.

February 22, 1943

Today's SS Bulletin describes that Norwegian saboteurs parachuted into Vemork, blew up critical machinery and experiments, and escaped into the Norwegian fjords. Since the facility was extremely well guarded, this mission could have been suicidal but it succeeded. Could there have been inside help? If so, the SS will take revenge. The nuclear bomb project is now set back by years.

February 23, 1943

Reinhard Heydrich is one of Hitler's most trusted and powerful SS generals. He is one of the planners of the Final Solution and was put in charge of the occupation of Czechoslovakia, Bohemia, and Moravia. This area is of particular importance to Hitler for its steel and armaments production. Heydrich has ruled with an iron hand and was feared by most Czechs.

We have read that Heydrich has been assassinated by two Czech resistance fighters named Jan Kubis and Jozef Gabcik. They hit his moving car with a grenade that exploded with splinters of steel into Heydrich's spleen and lumbar region. The SS tracked the assassins to a hideout in a church and at great loss of many men, the SS trapped them in the church's crypt and then killed them.

February 28, 1943

Germany lost sixty-three U-boats just this month. This is not sustainable and Germany cannot train crews fast enough to replace lost U-boats. It is amazing that the Navy has produced so many hundreds of U-boats and has been able to procure the raw materials needed to build these underwater vessels.

March 2, 1943

Naval Report: A huge battle in the Bismarck Sea against U.S. and Australian ships has resulted in a German Naval defeat.

March 3, 1943

Himmler, SS: Medical staff and patients of the Jewish hospital in Rotterdam have been transported to Westerbork. Their destination is Sobibor and the gas chambers.

March 4, 1943

SS Report: Transporting large numbers of Dutch and French Jews to Majdanek/Sobibor death camps.

March 5, 1943

I received a command from von Braun that Hitler wanted to meet me in person to discuss his intense interest in rocketry. I went (with the SS escort) to his bunker for a face-to-face session and a long lecture by him.

Hitler is convinced that there are various species in the human race and that interbreeding is sinful. He believes that the Germans had racial enemies and that his task is to kill them.

Frankly, I think it is an act and an excuse to steal other people's property and a way for his followers to terrorize defenseless people. He refers to his book Mein Kompf (my struggles) and the ceaseless strife of races as his essence. The weak are to be dominated by the strong and he "must preserve his species."

As he continues to talk non-stop, he refers to images such as God, prayers, commandments, and paradise so he can appeal to Christians. He is brilliant in a diabolical way, referring to the need to murder their races and reproduce Germans. He then transitions to Jews whom he plans to kill to "restore paradise" and claims he is "defending the work of the Lords" since Jews are a non? race and have "corrupted" civilization. He says that mass murder was a good act and would prevent capitalism and communism. He further states that laws have the purpose to codify his beliefs about race and that Germans would follow "the law." I am in shock that a mad man's fantasy is believed by a highly educated and "cultured" population. Perhaps a thousand years of German anti-Semitism has set the scene. Hitler shouts that Germans would always be victims as long as there are Jews.

Hitler referred to the first World War and believes that in 1918 Germans would not have been defeated if there were no Jews. He says he will accomplish World War II by conquest, starvation and murder of inferior races, which completely eliminate Jews and "their ideas."

Hitler then turned to science and his fascination with rocketry as a way to further his ambitions. That is why I am here and forced to listen first to this mad tirade that the German people have accepted and follow. He does not seem to grasp that Germany has lost the Battle of Britain Air War, is losing hundreds of U-boats, is occupying Western countries while he simultaneously diluted supplies and man power with an extended push on Russia. As a rocket guidance expert, I was able to explain why rockets can be effective weapons and he accepts my theories with great enthusiasm without realizing the massive resources needed to produce a rocket, and the uncertainty of even hitting a target many hundreds of miles away. He is also unaware of my ability to calibrate minute guidance settings that can cause rockets to malfunction in flight or bypass a target.

To Hitler, my scientific ability to help manufacture weapons had a purpose to help fulfill his racial rantings. To him, the technical achievement of the rockets is proof of racial superiority. Had he stopped to consider my being a descendant of Rabbi Moses Mendelsohn, he might have gone berserk.

March 8, 1943

Luftwaffe: Allied bombers are pounding Germany and this must cause the Luftwaffe to withdraw from other fronts to try to protect German cities. It is obvious that means eventual retreat on a broad scale. Before it is too late, Hitler must sue for peace or else he will destroy Germany. Some of the cities hit are Essen and Nuremberg.

March 10, 1943

Wehrmacht: Battles are waging in North Africa between the German Army's Rommel and the British Army's Montgomery.

Bulletin: The U.S. Army has just landed in Tunisia under the command of General Patton.

March 10, 1943

SS: The SS has diverted assets to the Greek island of Salonika in order to arrest an ancient Jewish community and send all the Jews to a death camp. With battles raging on four fronts, why would the SS divert assets to kill civilians?

March 12, 1943

Wehrmacht: German forces continue to retreat in Russia, but German armies are regrouping for another offensive.

March 13, 1943

Letter from a friend: A letter written to me in January miraculously made it to Peenemünde. My friend was with the German Sixth Army fatally trapped on the frozen outskirts of Stalingrad. He "blamed Hitler for demanding the Army advance while starving and freezing." "Death is certain." "Even if we could have escaped, we have run out of fuel." "There is no way out." "This is a lesson for Germany, but Hitler is crazed and will not listen."

March 15, 1943

Internal Rumor: Assassination attempt on Hitler during a flight has failed. This supposedly was planned by some top officers who believe the war is lost. Unfortunately, the SS guards discovered the explosives.

March 20, 1943

Himmler is furious that Bulgaria upset his plans for German trains to transport all of the 54,000 Bulgarian Jews to death camps. The head of the Bulgarian Orthodox Church persuaded the King to save the Jews and the Church sheltered Bulgarian Jews. The King dispersed Jews all over the country to make it hard to find them.

March 21, 1943

Internal Memo: Another assassination attempt on Hitler. It seems obvious that professional Army officers realize Hitler has made monumental errors and want to eliminate Hitler while there is still a chance to save Germany.

March 23, 1943

Wehrmacht- North Africa Corp counter-attacks U.S. Lines.

March 25, 1943

Rail cars are desperately needed for the war effort and to evacuate German troops from the east. Nevertheless, the SS continues to divert trains and rail cars to various ghettos and holding camps in order to take Jews to death camps.

A good example is France. When France fell in June of 1940, it was divided into Nazi-occupied France and Vichy France. France has a long history of anti-Semitism and blaming Jews for a variety of problems. The French churches bear some of the responsibility. Both France's established anti-Semitic laws and established many, many concentration camps. Now, in 1943, the French and Nazis continue sending trainload after trainload of Jews to the death camps.

March 27, 1943

My Family: I have made frequent demands to the SS handlers who track my work and travel to Mittelwerk that they must inform me of where my wife and son are being kept under guard.

They do not allow communication of any kind and I have never seen a photo of my son so I do not know what he now looks like. The SS assures me that as long as I research and produce rocket guidance systems, my family will be safe and taken care of. My son is almost nine years old and it has been five years since I have seen him and Julia. I miss them profoundly and worry that they will survive.

March 28, 1943

Wehrmacht- Eastern Front: The defeats at Stalingrad and Leningrad have been horrendous, but the Fuhrer has ordered a counter-attack even though we have lost over a million troops. I question his sense of reality... whether his blood lust has overcome any remaining sanity.

April 3, 1943

SS: The Polish people continue to fully cooperate with the SS in rounding up many thousands of Jews. The Poles are paid in sugar, zlotys, and keep the goods they steal from the Jews. All parts of Polish society are participating in this round-up of Jews and are complicit in condemning their Jewish neighbors to death camps.

April 5, 1943

Navy Bulletin: Spies in England report that the Allies appear to be diverting long-range bombers to the Atlantic. Also, they have learned that more sophisticated radar has been introduced which can detect U-boat conning towers from twelve miles away. To further cause concern, the Germans planted deep in British intelligence have concern that the British have cracked the Enigma code and will be able to anticipate U-boat movement. The British do not yet realize that German intelligence can decipher up to 80% of Britain's naval traffic, which until now has given U-boats an advantage.

April 7, 1943

Wehrmacht: North Africa, U.S., and British forces have linked up. This may be too much for Rommel to repel.

April 8, 1943

Report by spies in North Africa: A year after the Allies liberated French Morocco and saved hundreds of thousands of North African Jews from the Nazis and Vichy French, full rights for North African Jews have been reinstated.

April 9, 1943

Speer's armament office memo: A nuclear bomb could give Germany a quick victory, but most of the prominent physicists are Jewish and fled Germany. Werner Heisenberg did remain but was harassed by the Gestapo. Speer's agent in the U.S. reports that numerous German-Jewish physicists are now working in New Mexico on nuclear research.

April 10, 1943

Navy Bulletin: Albert Gemmeker, the Nazi commander of Westerbork Concentration Camp, has written an informative piece for the internal Nazi bulletin. He explains how he has created very livable conditions in order to lull the Dutch Jewish occupants into thinking they would be working. The civil environment is much like Theresienstadt, only much less crowded and more "relaxed." The reality is that Westerbork is a transit camp destined to send an estimated 100,000 Dutch Jews to their death. This is a sophisticated fa9ade and an effective form of deception.

April 12, 1943

Holland. Hitler continues to murder Jews throughout Europe and is pursuing Dutch Jews. Holland has a long history of a productive Jewish society that dates back to post-Inquisition settlers from Portugal and Spain. When Hitler was persecuting Jews in Germany, many families immigrated to Holland so that the Jewish population swelled to about 150,000. Since they lived in a relatively confined area, they were a perfect target for the Nazis. In recent months, the Nazi death squads have sent tens of thousands to the Sobibor death camp in Poland where no one survives. Other Dutch Jews are being sent to Auschwitz for forced labor and death. Many Dutch Jews were prosperous, so they became ready targets for the Nazi thieves and murderers.

Some of my colleagues believe that the Dutch shoreline will provide a logical launching pad location when Hitler targets England or other countries with the now advanced design rockets that are secretly in early prototype construction phases. MM

April 19, 1943

SS Poland: The SS has herded hundreds of thousands of Jews into the Warsaw Ghetto under the worst conditions. The ultimate goal is to send them all to death camps. Today the Jews in the ghetto have attacked the Wehrmacht. This gives the Waffen-SS the excuse to wipe out the Warsaw Ghetto.

April 22, 1943

Luftwaffe: Fourteen German transport planes attempting to supply the North Africa Corp have been shot down over the Mediterranean Sea by British fighter planes.

April 15, 1943

Wehrmacht Prison Report: Since the beginning of the Soviet invasion, the Wehrmacht has shot or starved to death over three million Russian prisoners. Personally, when the tide turns, it is obvious that the Russians will be ruthless in their revenge.

April 26, 1943

The German agent posing as a U.S. State Department official has reported that he attended a conference that occurred in Bermuda last month. British and American officials are well aware of the concentration camps and the killing of hundreds of thousands of Jews. They were advised by Germany that Germany was willing to stop the gas chambers and release a million or more Jews to go the U.S. and Britain. The British Foreign Office and the State Department decided not to press the Germans too hard, and, therefore, allowed the killings to continue. "They were afraid the Third Reich would stop the gas chambers and concentration camps and let the survivors immigrate to the west."

A related subject that has troubled me is the stance of the Vatican and Pope Pius XII. The Pope is supposed to be a force of moral leadership and can influence the vast Catholic populations in Europe. However, he has remained silent in the face of all knowledge of the murders of Jews and others in the concentration camps. Ironically, silence is in accord with what the Western Powers did at Bermuda. There are some that say the Vatican is surrounded by Italian and German troops and that silence is a way to self-preservation, but it seems unlikely that Mussolini or Hitler would be foolish enough to harm the Pope. In all fairness, there are rumors the pope has done numerous things to secretly save Jewish lives.

April 28, 1943

Wehrmacht: German and Italian forces counter-attack in North Africa.

April 30, 1943

The Bergen-Belsen death camp has been opened.

May 7, 1943
Wehrmacht: German troops are vacating various cities in Tunisia as British Army's advance.

May 9, 1943
Wehrmacht: Fifth German Panzer Army has surrendered in Tunisia.

May 12, 1943
Wehrmacht: All Axis forces in North Africa have surrendered. A huge blow to Hitler with the loss of men and tanks that should have been guarding Western Europe's flanks.

May 15, 1943
Waffen-SS: The Warsaw Ghetto has been destroyed and all Jewish defenders killed. (The use of vast Nazi resources should have been directed towards halting the Russian advance and instead have been used to kill Jews).

May 15, 1943
SS Report from Lithuania: There were 200,000 Jews in Lithuania when the SS arrived in 1941. Today, nearly the entire Jewish population has perished. Local collaborators have been most helpful to the SS. Many Lithuanians have helped send Jews to be executed so they could confiscate their wealth and possessions.

May 16, 1943
SS Warsaw: The Warsaw Ghetto uprising has been liquidated, along with 50,000 Jews who were burned, shot, or deported.

May 18, 1943
Wehrmacht Tunisia: American troops have broken Wehrmacht defenses and Germany has lost over 300,000 of our top-notch soldiers.

May 18, 1943
It seems that German Naval leaders have forgotten recent history as they

pursue a U-boat strategy to stop supplies from reaching Britain and as a way to fight the British and U.S. navies. As chronicled in earlier diary entries, the U-boats managed to sink more American ships than could be built, but then the Allies became much more sophisticated in hunting U-boats and the U-boat loses are becoming catastrophic.

Why do I refer to history of naval warfare? In the first World War, German U-boats had spectacular success starting in January 1916. Eventually, bad weather, underwater nets, mines, and depth charges, and destroyers decimated the U-boats and clearly destroyed half of Germany's U-boats, along with death to the crews. Had the German Navy learned a lesson from World War I, it might not have repeated the U-boat strategy.

May 23, 1943

Luftwaffe: Massive air raids by Allied bombers continue to wipe out German cities.

May 24, 1943

The German SS embedded in British Central Intelligence advises that aerial photos of the island of Usedom are being carefully studied. Usedom facilities are permanent so that Peenemünde is vulnerable to aerial bombing attacks.

May 26, 1943

Nazi Party Bulletin: Dateline, Krakow, Poland. From Governor Hans Frank. "We have been very busy with organizing the genocide carried out at nearby Auschwitz and other camps. We have deported the inhabitants to Kazimierz, the Jewish Quarter, along with 184 professors from Krakow University. Also, Salesian priests have been sent to Auschwitz. Some priests have been hiding Jews and Hitler has ordered us not to hunt these priests since he has an agreement with the Pope.

June 2, 1943

Wehrmacht: German assault on Sebastopol begins in an attempt to protect supply routes for the Army that is retreating further north and east.

June 5, 1943

Goebbels Radio Speech: Blames Jews for World War I defeat, for Bolshevism, for backing Roosevelt, for backing Stalin, for world domination, and for Wehrmacht losses. Goebbels rants that Jewish citizenship was a mistake and Jews must be exterminated. I find Goebbels to be absurd and demented. Germany is absorbing huge losses of soldiers on many fronts due to Nazi misguided policies and he is blaming a minuscule percentage of our country that has been "imprisoned" since the 1930s.

June 8, 1943

The lab has a great friend in Albert Speer, who has just appointed Gerhard Degenkolb to expedite rocket production. Degenkolb proposes to use three heavy industry facilities to build 900 rockets a month. I am aware that our Colonel Dornberger and Von Braun do not like Degenkolb since Degenkolb is a builder and engineer rather than a scientist who understands our research.

June 8, 1943

Waffen-SS: Report from Eastern Galicia. Russian troops are still three hundred miles to the east so extermination of Jews is being carried out with haste. In most cases the Jews are taken to the forest, shot, and thrown in death pits. Most children are thrown alive into the pits and bodies are thrown on top of them.

June 10, 1943

Dornberger has briefed us on the plan to build launching bunkers in Northern France. This is an effort to save a war that is virtually lost, so the bunkers must be completed rapidly and made to withstand bombing. The Eastern front was a disaster and American bombing raids on Germany are of increasing intensity.

June 10, 1943

Navy Bulletin: U-boats are being confronted by new Allied technology and aircraft, and losses are mounting dramatically. A very high percent of U-boats naval personnel are being lost.

Grand Admiral Karl Donitz has stated that U-boat warfare may now be impossible. To make matters worse for Germany, the English Channel will soon be unpatrolled by U-boats, which makes a channel crossing by the Allies an imminent threat.

June 11, 1943

SS: Heinrich Himmler has ordered the extermination of all the Polish Ghettos. His plan is to then round up all Jews in Amsterdam and ship them to death camps.

June 14, 1943

Interior Ministry: Counter espionage experts have revealed that Germany's minister in Switzerland is in constant touch with Allan Dulles of the U.S., an O.S.S. officer. The German is Fritz Kolbe, and he has been given access to all high-security documents. However, the Wehrmacht has altered the information so that Kolbe is passing on inaccurate documents. Kolbe is associated with the White Roses, an anti-Nazi German group. Their identity is known and SS will execute White Roses in "due time."

June 22, 1943

Our designers and engineers are working feverishly on the V-2 while very nearby other engineers are rushing to test the V-1. Foolishly, we do not talk to them or share research results. This is due to jealousy between the Army and the Air Force.

June 23, 1943

Internal Memo: One of the SS spies imbedded in the RAF command center reports that RAF recon has positively identified Peenemünde. At last, they have used the material I and others have smuggled out to the British.

June 25, 1943

Waffen-SS: Announced completion of the crematorium at Birkenau.

June 29, 1943

The head of the SS, Heinrich Himmler, has visited Peenemünde to inspect a rocket launching. The launch failed and this caused us to be very concerned. Why? Because it is well known that he controls hundreds of thousands of fanatical men and operated a "separate state" within the Third Reich. At lunch, Himmler talked about Hitler's war aims and tried to justify the colossal front in Russia which absorbed much of Germany's resources. We think that Himmler may have his own rocket testing site, so this visit is very suspicious.

June 29, 1943

Rocket guidance research: I have studied a system we call inertial guidance, which will give me greater control of ways to subtly sabotage our rockets. My work on inertial navigators consists of three grouped gyroscopes to indicate direction and accelerometers that measure changes in speed and direction and thereby guide the course of a rocket. My setting of these instruments will guide the rocket course but not directly to an intended target. The system should work in all kinds of weather and can avoid being jammed.

Early work on "IG" was done by German engineer, Max Schuler. I have refined IG so that it will guide the V-2 rockets against England when we get the V-2 operational. My access to the plans and production allows me to set enough of the guidance systems to hit, but most will fly over the targets.

June 30, 1943

Naval report: Intelligence advised that an Allied invasion may be forthcoming. The Navy has pulled U-boats back towards the continent in order to try to stop the invasion.

July 1, 1943

I was invited to join Dornberger and von Braun to meet with Hitler at his field headquarters in East Prussia. We showed him a launch film, review models and I explained the guidance systems. Hitler was most interested and assured us that the V-2 program will be elevated to the highest priority, including labor and materials. His expectations are unrealistic as to how many we can produce and his support may have come much too late. Hitler was very distracted by the reports of massive problems on the Russian Front.

July 3, 1943

SS contingents have been added to Peenemünde's security force. Since we have spies amongst us, this may be a good thing even though it injects Himmler's SS into our site.

July 5, 1943

Wehrmacht, Kursk: At Hitler's command, the Wehrmacht has amassed thousands of tanks to attack the Russian Army at Kursk. Wehrmacht reports during the preceding months stated that for the retreating Army, the high command needed a massive offensive against Russia. The Luftwaffe has been included and Germany has been producing many thousands of tanks and planes. Nine hundred thousand troops have been moved from the Western Front and based in Russia. Kursk is a strategic "bulge" in German lines, so it was chosen as this massive attack point.

July 6, 1943

Wehrmacht, Kursk: Russian intelligence and British intercepts have learned a lot about the Wehrmacht plans and have also amassed vast numbers of troops, tanks, and artillery pieces. It appears they have laid hundreds of thousands of anti-tank land mines in the path of Wehrmacht tanks. Yesterday, Russia launched a massive artillery bombardment which killed 25,000 German troops and impacted German morale. It appears Germany's plan has been compromised.

July 7, 1943

Wehrmacht, Kursk: Germany launched its attack with good Luftwaffe cover. Two hundred tanks have been lost along with hundreds of planes.

July 9, 1943

Wehrmacht, Kursk: Russia has put up a ferocious defense the past few days.

July 10, 1943

Wehrmacht, Kursk: Approximately two-thirds of German tanks have been lost, victim to land mines and anti-tank guns. The world has never seen such a massive tank battle.

July 11. 1943

The Allies have invaded Sicily in what appears to be a very lightly guarded area, since the main body of German troops had been shifted to a possible invasion in Spain. Also, the High Command miscalculated that there would be no Allied invasion of Europe in 1943 and sent hundreds of thousands of troops to the Russian front. The German intelligence was tricked and the Sicily landing means a strong Allied beachhead for moving into Italy, then Germany. This is a coup for the Allies since the high command knows that, at this time, German troops are more experienced and battle-hardened than the Allied troops and had they been at full strength could have easily repelled the Sicily invasion. However, the German command has lost sight of the fact that the German Air Force has been decimated and that the Allies dominate the skies.

July 12, 1943

Wehrmacht, Kursk: Germany tried a tank breakthrough fifty miles southeast of Kursk and it has failed. More tanks and men lost.

July 15, 1943

Wehrmacht, Kursk: Russia has launched a major counter-offensive.

July 19, 1943

Wehrmacht, Kursk: German Army is pulling back. Russian Air Force has stopped Luftwaffe's efforts and RAF is now harassing German troops.

July 25, 1943

Luftwaffe: Unable to stop Allied bombing of Hamburg. A million are fleeing and there is a loss of 20,000 German lives. The Allies are totally destroying Germany cities at will, yet Hitler continues to battle Allied armies. It is obvious that Germany is gone and we should stop the rocket work now instead of using vast resources in desperation.

July 27, 1943

Wehrmacht: Dozens of retreating troop trains are being sabotaged by partisans and they are then attacked by the Russian Air Force.

July 27, 1943

Heimich Himmler Bulletin: The SS reports that 2.5 million of Poland's Jews have been killed and a further million Jews in Northern Russia and the Baltic States have been murdered.

July 30, 1943

Bulletins have been pouring in about decisive German military disasters. These include Kursk on the Eastern Front facing massive Russian forces (supplied by the U.S.A.), North Africa and Italy. In addition, our lab has seen a detailed report regarding German Army drug use that is shocking. The report explains that Germany has a history of leading-edge pharmaceutical drug companies. They include LG. Farben, Bayer, and Merck. All of them have produced addictive drugs for doctors and flooded the German and world market.

During the early days of Nazi power, Hitler tried to depict drugs as a Jewish plot to weaken the nation. The truth is that much of the population is on drugs, including Hitler. The Army uses drugs to enhance troop performance. A product called Pervitin is popular throughout Germany.

The September 1939 invasion of Poland used Pervitin extensively to banish hunger, reduce fear, and make it possible for soldiers to keep going for days without sleep. When Germany attacked Holland and Belgium to force France and England to come to their aid, German troops quickly penetrated the Ardennes in Belgium and crossed Northern France to cut off the British and French. This daring maneuver had German troops going for days without rests. The obvious result of drug use allowed non-stop assault for three days. The French Army fell by total surprise, hence a speedy and ruthless defeat of the French and British armies.

However, for some unknown reason, German tanks stopped short of Dunkirk, which allowed many thousands of British and French troops to escape across the channel to England.

The report further states that, unlike the lightening quick invasion of France, Operation Barbarossa against the Soviet Union could not be won with the Wehrmacht's chemicals due to vast distances.

Further reports show that Hitler is laced with various drugs which no doubt contribute to his fantasies and extremely bad decision and loss of reality. This can only spell eventual and costly defeat for the Wehrmacht.

August 2, 1943

There are reports of constant Allied bombing raids on German cities. So far, the island of Usedom has been bypassed, but I am certain (especially due to the information I sent to the British) that the Americans and British are aware of the activity at Peenemünde.

August 15, 1943

German armies are in full retreat on the Eastern Front, with heavy casualties and abandoned armaments. As a student of history, I cannot help but think of comparing Hitler with Napoleon. Napoleon yearned for battles and was ruthless in pursuing conquests over much of Europe. This included Austria, Italy and Spain. He tried to destroy British trade with Europe to the point where the British declared war against France. Napoleon pursued British Allies Austria, Russia, and Prussia. His armies brutally controlled civilian populations, and he financed his empire by looting the entire continent, not unlike Hitler, killing Jews and others in order to confiscate their assets at no cost. However, when Napoleon made an alliance with Austria, he then made a catastrophic invasion of Russia, which is just what Hitler, however, has done. Both men were/are obsessed with world domination.

Napoleon was a tyrant who murdered his enemies without scruple and whose foremost interest was to promote himself–like Hitler. Both men have inflicted horrors on everyone in pursuit of "glory."

August 18, 1943

Last night Allied bombers held a massive raid on Usedom and Peenemünde. The Army's hope of new weapons to tum the tide of war has been completely shattered. Göring's Air Force had failed miserably to protect Germany. The bombing seemed to focus on the rocket research area, which confirmed my suspicions that British spies were working at Peenemünde. Scientists' quarters, the pilot factory, and the offices were obliterated. Last night the Army reported bombing of Berlin by planes that passed Usedom. So, the Usedom defenses were caught off? guard by this second, massive wave of Allied bombers. We assume that they flew in very low to the sea level so as to evade our radar. The Allied raid killed Walter Thiel who was our expert in rocket propellants and in the design of combustion chambers. He was the genius who designed a rocket motor with enormous thrust.

August 19, 1943

The German Air Force has admitted to being completely fooled by the decoy bombers over Berlin, which caused them to fly 300 night fighter planes against a bomber attack which did not occur.

This left Peenemünde completely without air protection. Since the British planned the bombing of Peenemünde for an hour after the decoy Berlin raid, the Luftwaffe fighter planes ran out of fuel and as many as thirty crash-landed.

My examination of the island requested by Dornberger revealed damage to the liquid oxygen plant, the power station, and the living complex of 3,000 scientific workers. Also, foreign workers who did forced labor had their settlement reduced to rubble. Von Braun lost a number of his close collaborators.

August 20, 1943

The Luftwaffe reports their Chief of Staff, General Hans Jeschonneck has been blamed for the Berlin/Peenemünde fiasco and has committed suicide.

August 22, 1943

The SS has established Battalion 101, which is composed of Polish political officers. They are instructed to kill Jewish men, women and children in Poland. I cannot understand how these ordinary men willingly carry out an extreme genocide. Their obedience to the SS orders causes these men to be murderers without qualms. A bulletin quotes one of the former policemen as "driving naked Jews directly into graves and shooting them"

August 23, 1943

Wehrmacht: Kharkov Russian troops have broken through German defenses. The Battle of Kursk has ended in Wehrmacht withdrawal.

I am certain Russia will now seek revenge and pursue German armies westward towards Germany. Wehrmacht has lost 500,000 men killed, wounded or missing, and much of the tank corps is destroyed.

August 29, 1943

Navy Report: Germany planned to use the Danish navy ships against the Allies, but Denmark has scuttled its fleet. Denmark has saved its Jews from Nazi slaughter by ferrying them to "neutral" shelter.

September 7, 1943

Vilna Ghetto: Several thousand Jews in the ghetto have been sent to the Treblinka extermination camp. The sick and elderly have been executed, while the balance will be used as slave labor.

The Allies are turning the tide of war against Germany and yet our leadership is intent on the genocide of innocent civilians. Before the British air raid, our lab had accelerated the research to perfect the V-1 and V-2, which now seems to me to be a desperate waste of resources. All the while, the Nazis are obsessed with exterminating all Jews throughout Europe.

September 8, 1943

Wehrmacht: U.S. General Eisenhower announces unconditional surrender of Italy. Our major ally is gone, so Germany must desperately fight to retreat in Italy.

September 9, 1943

Most German civilians I talk to are aware of the mass killing of the Jews and other atrocities. They know from the letters and photos sent by active-duty relatives and conversations with men on leave. They still seemed shocked by the Allied bombings and many regret that they have followed Hitler "over a cliff." However, none seem repentant about their own government's atrocities.

September 10, 1943

Propaganda chief, Goebbels, has convinced Germans that this war launched by Hitler is one of self-defense. His theme is that the French, Russian, British, and Americans are controlled by the Jews who want to destroy Germany. It is beyond comprehension how an educated population can believe Goebbels.

September 10, 1943

The easy victory over France a few years ago made Germans euphoric. However, by 1943, with enormous losses in the East, there are lots of second thoughts and bouts of unpopularity with the regime.

September 11, 1943

Wehrmacht: German troops now occupy Rome and by "special arrangement" are protecting the Vatican.

September 11, 1943

SS: We have liquidated the Jewish ghettos of Minsk and Lida.

September 13, 1943

Wehrmacht: Battle is raging in Italy. Allied forces advancing. Fierce battles, especially in the mountains.

September 13, 1943

Waffen-SS: In spite of the front-line war effort, the SS continues to open many more concentration camps. This is diverting valuable resources in order to commit murder.

September 15, 1943

Von Braun has convinced the high command and Hitler that development is complete and that we can start production. His enthusiasm has won Hitler's approval in spite of earlier criticism of the high cost and complexity of the rocket.

Technically the fuel the rocket uses is an ethanol/water mixture and liquid oxygen. It reaches a height of 80 km, the pumps are steam driven, and the tanks are specially produced metal alloy. The combustion of the fuel is at approximately 4,500° F, which produces numerous technical challenges in combustion chambers. My guidance system relies on four external rudders on the tail fins and internal motor vanes. There will be a gyroscope for the horizon and one for vertical guidance and lateral stability. We have been able to determine when the motor must shut off causing the flight curve and the horizontal angle to reach a precise target. All of this is subject to human calibration of key controls and that is where I am still secretly making my "statement" of resistance to the Nazi regime. There is also the possibility of using a beam guidance system but that will be rare.

The V-2 development had various problems that had to be solved. These included reducing tank pressure and weight, creating a lighter combustion chamber, specific cooling mechanisms, relays that can withstand vibrations, fuel pipes that reduced the chance of explosion, fins that avoided damage from expanded jet exhausts and fins that could control the V-2 at supersonic speeds. I think we could build four bombers with known technology for the price of one very complex rocket that might not do much damage after it hits.

The question is where to start production that is safe from Allied air raids.

September 18, 1943

Wehrmacht: Retreat continues on the Eastern Front due to withering Russian attacks.

September 23, 1943

Navy Bulletin: The U-boat fleet has taken a toll on the Allied supply lines by sinking numerous merchant ships. In the process, the British and Americans have hunted the U-boats by air and sea.

Recently, the loss of U-boats has increased dramatically. We know the British have the German Navy code and have changed their depth charge patterns and intensity.

October 6, 1943

SS Bulletin: Himmler announces acceleration of murdering of Jews throughout Europe. This will include sending Rome's Jews to Auschwitz. To date, there is no comment from Pope Pius. The ghetto at Riga, Latvia is to be targeted.

October 7, 1943

Himmler: From Germany's source within the U.S. White House. Four hundred American rabbis came to the White House yesterday to present proof to F.D.R. that the Nazis are murdering European Jews. F.D.R. turned them away.

That means the SS and German civilian collaborators can continue killing Jews as they wish and without any U.S. interference.

October 9, 1943

Wehrmacht Bulletin: German women by the thousands are being made an integral part of Hitler's machinery. They service the troops and his workers of every vocation in the occupied countries. There are thousands of German nurses caring for Wehrmacht wounded soldiers.

Some are stationed at concentration camps to aid in medical experiments.

October 11, 1943

SS Report: The SS Report boasts of keeping track of Jewish killing sites. This has required vast resources and been aided by local populations. In addition, the SS reports many German women have participated at the killing sites and as death camp guards.

October 12, 1943

Coded message to Wehrmacht from Nazi H.Q.: "Following the massive defeat of the Wehrmacht at Stalingrad, many German industrialists scrambled to get funds and gold out of Germany. The American Dulles brothers, who were clever traitors to the U.S., had close German connections and helped transfer funds to Swiss and Belgian banks. Some funds also went through the Vatican, as did gold that was shipped through the Brenner Pass into Italy. The Schroder Bank and Chase Manhattan Bank are deeply involved."

October 15, 1943

I have continued transferring to my contacts with British Army spies and SS messages received on the lab's "hot lines." Various formats are used to avoid detection. So far it has been a success and the word is that the British continue direct decoding. The messages divulge troop movements, supplies and the manpower situation.

Music is an integral part of the Mendelssohn inheritance, so at an early age I learned to read and write music. Today's coding is an "innocent" musical score. The notes then translated to letters, with sharps and flats and other musical symbols representing letter and code sequences.

October 19, 1943

War Production Bulletin, Mittelwerk: In 1942, Albert Speer, the German arms minister, appointed Arthur Rudolph to assemble the V-2 at Peenemünde. Rudolph proposed using concentration camp slave labor to overcome the German labor shortage. By June this year we already used 2,500 slave workers on an assembly line.

As I cautioned, the V-2 is very complex and each one must be specially tested. When the Allies bombed us at Peenemünde on August 17-18, we were forced to look for an underground production facility. There were already tunnels under Kohnstein mountain near Nordhausen, so Speer has contracted to produce 12,000 V-2s at the complex he called Mittelwerk. However, the SS has taken over V-2 production under the command of General Hans Kammler. He is known for having built gas chambers at death camps. Mittelwerk already has an extensive tunnel system that is wide enough for a rail car. Slave labor is provided by Dora, an Auschwitz sub? camp set up near the tunnels. Laborers must eat and sleep in the tunnels in crowded, dusty, diseased, and starving environments. All of our equipment from Peenemünde must be installed in the tunnels so I will have to spend time at Mittelwerk to be sure the assembled V-2s are operational.

I am told that the tunnels are to become widened and huge and also used to produce aircraft engines, V-1 flying bombs, synthetic fuel, and aircraft.

October 22, 1943

SS Bulletin, Sobibor: An uprising has occurred in which most of the SS guards were killed and three hundred prisoners escaped. The escapees were hunted and shot.

October 23, 1943

SS Denmark: The Danish King and the Danes have evacuated their small Jewish population at night by small boats across the waters to refuge in Sweden. Himmler is furious and wants to punish Denmark. It is revealed by the SS that this has been occurring over a three-week period and has had support from Danish church leaders who Himmler wants to punish. We know that during the 1930s Denmark refused safe haven to Jews and supplied the Wehrmacht with food. So, this rescue event has shocked the Nazi party controlling Denmark.

November 2, 1943

Allies Announcement: The Allies have issued the Moscow Declaration proposed by Winston Churchill. It states that German War criminals captured by the Allies will be sent to the countries where their crimes were committed for trial and execution (I doubt this will have an effect on the SS madmen).

November 8, 1943

Wehrmacht–Eastern Front: Kiev has been lost to Russian armies. Retreat continues.

November 10, 1943

Personal: Hitler and his advisors made a huge mistake to try to conquer the Middle East. I suspect that oil and control of the Suez Canal shipping lanes motivated this colossal expenditure of men and machines. It also presented an opportunity to kill Jews who were living in British Palestine. In fact, this genocide mentality may have been behind some of the losing battle plans.

Like the invasion of Poland, the Ukraine and Russia, the Middle East campaign took valuable resources away from the control of Western and Eastern Europe. When the U.S. came to the aid of Britain in the desert war, the German Army was destined to be overwhelmed.

Germany has tried to also enlist the support of Arabs, with special emphasis on Muslims living in British Palestine. Considering that Jews in Germany and elsewhere needed to flee the Nazis, the British have been cruel in keeping Jews out of Palestine except in very limited numbers. I wonder if this is to keep Muslims happy or to secretly aid Hitler's murder of Jews; or perhaps both.

We have just been shown a copy of a telegram that Heinrich Himmler sent to Amin al-Husseini, the Grand Mufti of Jerusalem. Husseini has been an active collaborator with the Nazis and broadcasts regularly from Berlin to urge the destruction of world Jewry. Himmler has thanked him for his efforts and pledge solidarity with Muslims in their "struggle" to kill Jews. There is no end in what the Nazis will do and say to recruit allies.

November 15, 1943

Nazi Memo: The American Jewish community has been pressuring the Allies to issue a statement on war crimes. They have now issued a publicized statement that Nazis will be held for war crimes against Poles, French, etc. However, Jews were not mentioned. Hitler sees that as an explicit signal that what he is doing to the Jews is acceptable.

November 18, 1943

High Command: Massive Allied bombing of Berlin. Hitler has moved H.Q. underground.

November 18, 1943

SS Confidential: Due to the massive Allies bombing capacity, it has been decided to build a series of tunnels in Lower Silesia. These will provide a safe haven for Hitler's central command, the SS leadership and provide manufacturing factories that are underground. The Lower Silesia location is out of bomber range at this time. Code name Riese.

There will be nine giant tunnels complete with entrances hidden by forests or other buildings. The labor is to be provided by captured and/or imprisoned concentration camp men. This will require the construction of camps to house the slave laborers. They will work in conditions similar to the Mittelwerk V-1 and V-2 tunnels. However, that means many will die as work proceeds and they will be replaced by other labor from camps and/or occupied countries across Europe.

This ambitious project must involve dozens of German companies, including Krupp. It needs steel, concrete, earth moving equipment, water supplies, sanitation, and communications equipment. All of the companies are fully engaged in these efforts and support the use of slave laborers. In the event of an Allied and Soviet invasion that establishes air bases on the continent, the Lower Silesia will not be within bomb range. Therefore, this Riese project has Hitler's approval to move quickly.

In order to avoid publicity, documentation will be kept to a minimum and upon completion all workers will be sent to their death at Auschwitz. It is expected to take two years for the work to be completed and ready to activate.

November 22, 1943

Navy: Extensive U-boat losses continue in the Atlantic.

November 23, 1943

Wehrmacht: The German high command has expected an Allied invasion of Europe to coincide with German defeats in North Africa and on the Russian Eastern Front. The problem has been to deploy troops where the invasion might take place. We have received a bulletin that a dead body washed ashore in Spain that had papers indicating the person was a British captain acting as a spy. His papers reveal Spain as the invasion point, so we assume German troops will be moved into position in Spain. They will easily be transferred from Italy.

November 20, 1943

SS Bulletin: The German spy planted in England's cabinet office reports Churchill is resisting an Allied amphibious invasion. His memory of England's disastrous attempt at Dieppe has influenced his thinking. Roosevelt is intent on a cross channel invasion, so it is now only a matter of where and when.

November 24, 1943

Foreign Ministry Report: The German spies who have infiltrated the Roosevelt Administration report that FDR holds anti-Semitic views which he expresses frequently in public. It is ironic that such a high percent of the U.S. Jewish population votes for him and his Democratic colleagues. With this knowledge of Roosevelt's antisemitism, Hitler feels very comfortable to continue annihilating the Jews of Europe.

November 24, 1943

SS Report: Heinrich Himmler has placed Haj Amin Al-Husseini, the Muslim Mufti of Jerusalem, in charge of recruiting Muslims to serve in the Wehrmacht. The goal is to recruit at least 150,000 Muslims. Al-Husseini is also to encourage the Muslims of the Middle East to kill Jewish neighbors.

November 25, 1943

The RAF is making concentrated bombings on Berlin and other German cities. This is significant in many ways. First, it means that Germany has lost conventional air power superiority. In that event, I believe Hitler will be even more obsessed with launching unmanned rockets to seek to intimidate the British. That helps our V-2 program.

Second, this bombing may make the German people more determined to unify under Hitler. How could a highly educated, cultured and scientific-achieving people believe the designs of gangsters such as Hitler, Himmler, and Goebbels? Clergy of Protestant and Catholic faiths are doing nothing. That includes Otto Dibelius, the Protestant Bishop of Berlin, and Catholic Bishop Konrad Graf von Preysing. There could be various events that influenced German Christian clergy, such as the loss of territory under the Versailles Treaty, or Churchill's rejection of Hitler's 1940 peace offer, or the "crusade" against "Godless Bolshevism." Nothing can justify the reports of the mindless slaughter of Jews and Slavs by the Nazis.

December 1, 1943

V-2 Production: Under the direction of Arthur Rudolph, the underground factory at Mittelwerk is now using 10,500 slave laborers supplied by the Dora camp. He has had his slaves do major tunneling by hand, living underground, working 12-hours shifts without ventilation, no heat, no toilets, and limited food and water.

December 3, 1943

Foreign Ministry: German spies report Churchill and Stalin are meeting in Tehran to map strategy for invasion of Europe. In the meanwhile, fighting continues in Italy and the German Army is putting up stiff resistance.

December 4, 1943

The German government has mastered the art of coercing organizations that might make Nazis look civilized. A prime example is the International Red Cross, which is under the direction of Jacob Burckhardt. He is a "classic" anti-Semite who thinks that the Nazis are a necessary evil.

The IRC has ignored pleas of help from concentration camp victims and issued statements that whitewash the Nazis in the eyes of the international press. In essence, IRC is serving Nazi propaganda purposes. In earlier diary entries I have mentioned how a year earlier the IRC knew about the Wannsee Conference's plan to exterminate Jews and did nothing to intervene. It is well known that Burckhardt is friendly with leading Nazis such as Adolph Eichmann and Joseph Mengele. IRC is based in Switzerland, a country that claims to be neutral but in reality has been cooperating with Hitler as a giant repository of stolen art and stolen funds.

December 5, 1943

The Nazis have tried to keep the concentration camps a dark secret from the German public and from world opinion. We, however, have just learned that a Polish officer, Witold Pilecki, actually got himself arrested and sent to Auschwitz in order to experience the extreme camp brutality and act as a witness to reveal the Auschwitz horror. After surviving three years of torture and brutality, he made a daring escape and has publicly revealed in unembellished frankness the horrors of the Final Solution. It is my strong belief that the world and German public has known all along what the Nazis have been doing for over a decade and simply turned away.

Shame on them since this indifference has given a free hand to these madmen. Now at least Pilecki's published accounts cannot be ignored.

December 8, 1943

I continue to visit Dora and Mittelwerk to inspect rocket assembly under the direction of Rudolph. There are now 10,000 slave laborers working underground. They are mainly Jews from all over Europe and captured Russians, Poles, and Czechs. As I observed in prior visits, they live underground and work twelve-hour shifts, seven days a week. There is no ventilation, no heat, no drinking water, and meager food rations. They sleep on bare rocks. There are no medicines and frequent beatings and executions. They are dying by the hundreds and are trucked to Dora for cremation. I am shocked by the barbarous conditions. Himmler's policy is to deliberately work the prisoners to death.

I was given a tour of Dora's medical facility and told that at most, camp German doctors have a free hand to perform medical experiments on their prisoners. There are prominent physicians stationed in camps who test altitude tolerance, immersion in ice tanks, testing typhus vaccine, etc.

It is clear to me that the Nazis and Wehrmacht have taken murder to a new sadistic level. The entire country of Germany has been industrializing murder to a mass scale, with a state objective of genocide. Germany is a killing machine. Back in the privacy of my own lab, I wept openly at the horrors perpetrated by Germany and resolved to dedicate my life to sabotage this regime and still remain alive.

December 9, 1943

Report from the War Production Bureau: Observers behind the Russian lines and our spies in the U.S., report massive supplies have been sent by the U.S. to restock Russia's arms and food supplies. Hitler was warned in 1941 that the U.S. has unlimited manufacturing resources and that is when he should have consolidated Germany's position by suing for peace. Now it is way too late to save Germany. The U.S. supplies to Russia are valued at tens of billions of dollars.

Arms include a volume of tanks three times the Soviet losses, 15,000 fighter planes, high octane fuel for the tanks and planes, communications equipment, 400,000 trucks, and raw material such as aluminum for Russia's own production for rail/road troop movement. The U.S. has supplied 400 locomotives and 11,000 rail cars. It is no wonder that Russia is now overwhelming the Wehrmacht.

December 10, 1943

Allied air power is dominating the skies and providing a distinct advantage to them. Germany possesses very accurate radar-guided anti-aircraft defenses that can hit some of the planes in the wake of strategic bombing raids. Our fighter planes are somewhat operational, but the U.S. possess a fighter known as the P38, which is a high speed, dual engine plane with heavy armaments that has been raising havoc with German fighter planes. The American bombers accompanied by the P38s have blanket bombed many cities, but in some cases, this has only made German "herd" more loyal to Hitler.

On the other hand, the tactical Allied air campaigns on German troops, oil shipping and targets in support of battlefield operations have taken a toll. The high command is pressing Rocket Central to make the V-1 and V-2 operational since Hitler is frantic to retaliate with the unmanned rockets.

December 11, 1943

Personal: I have been forced to aid the Nazi war effort and have seen the massive cruelty and cold-blooded murder committed by the German people. When the V-2 is operational and being used as a massive weapon, there will surely be many innocents killed. In order to survive with dignity, I must admit to bitterness and hatred for the people with whom I work.

December 11, 1943

I have constantly thought about the importance of being literate about historical events. An understanding of history provides a "roadmap" for my own family and a direction for our country. Hitler has re-written world history and completely ignored the lessons learned from unchecked aggression against other nations. Dictators of other eras have overextended and brought disaster on their nations. More recently, Napoleon failed and it is obvious that Hitler will fail in his massive conquests that have overextended German supply lines and manpower.

Madness will not prevail.

In the meantime, our rocket work has been supported so I continue to "keep my head down," prolong a final guidance breakthrough, and pray to survive. The only word that I hear about my immediate family is through the SS who assures me they are still alive and well and will be alright as long as I make progress in the lab and am "loyal" to the Nazis.

December 12, 1943

SS Bulletin: Hitler has met with Himmler and issues a statement that the Nazis will destroy a conspiracy against Aryans that is orchestrated by the Jews who are using Churchill, Roosevelt, and Stalin as their tools. This seems delusional to me. The published statement goes on to say that Hitler plans to conquer Europe first and then plans to attack the U.S.

December 12, 1943

Speer Production Report: Minister Albert Speer complains of a disparity of resources and production capacity between the Axis and the Allies. For example, the Soviets have produced 21,000 combat planes; England 15,000; the U.S. twice as many planes as Japan and Germany combined; Germany 10,000 planes. Speer is producing new tanks, such as the Tiger and Panther tanks.

Our inner circle at Peenemünde has discussed rumors that Hitler was told a year ago that production disparity means disaster. He has refused to listen and had the general who told him this executed.

Furthermore, Germany's oil resources are a fraction of the Allies' oil. And LG. Farben's costly attempt at synthetic fuel has failed.

Germany has persecuted the countries we occupy, which reduces the supply of badly needed natural resources.

Allied bombing has crippled German industry and hurt German morale. This is further proof that Germany should surrender soon.

December 13, 1943

The lab is very aware of spies from England, Russia, and the U.S. that have penetrated our supposedly secret research. They have mainly been searching for written reports that they can send back to their own rocketry programs. The SS has identified the spies in our lab and purposely not arrested them, but rather is trying to outsmart them. They are absolutely prohibited from attending flight trials, so they have no way to determine if the reports match the actual flights.

The SS has instructed us to be sure the actual and very detailed reports are left where the spies can read them and presumably photo them to convert to micro-film. The SS theory is that there is so much information that the spy countries will think that the reports are plants and not follow up on them or test the information. To date, the theory has worked and our spies report very little Allied rocketry progress in any one of the three countries. We do know that the U.S. has tried some experiments in Arizona and New Mexico, but are way behind Germany's program.

The American, Goddard, was an early leader in missile design, but that research is not too applicable to warhead types of rockets.

December 14, 1943

Report from America: It is now very clear that the U.S. has made a total commitment to the Soviet Union. The lend-lease program is providing massive amounts of arm, food, and other supplies to Russia via Alaska and across the Pacific Ocean. Also, the American Army is now seven million strong. The U.S. is producing more armaments than the three Axis combined. It is urgent for Nazi Germany to stop or it will be destroyed.

In addition to U.S. armaments, we have learned that Russia is producing 1,200 tanks per month. Another problem is that the U.S. has been bombing German cities around the clock, causing great destruction and loss of morale.

A year ago, Germany lost North Africa and Russia went on the offensive at Stalingrad. Nazi generals recognized this turning point, but Hitler refused to accept it and pushed "Victory or Death." I fear it is to be the death of a nation. The massive losses at Stalingrad changed the whole mood of Hitler's insane dreams and has created his fantasy of "holding firm."

December 15, 1943

High Command Bulletin: In the U.S. the Rockefellers control Standard Oil and have made billions by selling oil to the highest bidders. One of them is Nelson Rockefeller, who has strong financial ties to Germany and who has cleverly created a U.S. Government position with South America as his portfolio. In reality, he uses the position to provide refueling of Standard Oil for German submarines off the coast of South America. He also is close to many South American dictators and has influenced them to remain "neutral" and out of World War II. If Nazis need to flee the Allies, they can count on Nelson Rockefeller to help us find secure and prosperous havens in South America.

December 24, 1943

Intel Report: The Allies definitely plan to invade Europe and British General Montgomery is to be in charge of the invasion.

December 26, 1943

Navy: Battlecruiser Schamhorst sunk in Barents Sea. Many losses mount and U-boats need to protect the invasion routes.

1944

January 6, 1944

Wehrmacht: Soviet troops have advanced into Poland after having launched a December offensive in the Ukraine.

January 8, 1944

Allied planes are carpet bombing Germany's industrial cities. To help revive the spirit of the German people, Hitler is obsessed with using rockets to bomb London for retaliation and for the demented idea that guided missiles can force England to quit.

The Vengeance Weapon One (V-1) carries a ton of explosives and is powered by a pulse jet engine designed by our colleague, Prof. Schmidt of Munich. This noisy "buzz-bomb" can only fly at 360 miles per hour, which in my opinion, makes it a target for Allied fighter planes. It may kill people and start fires, but it will not be a meaningful weapon.

I have focused on guidance systems for the V-2. While I can create an accurate guidance system, I have also adjusted gyroscopes for temperature, altitude, and other variables to create a rocket trajectory that is "close" but not accurate enough to cause severe damage. An added trick is to affect the "feeding" of liquid fuel to the combustion motors. I can program a pinpoint breach of the system, which in one-tenth of a second causes intense fire and a destructive explosion of the rocket.

January 10, 1944

As I have described in an earlier entry, for the last four years the SS has assigned a "guard" to watch over me. It is obvious that the person is there to spy on me, make sure I am doing my guidance research and to keep me from defecting or transmitting information to the enemy. I will simply call him X as soon as possible not to reveal his identity. As time has passed, I have had some in-depth conversations with X where I have eventually revealed my revulsion with what has happened in Germany, the absurd cost of each V-2 rocket and the lunacy of our leadership. X has now advised me in "perfect German" that he is actually a member of elite British group called SAS that has seriously infiltrated the German Army inner circles and the SS. He even has the SS tattoo.

X has scientific training and at one time prior to World War II was sent to the U.S. to study with Professor Goddard, the rocketry pioneer. Therefore, he is well aware of what the V-2 rockets can and cannot do and aware that I can recalibrate various components to take the flight off course. He has confidentially briefed me on a British plan to provide misinformation to German spies so that my gyroscopes, fins, atmospheric pressure and temperature settings can be "accurate" and still overshoot or misdirect the V-2 contact points. Since the rocket descent from space towards a target is too fast for conventional anti-aircraft guns to hit, the recalibrations will act as a de facto defense and minimize the actual explosive damage. There will be some casualties, but they will be in sparsely populated locations.

January 12, 1944

Wehrmacht: War production headed by Speer has been short of technical manpower to work on developing the V-1 and V-2. Therefore, Speer has brought Polish scientists to work here and at Mittle. Many of these Poles are part of an Allied espionage organization that is transmitting German secrets on the V-1 and V-2 to the Allies, and I have been secretly providing them with information from my lab. We hear that when members of this resistance organization are arrested, the Gestapo tortures them and then sends them to a death camp.

January 12, 1944

The SS has insisted that our scientific group must visit concentration camps as proof of our loyalty to Hitler's plans for world domination. What I have been forced to witness at Dachau makes me believe that the guards are sharing a mutual desire to operate an exterminator machinery.

January 12, 1944

The SS has established another concentration camp at Krakow-Plaszow. (This diversion of resources and personnel to hundreds of camps will weaken German defenses). It is Himmler's maniacal obsession and strategy.

January 13, 1944

A command bulletin advises that advancing Russians and Allied forces may discover German war crimes and is now ordering a huge cover-up of atrocities and mass murder. I have searched for specific examples since life in the rocketry lab is sheltered by comparison. In Lithuania, Poland, the Ukraine, and elsewhere, the Army slaves had to dig deep pits which were then piled high with executed corpses. The mass shootings may have killed as many as two million Jews across Eastern Europe. These mass killings started when Jews were no longer imprisoned and instead exterminated.

The cover-up of these civilian mass murders will be to exhume the bodies and burn them in pyres around the clock. This sickening program confirms the horror of Nazi Germany's useless existence.

January 14, 1944

American Source: The German, Albert Einstein, left Germany in the late 1930s and became an American citizen. Since that time and to the present, he has been writing to the State Department to stop the bureaucratic regulations that are keeping hundreds of thousands of worthy people from seeking refuge in the U.S. It seems to me that this has been futile since between 1941 and today, Germany has murdered millions, including almost three million in 1942. It is now too late and the American State Department can take much of the blame.

January 15, 1944

Memo from our spy in England: Relocated Jewish scientists in England, Rudolf Peierls and Otto Frisch, have made progress towards a nuclear bomb. In collaboration with Klaus Fuchs, they have proved that fission is possible. This news has upset Wehner and he has convinced Hitler that we must accelerate the V-2 program and launching to counterbalance the nuclear threat, and attempt to aim at British uranium research facilities.

January 20, 1944

Personal: Leningrad. The end of Germany is in clear sight for anyone to see, except Hitler who is obsessed with Communism, Stalin, and it seems like all of Eastern Europe. His obvious plan is to destroy and brutalize everything east of Germany and in the process kill every Jew he can find in Poland, the Ukraine, Russia, etc. To this end, he used Poland as a staging area to invade the USSR in 1941. The invasion moved with lightning speed until the Nazi armies reached Moscow and Leningrad. At that point, Stalin was starting to receive arms and equipment from the vast resources of the U.S. via Alaska to the frozen east coast of Russia, then transported westward.

The siege of Leningrad started in September 1941 and the Russians put up a determined resistance, along with the civilian population starving and freezing. We believe the relentless German bombing, shelling and starvation, produced 800,000 civilian deaths, and probably as many Russian soldier deaths, along with hundreds of thousands of German soldier deaths. The winter of 1943 was especially cold and by January 1944 the German trucks and tanks had frozen oil, their guns would not work and only flame throwers could be used as weapons. So, in January 1944, the Germans retreated and were either frozen or slaughtered by the Russians seeking revenge.

To add to Hitler's stupidity, the resources tied up on the Eastern Front along with many divisions of troops, had diverted his reinforcements badly need in and around Germany. Now these troops and equipment were totally lost. It is clear that the prolonged invasion of Russia will lead to Germany's defeat; sooner rather than later.

As a descendant of Felix Mendelssohn, I have been very aware of music in Germany and throughout Europe. An important footnote to the siege of Leningrad is the 7th Symphony written by Dimitri Shostakovich. It was intended to raise the spirits of the soldiers and civilians facing Hitler's vast

Army. It embodied the siege and served to keep Russians determined and in the battle. It was truly an anthem of survival for Leningrad.

January 22, 1944.

Allied troops that had landed in Italy created what is now a serious Italian Front that is dividing Wehrmacht' s ability to stabilize a defense in the east and west.

January 22, 1944

Luftwaffe Report: To retaliate from the RAF bombing of Berlin and Magdeburg, four-hundred and forty-seven German bombers were sent to attack London. Luftwaffe is low on fuel, but still has a large fleet of bombers.

January 29, 1944

Internal Peenemünde: The work on the V-1 flying bomb had proceeded near our V-2 rocket labs. There had been no contact between the two projects even though there was interchangeable technology. It is clear that jealousy has slowed design and production of this massive weapons program that is already too late. I believe that more than six months ago the war was already lost.

January 30, 1944

Internal: Just months ago Hitler had given the V-2 program top priority for production at Peenemünde. He thought it could change the war. Then, August 19, 1943, Peenemünde was seriously bombed and we had to move production into the mountain. During the Peenemünde raid, we lost numerous scientists and our air protection never arrived to help ward off the Allied flying Fortresses. The British had attacked Berlin in order to draw off our protection and Peenemünde was devastated. A brilliant diversion.

January 31, 1944

Spy report from London: The Allies have planned an invasion of the continent and postponed it until this summer.

February 1, 1944

Memo from the German implant in the White House: In spite of the continual pleas from the American Jewish community, President Roosevelt has taken no action to save Jews. He has refused bombing the concentration camps, which might put them out of business. Therefore, our spy is recommending that Wehrmacht troops be stationed near the concentration death camps as a way of avoiding Allied bombers.

Personal: With Hitler's intent to eliminate European Jews, it is Roosevelt's inexcusable failure to bomb the death camps. The world knows what is happening and, even now, the SS is trying to accelerate the deaths of hundreds of thousands of Hungarian Jews. We know that many American diplomats were openly anti-Semitic. Roosevelt could have persuaded his congress to lower immigration barriers to provide a haven for refugees from Hitler. To date, we also know the Nazis have murdered almost five million Jews and in the face of certain defeat will be fanatical to murder more Jews.

February 3, 1944

Visit to Mittelwerk: I met with Arthur Rudolph, the head ofV-2 production. He is actively driving slave laborers to work around the clock to produce V-2 rockets. We argued about the risk of fatigued and dying workers creating highly technical rockets to precise standards. He claims he has no other alternatives and must accept the fact that some of the V-2 rockets will be defective.

The Mittelwerk tunnels are over a mile long, twenty-one feet high, and 30 feet wide. My V-2 production occupies half the space, with V-1 and aircraft engines produced in the heart of the tunnels. Railroad tracks run through the tunnel and there are halls for assembly and testing rockets. A V-2 to be assembled is loaded on a railroad cart and moved from north to south so parts can be added. At the final hall the ceiling is fifty-feet high so a V-2 can be lifted vertically by a crane. This allows for final inspection, including my gyroscope guidance system.

First, the center of the rocket is assembled with alcohol and oxygen tanks. Next, the propulsion section and then the tail section and fins are attached. Finally, the guidance compartment is attached to the missiles' front. Warheads are separate and attached in the field.

Allied bombing is causing a disruption in Germany, so it is a miracle that parts with close tolerances come from various sub-contractor sources and all seem to meet the stringent specifications. The halls in the tunnels contain metal working equipment and serve as inspection areas.

After assembly and final inspection, the V-2 rockets are ready to be transported to launching sites.

It is well known that some of the slave workers performed passive sabotage such as loose electrical connections and cold welds that could come apart during flight. The SS guards are quick to harm any worker found sabotaging a V-2.

As I left Mittelwerk to return to Peenemünde, I am haunted by having seen slave laborers half? crazed with hunger and treated as sub-humans. It is beyond human understanding.

February 10, 1944

Our spy at MI6: Last year British anti-aircraft guns shot down a high percentage of our bombers. Our V-1 drone airplanes are now attacking London, but 70% are being shot down. The reason is that Britain developed a rear-guided anti-aircraft shell that explodes in the vicinity of our planes without the need for a direct hit. Had Luftwaffe developed a proximity fuse we might have stopped Allied bombing of German cities.

February 11, 1944

Our sources in Washington tell us that President Roosevelt despises the French General de Gaulle and does not trust his motives. The American Army generals consider De Gaulle to be a "Petain in sheep's clothing." He is not trusted with top-secret information.

February 12, 1944

Report from the Eastern Front: Hungarian Jews have been used as slaves since 1942 to support the German Army's invasion of Eastern Europe.

This forced labor had advanced with the Wehrmacht and now supports the Wehrmacht in full retreat.

February 12, 1943

Navy Report: U-boat losses are mounting. Lack of manpower has also created a scarcity of trained crews.

February 15, 1943

Luftwaffe and Wehrmacht: Massive numbers of British bombers are demolishing Berlin on a nightly basis. Simultaneously, the Allies are attacking German fortifications in Italy.

February 17, 1944

Theresienstadt: The SS journal bulletin of yesterday actually brags about exterminating Jews and using a brilliant cover-up. It is conceived of by sick and devious criminal minds that have brain? washed and influenced an entire nation of supposedly educated and sophisticated citizens.

The location is Theresienstadt, one of many Nazi Germany concentration camps. The SS has been using it as a gathering place for Jews from Czechoslovakia, Austria, and Germany for deportation to the death camps of Poland, especially Auschwitz. It was a town of a few thousand people that now has 58,000 people squeezed into every meter of space; that means death from disease and starvation is rampant. The SS claims that over 140,000 victims have been "processed" at Theresienstadt.

The SS writes of using this camp to show the Red Cross that they were treating Jews well. Before inspections, the grounds would be cleared, barracks rearranged, soccer games and symphonies performed. My opinion is that the Red Cross knew what was happening and went along with the SS charade.

February 17, 1944

SS Bulletin: SS Chief Himmler has written about creating medical experiments at these camps in order to advance his obsessions with racial "utopia." This has included artificial insemination, sterilization, and pairs of twins operated on by Josef Mengele. Most twins were murdered and used for autopsy. Himmler and Mengele experimented with forced seawater drinking, freezing, injecting tuberculosis and decompression chambers. Himmler says many German physicians willingly have participated in euthanasia programs.

Mengele is seeking a way to genetically produce Aryan babies. He has used painful and incapacitating drugs, injected children with diseases, and performed surgery on them, including amputation without anesthesia. These experiments are horrible. Mengele is clearly a man who has no soul.

February 18, 1944

Internal comments: Teams comparing the V-1 and V-2 have finally realized that the V-1 has drawbacks. It is slow at 500 kph and with a lower ceiling that guns and planes can shoot. The V-2 has a 150 km ceiling and a speed of 1,500 kph, so there is no defense against the V-2. And the V-2 is mobile and can be launched from any place. However, the V-2 is so complicated that it costs a hundred times the V-1 cost and is very sensitive. That sensitivity makes it easy for me to calibrate slightly "off course" controls. Also, the supply of large amounts of alcohol and liquid oxygen needed to fuel a V-2 are very limited.

February 20, 1944

Luftwaffe: American bombers are attacking our facilities that produce war materials.

February 21, 1944

Control Command: Germany's nuclear program is finished. The Norwegian ferry with our heavy water drums from the Vemork hydroelectric plant has been sunk by saboteurs. This means my V-2 program will require undivided attention as Hitler's last hope for a weapon to win this war.

Wehrmacht: Sabotage has been an ongoing problem throughout German-occupied Europe, especially in Poland, Yugoslavia, and France. Wehrmacht's nuclear program to develop a nuclear bomb has been in research for many years and is dependent on heavy water from Norway's

Vemork hydroelectric plant. Yesterday, Norwegians sabotaged the program by sinking the ferry Hydro that was carrying rail cars with drums of heavy water from Vemork. This has ended the Wehrmacht's nuclear program but means that my V-2 program will receive all the resources needed to make the V-2 the last hope.

March 1, 1944

Navy: Continued U-boat sinkings. The Allies have developed a sonar system that locates our U? boats. The losses cannot be sustained much longer.

March 5, 1944

Berlin/Luftwaffe: U.S. bombers have joined British bombers in massive raids that are destroying Berlin and killing thousands.

March 6, 1944

Himmler bulletin: The SS has been ordered to kill children as a first priority. Himmler: "That is the most efficient way to eradicate future generations."

March 20, 1944

Hungary has just been occupied by the German Army. This is the last major Jewish community in Europe and numbers 800,000. It is now in line for the same ruthless treatment meted out to Jews elsewhere in Europe. As we have seen throughout the 1930s and 1940s, America has left its doors closed to Jews, which gave Hitler the confidence to pursue his plan to kill every Jew in Europe. This removed the hope of Hungarian Jews to escape to America.

Much closer to Hungary is British-controlled Palestine, but since 1939 the British White Paper has kept all but a few Jews from the Holy Land. Despite anguished appeals from Jews around the world, Winston Churchill refused to alter the White Paper policy, and his foreign office has undermined opportunities to rescue Jewish refugees from the Nazis. This policy is a death sentence for Hungary's Jews.

March 24, 1944

Allied bombers continue to pound Germany. The entire Nazi and SS commands are now functioning from underground shelters. They continue to refuse surrender while there is still some of Germany remaining.

March 27, 1944

SS: Even though resources are needed for the Wehrmacht battles, the SS is deporting Jews from France, Lithuania, and Latvia and sending them to death camps. This is using vital fuel and transportation.

March 31, 1944

Hungary: The Hungarian government is working closely with the occupying Nazis and has ordered all Jews to wear yellow stars of David.

April 3, 1944

Luftwaffe Memo: The U.S. Air Force has been shooting the Luftwaffe out of the sky so that we can no longer protect our troops and strategic factories, such as synthetic fuel plants.

Nonetheless, Germany can still produce armaments. The V-2 production from deep within a cave is evidence Germany is still producing vast amounts of armaments.

April 4, 1844

Goebbels Propaganda Report: Haj Amin al-Husayni, the former grand Mufti of Jerusalem, has been in Berlin since 1943 broadcasting anti-Semitism and anti-Zionism. He has been used by Goebbels to incite in Arabic to Arab societies. The message is "kill the Jews." He is using communications to support genocide.

April 8, 1944

German intelligence reports from the German spy embedded in the inner American White House staff tells us that America and Britain have an atomic bomb project proceeding on a crash basis. Whoever will possess such a destructive weapon will win this ghastly war in short order. The German facility in Norway that was working on a bomb has been destroyed by Allied bombs and by saboteurs. The German scientists who are knowledgeable in nuclear fission include Teller and Einstein. Both, and other great scientists, are Jewish and have long ago fled the Nazis to find refuge in the U.S. The very people who might win this hopeless war are the ones that Hitler has persecuted.

April 10, 1944

Wehrmacht: Soviets continue to advance. Odessa has just been liberated.

April 15, 1944

Hitler directive: Progress on the Piese Tunnels in Lower Silesia has been very slow. As the Russians approach and the Allies may invade soon, these tunnels must be completed.

Construction will now be supervised by the Todt Organization with high priority to transfer concentration camp prisoners to the tunnels. The SS is authorized to guard the prisoners at the tunnel worksites. A.H.

April 16, 1944

The Jews of Greece are being transported to Auschwitz.

April 16, 1944

Himmler has continued his policy of requiring the scientists in our lab to visit concentration camps so that he can display his diabolical concepts of extermination. Traveling from Peenemünde to the required visit to Bergen-Belsen is a waste of time and exposure to Allied planes, all at a time when German forces are retreating Westward in great numbers and fighting continual battles.

As our group approached Bergen-Belsen there was the smell of rot and excrement that grew stronger. SS guards were at the gate and stationed at the perimeter of the fences. There were machine gunners in watchtowers. What we saw was a surreal scene of wandering, ghostlike humans who were starved and half naked. Piles of dead bodies were everywhere and then we came upon a huge pit with dead, rotting bodies.

We were introduced to Josef Kramer, the camp commandant. He introduced us to Irma Grese, the warden in charge of women prisoners. I could not believe that they were smiling and proud of the nightmarish conditions we were witnessing. The word "witness" is important, since when this war comes to an end all of Germany should be "put on trial" and witnesses testify to the brutal and heinous way that Nazis have treated other humans. It was clear to me that even if a person could survive one of the many Nazi concentration camps that their lives would be ruined forever and it would be next to impossible to survive this horror and again lead a normal existence.

Kramer took us into one of the huts. Gloomy. A stench. Dead bodies lying next to starved and barely alive people. We were totally shocked and when we exited the hut, we saw a guard beating an inmate and then witnessed a woman being shot in the head because she reached for a rotted piece of a plant next to the security fence. I could not wait to leave and travel back to Peenemünde even though I am aware that the advancing Russian Army could soon be there.

Before leaving Bergen-Belsen, Kramer made a point of telling us all that he and all of the SS were under orders at the hundreds of occupied killing sites to make Jews suffer before killing them.

April 18, 1944

Germany has invaded the Greek Isles and commenced the round-up of ancient Jewish communities. The tide of war in western Europe is clearly against Germany, yet precious resources and manpower are being expended to arrest defenseless communities. Clearly, this is a cowardly obsession that has no justification. Corfu, Athens.

April 20, 1944

Washington D.C. Report: Germany's spy in the Roosevelt Administration reports that numerous advisers have recommended to President Roosevelt that the railroad tracks leading to concentration camps and the gas chambers shown by aerial photos be bombed by U.S. bombers. The targets are near industrial sites already being bombed or flown over. The SS has already killed 5,000,000 Jews and, had this bombing been done a year earlier, it could have saved millions of lives, both in the camps and victims destined for the camps.

Roosevelt has refused the bombing and SS Himmler accepts that as his go ahead to rush Hungarian Jews to Auschwitz. Greenlight thanks to F.D.R.

April 29, 1944

Albert Speer Bulletin: The working conditions at Mittelwerk are so deplorable that it will be impossible to meet the planned rocket production. Therefore, the camp at Dora has been expanded with sanitary facilities, water, and food. Prisoners must be transferred from the tunnels to Dora. In the tunnels and at Dora, security is to be very high.

April 30, 1944

Mittelwerk, Dora Report: We still have imperfections in the rocket and many explode upon takeoff. I have been very slow to correct my guidance flaws so that the trajectory does not stay on course.

May 2, 1944

SS published statistics, Lithuania: At the start of the 1941 push east by the German Army there were 235,000 Jews in Lithuania. Today, it is estimated that only 2,000 to 3,000 survived.

May 8, 1944

Hitler is furious that the Luftwaffe has lost the battle of the skies over Britain and that his fighter planes are getting shot out of the sky.

He has now become obsessed with the use of rockets to inflict terror on Britain. This obsession plays right into my plan to sabotage the guidance systems in such a way that cannot be detected by my colleagues here at Peenemünde.

What it involves is precise, miniscule deviations in my formulas, depending on assumed target destination, rocket trajectory, and atmospheric conditions at that moment in time. There will still be great damage inflicted upon facilities that are important to the British work restrictions effort.

On occasion I must direct a hit on some enemy facilities in order to maintain my credibility.

May 12, 1944

Wehrmacht: German troops surrender in the Crimea. Russian forces are overwhelming German troops and are heavily supplied by the U.S. while the German Army supply lines are stretched thin.

May 13, 1944

Family: My son is now 10 years old and the SS still refuses to let me know where he and my wife are located and will not allow communication. With increased daily bombing by the Allies, I am concerned for their safety. The "hint' is that they are in a remote location that would not be targeted by the Allies.

May 14, 1944

SS Bulletin, Terezin: Adolf Eichmann has hosted officials of the International Red Cross at Terezin concertation camp. We know that the camp is an overcrowded transit terminal for sending people to their death at Auschwitz. For this occasion, Eichmann has staged gardens, soccer fields, a choir's performance of Verdi's Requiem and other tricks to dupe the IRC. It is widely known that Eichmann has carried out assembly-line mass murder and the IRC is going along with him.

May 18, 1944

SS: Since March, 430,000 Hungarian Jews have been deported to Auschwitz to be murdered. This is in spite of the efforts of neutral diplomats who have saved approximately 100,000 Hungarian Jews. Even though Germany is in need of trains to transport equipment to the front, Nazi ideology centered around killing every Jew has taken a priority. The SS is using technology and industrialization to efficiently murder Jews.

May 20, 1944

Nazi Archival Report: "Property theft is an integral part of the genocide against the Jews. In art alone, we have taken 73 Rembrandts, six Da Vincis, 90 Picassos, 63 Renoirs, 53 Matisses, and 19 Monets. These are the "stars" of 22,000 stolen paintings, including those taken from the Netherlands, Belgium, Italy, and Russia."

With the tide of war going against Germany, I suspect leading Nazis will now hide valuable paintings for possible illegal sales following this war.

May 23, 1944

SS Bulletin, Einsatzgruppen: Himmler is so obsessed with killing Hungarian Jews that he has ordered 10,000 per day to be shipped to Auschwitz for immediate killing. The trains he has commandeered for this mass killing are needed by the Wehrmacht for movement of troops and supplies and ammunition. However, Himmler does not care that he is jeopardizing the war effort. This orgy of death is well known to the Allies, so I wonder why they are not doing anything to stop it.

An eyewitness working at Birkenau has told us that Himmler is getting low on poison gas so has reduced the amount used in gas chambers. This means that the victims have a slower death. The Einsatzgruppen soldiers are tossing small children into the crematorium fires without gassing first. This is a horror beyond the worse imagination. As the father of a 10-year-old son, I fear that he is held captive by the SS in an unknown location.

May 24, 1944

Personal: It is no wonder that Hitler and Himmler created a vast system of death camps and thought they could do whatever they wanted. The countries of the world refused asylum to European Jews, even on a temporary asylum. Moreover, these countries refused to issue declarations condemning the killings and certainly did not warn Hitler to stop. Allied air power can easily reach the camps and could have bombed rail lines and gas chambers. However, Allied bombers did not touch the camps.

May 25, 1944

Einsatzgruppen Archives: This special SS group has kept meticulous, typed records of work and has "proudly" distributed to all Nazis. It details just some of their horrid details: Executing Jewish children. Cutting eyes from captured enemy soldiers. Creating violence and destruction across Europe. Two hundred thousand Germans euthanized. The Croatian Ustase trying to outdo the Einsatzgruppen. Almost six million Jews murdered, including 34,000 at Babi Yar, the Ukraine; moving eastward and killing eleven million. The list goes on.

May 27, 1944

Mittelwerk: My frequent visits to Mittelwerk are to meet with Arthur Rudolph who is in charge of the V-2 production. His use of thousands of slave laborers is risky since any one of them could sabotage an assembly line. They are housed at the nearby Dora Camp and Rudolph tells me thousands are dying. Rudolph is a very close friend of my boss, Wernher von Braun, and claims that love of rocketry and friendship with Wernher are the reasons he became a Nazi. The time Rudolph has spent in the tunnels has taken a serious toll on his health and aging process.

Rudolph confidentially tells me the war is lost and that when the time comes he will hide out in Bavaria.

May 28, 1944

Himmler SS: With Russian and the Allies advancing on all fronts, Germany has no defensive strategy. The SS has formed "Squad 1005" to locate the mass graves of the millions murdered, exhume the corpses, and bum the evidence of the mass murder.

June 3, 1944

Wehrmacht: "Regarding resistance operations, the BBC has broadcast some very strange sentences which we believe are a signal for an invasion to come. Soon thereafter sabotage events occurred throughout France. Communications have been cut, trains derailed, and ammunition depots destroyed. Wehrmacht will be on full alert, especially at all defense installations overlooking beaches and harbors.

June 4, 1944

Personal: It has been reported by the Nazi Party that Germany has looted painting masterpieces all over Europe. The Russians are doing the same, plundering as they advance west. The Party is also gloating over the wanton destruction of historical Synagogues throughout Europe in an effort to obliterate Jewish culture. Contrary to the Nazi looting, we have been warned that the U.S. 5th Army has a special unit called the Monument Men, with a charge to save art and cultural monuments.

June 6, 1944

Wehrmacht: The Allies have landed on the northern coast of France and a fierce battle is raging with heavy losses on both sides. This Normandy invasion opens another front against the Wehrmacht. France has been occupied for four years and now may be lost to the Allies' armada. Italy is all but lost and the Russians are moving westward. Hitler is a fool to continue sacrificing Germans.

The Allies have dominated the skies, so with no air support the Wehrmacht is doomed. The Allies' massive invasion has taken the Wehrmacht by surprise and exposed a disastrous failure of German leadership with no coherent plan to fend off the invasion. Hitler has delayed decisions and has made irrational decisions that are not compatible with the conditions at the front lines.

Hitler is emphasizing the secret "V" weapons which we all know are too late, too few.

June 7, 1944

Himmler Report: High praise for Franz Stangl for commanding Treblinka, the Third Reich's most efficient death factory. Stangl has claimed 900,000 deaths.

June 8, 1944

For many months a representative direct from Hitler's command has been a frequent visitor to my lab with the assignment of reviewing my calculations to understand why V-2 rocket tests sometimes produce an inaccurate flight path. He is Colonel Claus von Stauffenberg. Evidently, he had looked into my family background and as we met frequently, we developed a confidential rapport and mutual trust. Claus explained that many high-ranking Wehrmacht officers did not agree with Hitler and the Nazis and felt compelled to prove to the world that not all Germans are Nazis. He and I agreed that by mid-1943 the tide of the war had gone against Germany and that with the huge losses on the Eastern Front in early 1944, that continuing the war was insanity.

Therefore, Claus and others planned to assassinate Hitler, seize control of the government from the Nazis and the SS, and then negotiate a peace with the Allies. He also explained that the Allies now controlled the skies and had many thousands of heavy bombers that could totally eliminate Germany's major cities and set Germany back into the prior century. He said that German spies reported that the Allied commanders will seek revenge and punishment for the inhumane behavior and wanton civilian murder perpetrated by Germany. A further explanation of this plot is to try to prevent a Soviet invasion of Germany, since the Soviet Army is now rapidly moving west and, understandably, will show no mercy for Germans after being brutally invaded and occupied in recent years.

June 9, 1944

Wehrmacht: The battle of France is massive and the Soviets continue to attack from the east.

June 10, 1944

Peenemünde: The V-1 program has made its first attack on Britain. I am still working on V-2 production and guidance systems.

June 11, 1944

Observations of the International Committee of the Red Cross, based in Switzerland.

When I have visited Dora and Mittelwerk and witnessed the inhuman conditions, it seemed obvious that the ICRC was missing in action to aid the slave laborers. Research of the ICRC revealed that they have been aware of the atrocities committed by the Nazis and have been silent and ineffective out of fear that Germany will invade Switzerland.

Records also show that soon after the 1942 Wannsee conference, the ICRC was briefed on German plans to murder the Jews of Europe. They did not speak out and provided little or no assistance to the Jewish populations that were trapped by the SS. The record further shows that in some instances ICRC did try to send packages to some of the concentration camps but the German Red Cross refused them. As of right now, the ICRC has been pressed to try to help the Jews of Hungary. This is too little too late, since the SS has already bragged of sending 400,000 Hungarian Jews to Auschwitz.

It is obvious to me that Germany has lost this war and should sue for peace right now. The ICRC has the ability to issue travel papers to displaced people and I worry they will issue these "freedom passes" to Nazis, who will surely try to escape the wrath of the people they have persecuted. MM

June 13, 1944

German Command: The flying bombs (V-1) have been launched; four of them reaching English soil. This is a first and the secret weapon is now operational.

June 14, 1944

Personal: We have been buying precision V-2 parts from JAB, owned by the Reimann family. They are also producers of the chemicals used to mass murder concentration camp prisoners. The JAB Company has been sending war equipment for German armies for a hundred years. They also are managing the Harz Mountain production. I believe the Reimann family is taking money and gold out of Germany and depositing it in Switzerland so as to have a huge capital base to invest after this war is over. JAB was founded in the 1800s by Johann Adam Benckiser.

June 16, 1944

Wehrmacht report from the invasion fronts: The Allies have landed a million men and 500,000 tons of material. Hitler cannot be persuaded to relinquish operational attacks and has relieved von Rundstedt of his post.

June 24, 1944

Wehrmacht: Soviet troops in the east and U.S., British, and Canadian troops in France staged simultaneous attacks on German armies. Germany cannot defend and supply two fronts.

June 24, 1944

A Soviet summer offensive continues moving through Eastern Europe. They have just liberated the Majdanek death camp.

June 25, 1944

Himmler Confidential: In Holland at the Westerbork Camp there had been instituted a plan to create a luxury environment to lull the Jews before sending them to be murdered. This facade will facilitate the transit of Dutch Jews to death camps in Poland, just as the SS enlisted local Poles in Poland to commit programs. The SS plans to ask local Dutch to identify Jewish neighbors.

June 26, 1944

Wehrmacht: The Red Army has encircled the Wehrmacht in Belarus. Because the Allies have been bombing German cities, the Luftwaffe has pulled from Belarus to try to defend Germany. As a result, Russian planes have dominated this battlefield, with great loses to the Wehrmacht.

June 27, 1944

Wehrmacht: Battle continues in France. Despite loses, the Wehrmacht is staging some offensives. Hitler has summoned General Rommel to Berchtesgaden.

June 28, 1944

Wehrmacht Intercept: An American message from Washington to all troops was intercepted. It ordered all advancing troops to respect and protect artwork and civic buildings. (I wonder why the Allies did not focus on seizing the SS concentration camps to save human lives, as well as artwork.)

June 29, 1944

V-1 Report: As of today, 2,000 V-1s have been fired.

July 1, 1944

Twenty-four-hour production of V-1 and V-2 rockets has been increased at the expense of a high death rate by the Army's slave labor. Hitler has desperately reacted to last month's Normandy invasion by ordering thousands ofV-1 and V-2 rockets to be fired at London. The folly of this illogical order is firing at a civilian population across the channel instead of at the Allied armies that will be advancing toward Germany. I have continued to travel into the Dora Mountain cave rocket factories to supposedly be assured of production rates. The Army is not aware that this gives me the chance to adjust guidance systems so that the rockets overshoot their intended targets.

What is being kept secret is Hitler's order to develop a long-range rocket that will hit New York City. This is a diversion of time and resources, but this mad man is bent on revenge and on punishing civilians.

July 5, 1944

From the Eastern Front: Hitler's mad obsession with destroying Russian communists is now in total ruin and German armies are in full retreat. These defeated armies are under scorched earth orders and turning entire areas into dead zones. The towns of Bialystok, Slutsk, Baranowitz, Wolkowysk, Sekokard, and many others are totally demolished. This constant perpetration of atrocities has lessened Germany's chances of survival. Previous resources are diverted, armaments are being compromised, as in German armies' ability to react quickly.

July 6, 1944

Luftwaffe: The V-2 flying bomb was unleashed on London and is killing thousands.

July 7, 1944

Wehrmacht: Allied forces are advancing. U.S. Generals Patton and Eisenhower establish headquarters in Normandy.

July 8, 1944

SS, Auschwitz: So far over 400,000 Hungarian Jews have arrived and immediately are gassed to death. Their money and valuables are sent to Berlin.

July 12, 1944

SS Memo: Various concentration camps are being evacuated to destroy evidence from advancing Allied forces. The Resianskodt has been evacuated and the 4,000 people that were still there have been sent to be gassed.

At other camps, the prisoners are moved by death marches, which few will survive.

July 18, 1944

Luftwaffe: U.S. and British bombers continue to pound Germany and German-occupied French towns.

July 20, 1944

Rocket Testing: The launching pad at Waffen had been destroyed by fly fortresses. It was not robust, so a new launching bunker in Wizernes was to be hidden underground. However, constant bombing has delayed its finish and launching must take place at various locations. My colleagues do not realize that I had leaked the pad location to Polish underground operatives who then relayed the locations to Allied command via Spain.

July 21, 1944

Details of an attempt to kill Hitler are pouring in from Hitler's command to our official communication network. On July 20th there was a bomb planted by Colonel von Stauffenberg (who had been assigned to oversee my work at the lab and became a trusted confidant), at a military conference at the Wolfsschanze. At 12:42 p.m. the bomb exploded, killing three officers and wounding approximately twenty others. Hitler and many others survived because the bomb was placed behind a table leg which shielded Hitler. Stauffenberg had left the conference room and was headed back to Berlin, mistakenly thinking that Hitler was dead. A lot of confusion occurred since many of the plotters learned that Hitler was still alive. Heinrich Himmler took control of the situation and took steps to regain control in Berlin.

General Fromm took control in Berlin and arrested Stauffenberg and other high officers who were part of the plot. They were given a "trial" by Fromm and executed forthwith. It seems obvious that Hitler will be making arrests of thousands and then executions since a plot of this magnitude must involve thousands. I will of course remain silent about my knowledge of a possible plot.

My sources have explained that the plan was to seize control from the Nazis and quickly make peace with the Allies. Many officers want to show the world that not all Germans are like the Nazis. They say that there has been a plan dating back to 1938 to overthrow Hitler, but it had been delayed due to Hitler's general popularity and a lack of will by the western powers to confront Hitler until it was too late.

By mid-1943 the tide was very much against Germany and a plot by von Stauffenberg intended to stop the war before Russia reached Germany. Himmler suspected a plot so by mid-1944 the assassination attempt had to proceed. In early July, there was a number of aborted attempts.

Finally, on July 20th, the bomb was detonated, but Hitler survived.

July 21, 1944

SS Himmler: Following yesterday's assassination attempt, H.H. has been made Commander in Chief of the Army.

July 22, 1944

SS, Himmler: H.H. has appointed SS General Hans Kammler to head my V-2 operations. This means increased resources for the V-2, but Kammler has a ruthless reputation and may drive the V-2 workers relentlessly.

July 23, 1944

Nazi Party–Re: Resistance: Further investigation of the July 20th plot reveals a network of resistance throughout Germany. This small minority of Germans will be arrested and quickly "eliminated" since most Germans revere Hitler.

July 23, 1944

SS bulletin about the Greek Isle of Rhodes: The Isle of Rhodes has an ancient Jewish community dating back to C.E. Therefore, Herr

Himmler deems it high priority to destroy the Jewish community and its culture. All Jews have been rounded up and are being sent to death at Auschwitz.

July 24, 1944

Luftwaffe Diary: Germany has launched thousands of V-1 bombs from French sites to attempt to destroy London. In retaliation, the Allies have bombed launch sites for many months and have killed or wounded hundreds of soldiers working at the launch sites. There have been heavy Allied losses, with dozens of aircraft shot down.

July 24, 1944

SS: The following military resistance figures had been arrested and quickly executed in addition to Stauffenberg: Ludwig Beck, Erwin von Witzleben, Gunthere von Klug, Erich Hoepner, Hans Oster and Fredrich Olbricht. (While the SS considers these officers to be traitors, I consider them to be heroes.) Hitler has sent a message from his underground command center that most Germans will follow him to the bitter end.

July 25, 1944

Wehrmacht: Wehrmacht engaged Canadian troops and inflicted thousands of casualties on them.

July 26, 1944

Peenemünde, Wehrmacht Assessment: After our first V-2 rocket hit England, he is waiting for an assessment by our spies in England.

July 27, 1944

Peenemünde research notes: Many test rockets are exploding in mid-air. I have observed that the great heat from burning liquid fuel and the strong vibrations are bursting the fuel tanks. The underground slave factory at Nordhausen will now insert steel sleeves on the fuel tanks in order to solve that problem. This is per Hans Kammler's directive.

July 30, 1944

SS: The SS continues deporting Jews by the tens of thousands from all over Europe to Auschwitz. The rail cars and fuel are needed at the fronts to battle Russian and Allied armies. Instead, they are being used to kill Jews. Madness.

Even though defeat is likely, the German Navy is sending ships to various Greek islands to capture Jews to transport to death camps.

August 2, 1944

Wehrmacht: Yesterday the surviving Jews of the Warsaw Ghetto have revolted against the five? year occupation by Nazi Germany.

The Soviet Army is on the outskirts of Warsaw so it is assumed they will join the Poles. So far, the Soviets have not made a move.

August 3, 1944

Visit to Mittelwerk: I continue to meet with Hans Kammler, the designer and builder of numerous secret weapons facilities. He is a high officer in the SS, responsible for creating German extermination camps and is now in full control of production ofV-2 missiles. His design of Mittelwerk has all the markings of an extermination camp, except it is producing V-2 rockets and other weaponry.

August 6, 1944

The Army command reports that with the Soviets advancing in Poland, the situation in Warsaw turned violent a few days ago. The underground resistance Polish Home Army rose up in Warsaw and for the past few months has been fighting the German Army block by block. This action naturally diverted troops from the Eastern Front and made the Soviets advance easier.

As I have entered in the diary many times, the Army's approach to civilian resistance is totally brutal. The Army bulletin brags about destroying half of Warsaw and executing 100,000 Poles. In addition, Polish men by the thousands are being sent to work as slaves in German factories. This allows the Army to force German males from teenage to advanced ages to serve in the Army. If there is an end to this war, it seems impossible for Poles to ever trust a German.

It is ironic that the few surviving Jews in Warsaw who volunteered to help the Polish Home Army were either driven away or murdered, a horrible reflection on the PHA and on Polish anti? Semitism.

August 7, 1944

Wehrmacht: Hitler has ordered another major counter-attack at the Allied troops near Ardennes.

August 8, 1944

Wehrmacht: The July 20th assassination plotters were tried yesterday under the leadership of Roland Preisler. It lasted a few hours and then the accused were "hung like cattle." The Gestapo has arrested 7,000 people so far and will execute most of them.

August 8, 1944

Gestapo: Klaus Barbie, Gestapo head in Lyon, France, has transferred to Auschwitz. (Waffen SS troops continue massacring Jews at a time when these troops are needed on the front lines.)

August 9, 1944

Wehrmacht: Allied forces have landed on the French Riviera. This opens still another front. Time is running short.

August 10, 1944

SS, Himmler: Another mandated visit to his camps. This time, Ravensbruck camp for women, where women are used as slave laborers and worked until they drop dead. Ravensbruck is a true example of Nazi barbarity. Those women who give birth have their babies taken at once and left to die or be eaten by rats. I witnessed a truck full of bodies. A return to Peenemünde to work on the V-2 will be a relief. From Ravensbruck, I visited Guben with a purpose. Women were in a factory producing radio equipment for aircraft and for the V-2. This was a perfect opportunity to whisper to one of the slave laborers about a way to sabotage the equipment.

August 13, 1944

Today's Gestapo Bulletin states that they have just executed Suzanne Spaak. She is a Belgian heiress who lived in Paris. The Gestapo accused her of saving Jewish children from being deported to death camps and for collaborating with resistance groups. Nazi records show she was arrested last November and kept in solitary confinement at the Fresnes prison until her execution. My personal questions are how could trying to save the lives of innocent children be a crime? What kind of people would kill children and why is Germany wasting resources on murdering innocents when we all know that Allied armies are close to liberating Paris?

August 15, 1944

Wehrmacht: Soviet troops continue liberating cities in Eastern Europe and the Balkans. Allied forces continue to push through France and Belgium. The German divisions are being destroyed.

August 16, 1944

Luftwaffe: The Junkers Ju 287 jet has been flight-tested. This is a waste of resources since the Allies control the skies.

August 25, 1944

Goebbels Announcement–total mobilization: All men between fifteen and sixty are to be drafted. Armaments production to be accelerated to the highest figures under the direction of Albert Speer. This will exhaust our resources, but is necessary for "the last battle." Fuel for the thousands of tanks and planes will be sparse. Raw materials will be depleted.

Hitler is still furious about the assassination attempt and has had the Gestapo arresting thousands of plot suspects. In the process, the Gestapo has found material related to a number of other plots, and has arrested those people involved in attempts unrelated to the July 20 explosion. The Nazis passed a law implicating the innocent families of plotters, so even remote family members are being arrested. To date, approximately 7,000 have been arrested and of those, 4,900 have been executed without a trial. This represents a desperate attempt for the insane to wipe out the sane. With Allied forces now having invaded France and with Russia moving swiftly westward, this is another example of Hitler using resources for revenge that should be deployed on the battlefield. Our V-2 program has been untouched by the assassination turmoil, so we are just "tending to business" and moving the rocket program along.

The Gestapo is using this incident to round up people they do not like by accusing them of being part of the plot to kill Hitler and take over the government. They are sent to a "people's court," swiftly tried and then, according to Hitler's orders, "hanged like cattle." Many of the more prominent plotters like Kluge and Tresckow have committed suicide. General Fromm was the one who took control of Berlin from the plotters, and even he was arrested and shot by a firing squad. Hitler has also required every member of the military to take a new oath of loyalty, which seems like a total waste of time. There are rumors that the very popular Field Marshall Erwin Rommel knew about the plot but did not participate. That would have been impossible since a few days before July 20th his command car was strafed by an Allied plane, which sent Rommel to the hospital with serious wounds.

August 26, 1944

Wehrmacht: Yesterday the Wehrmacht retreated from Paris and the Allies liberated Paris.

August 27, 1944

Personal: The Nazis have done such a thorough job of propaganda on the German people that even as defeat is looming, most Germans believe that exterminating Jews and Poles is necessary for their "security." This is in spite of daily bombing by the Allies that has destroyed most major cities.

August 28, 1944

Himmler SS Memo from Budapest: The SS has been very busy transporting hundreds of thousands of Hungarian Jews to death camps.

A situation has arisen whereby a Swedish diplomat named Raul Wallenberg has caused the SS a huge problem. He has established safe houses and issued false Swedish identity cards to most of the remaining Jews. We estimate he has been in active contact with 100,000 Jews who Himmler wanted to send to Auschwitz. With the Soviets rushing west towards Budapest, the Nazis may be prevented from arresting the remnants of Hungary's Jews. H.H.

September 1, 1944

German Spy in U.S. State Department Reports: For many months Jewish leaders have continued to make the case for destroying death camps. Today, Secretary Richard Law has advised them that "technical difficulties are involved and we must refrain from bombing the camps."

September 3, 1944

State Department info intercept–John J. McCloy: "Operational troops cannot be diverted to liberate the Jews." Himmler: "Further, approval from the U.S. State Department." Also, Germany destroyed the Warsaw Ghetto with Russian armies nearby, and they did nothing to help save the Jews."

September 4, 1944

SS: Transports of Jews continue from areas in Europe still controlled by the S.S.A. Diversion from the war effort that is fueled by hate and futility.

September 6, 1944

First firing report V-2: The Allied advance has forced relocation of launch pads. Kammler chose the heavily populated Hague, thinking Allied bombers might avoid populated areas. Each huge rocket needs special tractor trucks, firing crews, three tankers, an electric generator truck, plus staff cars. All this equipment makes a pad noticeable from the air.

September 8, 1944

V-2s fired at London.

September 8, 1944

Germany has begun to use the rocket-propelled V-2 guided missile which our Werner von Braun team has worked on for almost a decade and for which I have designed the guidance system.

Since I am in charge of setting those very complex machines, it is at this point that I can register my secret protest against the Nazis and their persecution and enslavement of millions.

We have a goal of sending thousands of V-2 to destroy London. What Hitler has not considered is that the RAF can retaliate and wipe out entire German cities.

The forty-six foot long, terrifying V-2 is so complicated that it has 30,000 parts. Imagine if just one or two parts are made to malfunction, or "incorrect" wind, payload and weather conditions are entered into the guidance system, then the rocket may implode in flight or miss a target. The V-2 is silent and travels 3,600 mph. It is not vulnerable to being shot down.

September 9, 1944

SS Himmler Commands: Himmler, as I noted in last month's entry, sadistically has required top members of the V-2 design team to periodically visit his "creations," the concentration camps. I still think about Ravensbruck, the camp for women. The camp commandant actually bragged about the brutal environment; trucks full of dead women who have been worked to death; pregnant women forced to abandon their babies and newborns left to die of starvation or be eaten by rats. Typhus and dysentery are rampant. The sick and starved women work twelve-hour shifts at a Seimens' plant. They are dehumanized and die in droves to be carted off by the truckload. The visits to the camps leave unforgettable impressions of intentional brutality and may be designed to keep our team working diligently.

September 12, 1944

Wehrmacht: Allied troops have entered Germany as the Russians push from the east. The Siegfried line has fallen.

September 17, 1944

Civilian populations in occupied countries are rebelling and striking against German occupiers.

In Slovakia, the resistance movement has taken two airfields, and Russia is flying in arms and supplies to Slovakia and Soviet partisans.

September 18, 1944

Allied bombers have been destroying German cities. Nazi propaganda and German public opinion are stressing “moral equivalence” by saying that death camps and shooting pits are really no different than the bombing.

September 22, 1944

Intel Report, Wehrmacht: The V-2 launches at London have caused British General Montgomery to lobby Eisenhower to concentrate on liberating Holland to eliminate the launch sites. The V-2 has killed 6,000 and wounded 40,000 and Britain is afraid the V-1 will do the same. So, the U.S. and British have diverted many divisions and thousands of paratroopers to “liberate” Holland and stop the V-2 attacks on London.

(Personal: We know Roosevelt and Eisenhower refused to bomb the concentration camps and save hundreds of thousands of Jews. Now, to save 10,000 Englishmen, a vast armada has been diverted to battle German Panzer Corps.)

September 29, 1944

Wehrmacht: In spite of massive Allied advances, Hitler still insists on counter-attacking at Arnhem in the Netherlands. The Wehrmachtjust beat back a British force. Well in advance of the September 17th airborne attack by two U.S. divisions and one British division, we had broken Allied codes and were well organized to resist their advance. Unlike other Allied advances that followed heavy artillery cover, it appears that the British at Arnhem had very little artillery support. Our intelligence tells us that Field Marshal Bernard Montgomery planned the air drops and made serious mistakes, including inadequate force concentration. Credit goes to General Model, who has refused to follow Hitler and Himmler’s orders.

October 1, 1944

Arthur Rudolph has been at Mittelwerk for more than a year and has insisted that I make frequent visits to be sure that the guidance systems of the V-2 are being properly assembled. When Peenemünde was bombed on August 17th last year, the high command and Hitler decided to move the production to an underground factory. Construction of a million square foot cave was started at once by slave labor in a gypsum mine near Nordhausen in central Germany. A branch of the Buchenwald concentration camp was established in the interior of the mountain and is called Dora/Mittelwerk.

Slave labor is used for the factory and there are thousands at work at any one time in the cave. The conditions are deadly, with no air, no sanitation, freezing cold, lice, filth, miserable lighting, no real rest, and almost no food. It is no surprise that the slaves are dying by the thousands and that the stench is not to be imagined. Here we are dealing with a highly technical 46-foot long, 28,000-pound instrument of death under conditions that can cause any human to make mistakes in assembly and calibrations. It is a perfect setting for sabotage that will only be evident once the V-2 is in the air. The gyroscope guidance technology that I designed requires precise assembly and I doubt that can be achieved in these conditions. The monsters of the SS and the Army who have conceived this factory in hell may have outsmarted themselves.

The choking dust and fumes in the tunnels, beating, starvation and disease have taken an enormous human toll. If workers do not produce, they are beaten and hanged by brutal SS guards. Many are dropping dead from exhaustion. Anyone too young to work is beaten to death.

When I have had to visit Mittelwerk, it has been possible to adjust certain rocket calibrations so that when a V-2 is fired it will disintegrate. I know that many of the slaves have sabotaged the V-2 in various ways.

October 2, 1944

Swedish Radio Broadcast: Last night thousands of Danish Jews were saved by the heroic efforts of Danish fishermen and boat owners ferrying them to Sweden to avoid being rounded up by the occupying German SS in order to send them to death camps.

Danish courage and Swedish generosity gave indelible proof of human values in times of barbarism. The world should remember.

October 3, 1944

Wehrmacht: Yesterday, Nazi troops crushed the Warsaw uprising, which has killed 250,000 civilians.

October 3, 1944

The U.S. and Britain continue to blanket German cities with incendiary bombs. This has burned thousands (if not millions) of civilians and laid waste to much of Germany. It is my fear that Hitler and his generals will continue this hopeless war until the last civilian is dead. They have committed mass murder throughout Europe, so I guess they are now in a panic that they will have to stand trial.

October 4, 1944

Warsaw Bulletin: The Red Army simply looked on as Warsaw revolted against the Wehrmacht. In these last sixty-three days, more than two hundred thousand people have been slaughtered, and Warsaw has been reduced to rubble.

October 7, 1944

Luftwaffe: Allies continue bombing of numerous cities.

October 8, 1944

Auschwitz–Birkenau: Jewish prisoners' uprising has burned the crematoriums.

October 15, 1944

Personal Note: Hitler continued to suspect Rommel, one of Germany's best generals, of being part of the plot to assassinate him. Rommel was given the option of the people's court or suicide. Rommel knew that the court was certain death and committed suicide yesterday. This is yet another example of Hitler's insanity. Right at the time the military needs Rommel's leadership, he is forced to commit suicide. The rumor is that Rommel's family would not be arrested if Rommel killed himself.

October 16, 1944

SS Bulletin from Hungary: A large political party, the Arrow Cross, has collaborated with the SS and now has power in Hungary.

October 19, 1944

Wehrmacht: Soviet troops invade Czechoslovakia. This puts the Soviets in a position to push into Germany. U.S. and Canadian forces pushing forward on the Western Front, approaching Aachen. Wehrmacht has a large Army at Aachen that will be trapped and forced to surrender.

October 20, 1944

Mittelwerk: Sabotage has hampered the V-1 and V-2 offensive against Britain. Prisoners have slowed production, welders have made mistakes, defective wiring has been assembled, and almost completed weapons have been damaged. I personally have been allowed to recalibrate some of the gyroscope settings to slightly cruise off target. Gestapo and SS infiltrators have arrested many of the saboteurs, and there have been numerous public hangings and mass execution.

October 21, 1944

Wehrmacht: So many troops have been lost fighting the Allies that we must now start recruiting teenage boys as young as thirteen for the defense of Germany. They will receive minimal training and be put into battle. Also pressed into the Army will be older men. These new soldiers will form a defensive position.

October 21, 1944

V-1 Report: Production has accelerated. Wachtel is launching at Brussels and Antwerp. Powerful but much too late to tum the Allied tide.

October 23, 1944

V-2 Report: We have launched 43 rockets at Norwich, England and only two reached the targets. My calibrations are working in order to throw the rockets slightly off course.

October 23, 1944

Wehrmacht: A bulletin has been issued by the Army to caution us regarding spies from the American Army. Evidently, in 1938 and 1939, some of the young German Jewish men were released from camps such as Dachau or escaped Nazi Germany and were able to relocate to the USA. When Germany declared war on the U.S.A. in December of 1941, these men became enemy aliens, but were quickly recruited by the U.S. Army and trained as spies, as decoders, and as interrogators for captured enemies. They eventually were trained exactly as if they were in the German Army and outfitted in German Army uniforms. We are told that since their families have been exterminated by the SS, they are willing to take extreme risks as they seek revenge.

Their German language is perfect because they are native-born Germans.

There have been numerous battlefield setbacks and that may have been due to these spies who have access to German battle plans. Or, the interrogation of captured German soldiers maybe revealed vital information. These spies may have also had the Enigma codes to pass on for decoding messages. Our rocket lab is especially vulnerable since many of the Jews who escaped had physics and chemistry degrees and could easily have been assigned to the vast lab and test facilities working on the V-2. I do not know their identity, but must try not to have contact with them since I do not want anyone to know of my guidance system design “adjustments” that will destabilize the V-2.

October 30, 1944

Peenemünde: Göring has come to Peenemünde to listen to a Dornberger lecture and witness a V-2 launching. Göring seems jovial and distracted. German armies are being pushed back on every front and Göring is talking about a post war party. He must be delusional.

The massively expensive V-2 secret weapon is just too late. I can take some credit for this since slave production can "take time" and Hitler is still proclaiming Germany "will win."

November 5, 1944

Kammler of the SS has had control over V-2 research and has infiltrated his own men to watch our every step. Kammler has also frequented Usedom/Peenemünde to give Dornberger a bad time. However, von Braun has been left alone as "indispensable."

November 10, 1944

Trouble: General Dornberger has been advised by Field Marshal Keitel that von Braun and Reindel have been arrested (which makes me very nervous). The Gestapo evidently is accusing them of sabotage.

November 12, 1944

Navy: The RAF has sunk the battleship Tirade which was at Tromso Fjord, Norway. Estimated 2,000 sailors killed.

November 15, 1944

Von Braun Saved: Dornberger had Albert Speer put in a plea direct to the Fuhrer for Von Braun's release, along with his team. The war is going badly, yet German leaders are wasting their energies fighting each other.

November 16, 1944

SS Bulletin from Hungary: SS has begun the systematic extermination of all Jews outside of Swiss and Swedish safe houses. Thousands are to be frozen to death on forced marches. The remaining are to be shot and thrown into the Danube River.

November 21, 1944

V-1 Report: Hitler has been impressed with the V-2's destructive power and he ordered increased launches aimed at London. This has brought Allied air raids in an attempt to destroy the launch pads.

November 22, 1944

Personal: It is obvious that Germany cannot hold out much longer. Massive Allied and Russian forces are now in place and moving toward Germany. Hundreds of SS and Nazi officers are rushing to the Vatican to get false papers and escape. The Catholic Church has a long history of anti-Semitism, such as maligning Jews as with blood libels, "Christ killers," a 500-year inquisition, the Crusades, etc. Therefore, the Vatican is protecting Nazis who are fleeing crimes against humanity.

November 23, 1944

Wehrmacht Research Division: A paper has been issued relating to Germany's research to develop an atomic bomb. The decision has been made to drop work on a bomb. It is too expensive at a time of German retreat and it is doubtful that the Allies can produce an atomic bomb.

November 24, 1944

Heinrich Himmler official direction: "The murder of Jews remaining in concentration camps is to be halted and gas chambers and crematoria destroyed."

Personal reaction: It is known that Hitler has ordered the annihilation of all Jews, so that Himmler's order is against Hitler's orders. It is known that Himmler is friendly with Swiss politician, Jean Marie Musy, who is a Zionist. It is very possible that Musy convinced Himmler to stop the murders. Himmler may be trying to save himself from being tried as a murderer.

However, he will be saving thousands of lives and will be at odds with Hitler.

November 24, 1944

SS Orders: Since Himmler has ordered Auschwitz and its gas chambers and crematoria to be destroyed. It is clear that he believes that the Allies will bring charges of crimes against humanity and he wants the SS to destroy the evidence. I know that there have been so many hundreds of camps and ghettos that Himmler is a fool to think he can hide SS evidence.

November 25, 1955

Rocket Command: A V-2 which I had diverted from hitting central London has exploded at a store in Deptford, killing many shoppers. However, that outcome is much less destructive than hitting central London.

November 27, 1944

SS Bulletin: Himmler is now concerned about the criminal evidence of the camps and has again ordered the destruction of Auschwitz and Birkenau crematoria.

November 30, 1944

The Kaltenbrunner Report: We have copies of an inquiry into the July 20th assassination attempt which states that Pope Pius XII was a conspirator. (This may have been in retaliation for Hitler's 1943 plan to kidnap the Pope.) The very popular General Rommel was implicated, and, as I have noted, Hitler gave him the option to go to trial or commit suicide. He committed suicide in October.

December 4, 1944

SS: Many thousands of Hungarians have been put on a death march that is simply intended for mass murder.

December 5, 1944

Wehrmacht: Army demolition teams are destroying Rhine dikes in an attempt to cause flooding and impede Allied advances. As German troops fall back, they are stealing everything they can carry.

December 16, 1944

V-2 lab: In coordination with the German offensive, we are ordered to fire V-2 rockets at Allied supply lines in Belgium. A hit on Antwerp has killed hundreds.

December 16, 1944

Command Bulletin: A decision has been made to take a late gamble by mounting in the Ardennes a large scale, unexpected assault on Allied forces in northern France. German generals believe that the British Army leadership is lacking in judgment and that British armies may be vulnerable. They also are convinced the German fighting formations and tanks armament is superior to the Allies and will allow for a substantial break through the British defense lines.

Until 1944, America has had a relatively small number of troops in Europe, but their build-up in recent months may prove to be a problem for this Ardennes offensive. Hitler made the decision to move troops from the Eastern Front to the Ardennes. This gives Russia a much easier path to Berlin. One thousand German tanks moved forward to surprise the Allies. However, German air support is non-existent.

December 17, 1944

V-2 Command, Kammler and Wachtel: Hitler has given further explicit orders to fire V-1 and V-2 at the Port of Antwerp. Due to my "adjustment" of flight path, the Port is being missed.

However, this means civilians will suffer direct hits. Five-hundred-and-sixty-seven people were killed at the Rox Cinema due to a V-2 direct hit. Hundreds of rockets will also be aimed at London.

With 16 launch pads, Wachtel estimates he can launch over a thousand missiles to try to impede Allied advances.

December 17, 1944

V-1 and V-2 Report: Hitler continues to focus launches on the Port of Antwerp to try to destroy supplies corning to Allied armies.

December 17, 1944

Ardennes, Wehrmacht: Seven panzer and 13 infantry divisions have concentrated and attacked on a 61-rnile wide front. So far more than 7,000 Americans have been captured. Wehrrnacht general saw that two U.S. divisions had not crossed the Rhine and had left German troops at their rear. This presents an opportunity to attack the Allies and completely surprise them. The weather is brutally cold, but German troops transferred from the Eastern Front are used to cold conditions.

December 17, 1944

Wehrmacht–Wacht am Rheine: Hitler has launched a brazen offensive of 200,000 troops against 100,000 American troops. This is an offensive effort to smash thru Allied lines near the Ardennes Forest in Belgium, advance to the coast, and stop Allied supplies from landing. The orders are to kill all prisoners and inflict as many casualties on the Americans as possible. SS troops have been supplied with drugs that will allow them to fight for days without resting.

Germany will decide the location of the fight and set the pace of the battles.

Also, to the Wehrmacht's advantage is the foggy, overcast weather that has hampered Allied advantage in the air. German retreat following the Allied invasion destroyed ports and railways, so that now the Allied troops will have difficulty being supplied.

Personal: Massing 200,000 troops and equipping them for a harsh winter has meant pulling divisions from the Eastern Front and Italy, and allowing the Russians to advance. While Germany may temporarily have success in Belgium, this frantic offensive will expose the Eastern flank and lead to major territory losses.

December 20, 1944

Wehrmacht: The battle plan is working and Wehrmacht has surrounded the U.S. 101 Airborne Army.

December 21, 1944

Wehrmacht: Vast numbers of American troops have surrendered. Waffen SS are ordered to murder all Americans as has been the case on numerous occasions when Germany has captured prisoners.

December 26, 1944

Wehrmacht report, Bastogne: The U.S. Army has repulsed the Wehrmacht offensive. German tanks and cars ran out of petrol. America's vast material advantage was decisive. Hitler had committed 400,000 men and 1,400 tanks. Losses here alone were 80,000 men. The U.S. counter-offensive was led by General George Patton.

Hitler's gamble on the "Bulge" attack has added to Wehrmacht losses, which now approach 400,000 casualties. Even with our new, very young and poorly trained conscripts, this war is lost. Allied air power was instrumental in destroying tanks. Luftwaffe support was non-existent. Also, many German tanks and other vehicles ran out of petrol.

December 27, 1944

Our lab continues to be wired into the top echelon of military intelligence so that I can discreetly read incoming bulletins. Based on many hundreds of bulletins, I have formed a personal opinion about the Vatican and it is not pleasant. I continue to believe the Church has collaborated with the Nazis for many reasons, even though on a local level there have been instances of clergy and church members who tried to help and hide those hunted by the Nazis. The evidence creates this pattern by a Church supposedly dedicated to Godly ways:

> The Nazis, so far, have not occupied the Vatican. Perhaps Pope Pius XII is dealing with the devil in order to protect the Vatican.
>
> The Pope has not forcefully spoken about the killing of massive amounts of Jews and others, even though this has been common knowledge.
>
> In the Ukraine, an entire Nazi Ukrainian Catholic division fought alongside the German Army and was active in committing atrocities.
>
> One of the most notorious concentration camp commanders in Croatia is a Catholic priest.
>
> The Vatican Bank has been dealing with the Nazis, including stolen Jewish art and insurance policy collections of people sent to their death in Auschwitz.

To any observer, the great losses of the German Army on the Eastern Front and limited resources compared with the U.S., it seems obvious that Germany cannot win this horrible war that it thought would be an easy world domination. I believe that numerous Nazi officials and Army high officers are preparing to escape with the loot they have stolen from Jewish families and from many towns they have ransacked. What appears in the bulletins is a department in the Vatican that is run by priests in order to hide Nazis and prepare an underground "railway" to spirit Nazis to Catholic dominated Central and South American countries and to Arab countries who have predominantly collaborated with the Nazis and joined in anti-Semitic public diatribes.

1945

January 1, 1945

Luftwaffe: Still operative raid on Eisenhauer (Allied) airport.

January 2, 1945

Luftwaffe: Allied air raid on Nuremberg in retaliation. Unable to defend.

January 4, 1945

Wehrmacht: Allies advance in France. Churchill visits France.

January 4, 1945

SS: Resistance fighters in Amsterdam have been captured and executed.

January 7, 1945

Wehrmacht: German victory in Ardennes. Massive number of Allied troops captured.

January 8, 1945

Von Braun Memo to MM: With defeat certain, SS General Karl Wolff is forming a secret society and asking us to join. Wolff's theory is that the Western Allies are so obsessed with communism that they will not pay close attention to the violent crimes committed by the Nazis.

Wolff is in touch with U.S. generals in order to sign a surrender in Italy. He claims that Mengele, Himmler, Eichmann, Brunner, and leaders of Einsatzgruppen have joined his plan to escape from the Allies or trick them if there are trials.

January 10, 1945

Personal: There have been constant bombing raids by Allied planes. The end result is that much of Germany is now a pile of rubble and the Nazis have brought disaster to this country and much of Europe. In effect, the "lights have gone out" so to speak in most of Europe. England and the U.S. are joined with the Soviet Union, but I sense this is only a union of convenience to combat Hitler. The collapse of Germany is imminent and then it is clear that there will be a conflict between East and West. Germany has inflicted a horrible price on Eastern Europe and the Soviet Union will demand revenge and restitution. A new battle of titans will go on for many decades.

January 10, 1945

Directive from SS to Schutzpolizei to Karl Jaeschke, Commandant Schiliersee.

Personal: A reading of the directive from Himmler adds to the unbelievable, twisted, mindset of the SS. With the rapidly approaching Russian and US troops, Himmler wants to "hide" evidence of German atrocities by taking female slaves from camps and marching them on a death march. His objective is to force the women to march long distances every day without protection from the weather, and on little or no food or water. He believes that they will die along the way, or at his instructions be shot for walking slowly, or trying to escape.

The plan is to march the prisoners toward Germany for as long as it takes, covering 20 km per day. Any survivors of the 900 km death march are to be left with Czech or German villagers. Himmler assumes few will survive and therefore there will be few to bear witness against the SS.

January 12, 1945

Wehrmacht: Allied forces have regrouped and Wehrmacht retreating in Battle of the Bulge.

January 12, 1945

Wehrmacht: Red Army offensive on the Eastern Front has crashed through the Wehrmacht lines. The entire front from Balkans to the Carpathians is in retreat. The Russian infantry outnumbers us 11:1, tanks 7:1, and artillery 28:1. It is an avalanche Germany cannot resist.

January 13, 1945
Wehrmacht: Soviet offensive on Eastern Front accelerates. Uncertain how long Wehrmacht can sustain two fronts defense. Our divisions are depleted, soldiers exhausted, and the Luftwaffe is very low on petrol.

January 16, 1945
SS: Ravensbruck is to become an extermination camp. The SS will install gas chambers to eliminate thousands. Ludwig Ramdohr will direct the urgent elimination of all evidence and is permitted to torture his prisoners for interrogation purposes.

January 17, 1945
SS: Fear of Allied war crimes charges orders to clear out Auschwitz and related evidence.

January 18, 1945
Wehrmacht–Warsaw, Poland: Total retreat after destroying the city. Russians and Poles occupy.

January 20, 1945
Wehrmacht: The Hungarian government has concluded an armistice with the Allies. Wehrmacht retreats. Russian troops occupy Pest and Buda.

January 20, 1945
German military casualties have been horrific. It is obvious that the Allies will win, yet Germans continue to follow Hitler's order. This month alone, the German Army may have lost hundreds of thousands. We know that since the start of the war, German military deaths are over four million soldiers, plus badly wounded.

January 21, 1945
Personal: As I contemplate the final stages of this massive World War and the misery and death it has wrought, it seems in hindsight it could have all been avoided. Going back to 1933, when Hitler came to official power,

most of the world "looked the other way." In 1936 when Hitler remilitarized the Rhineland, Britain and France did not call his bluff. In 1937, Chamberlain of Britain was a proactive appeaser and he did not oppose "change in the status quo in Europe."

This was evidenced by his abject surrender at Munich without which the war and holocaust could have been avoided. So, Austria, Czechoslovakia, and Danzig fell into Nazi control in 1938. There were even prominent figures such as the Prince of Wales, who openly admired Hitler. Unseemly scenes of violence against Jews were accepted in London and the U.S. Then came Kristallnacht, and Poland, and France, and on and on.

The true character of Hitler and the Nazis was ignored by the world and perhaps denied. Appeasement is the culprit.

I have attempted to understand how all of Germany could be influenced by leaders who have committed unspeakable crimes against other humans.

Sociopaths? Enthralled by Hitler? Sadists? Murderers? Brainwashed? Following orders? All of the above. What I have witnessed at high-level V-2 briefings of Göring, Hoss, Ley, and Streicher is that they are perverts, dope addicts, and liars. Hans Frank wore lace panties. Göring traveled with a young boy. Ley was a pervert. Screaming grandstanders have destroyed a nation.

January 23, 1945

Navy Report: Admiral Donitz has launched a last-ditch plan to save German ships and confront Allied Navies.

January 27, 1945

SS Report: Auschwitz is being overrun by Russian forces. The SS are escaping as Russians liberate Auschwitz and Birkenau.

January 27, 1945

SS Himmler memo to V-1 and V-2 leaders and Wehrmacht generals regarding Bergen-Belsen. In an effort to exterminate Jews, they have been gathered from all parts of Europe to come to Bergen-Belsen. Disease, starvation, death marches, exposure, and exhaustion have killed thousands, even before the gas chambers. Josef Kramer, formerly from Auschwitz, has been the Bergen-Belsen commandant. It is only a matter of time before Bergen-Belsen will be liberated by Allied forces.

January 27, 1945
Soviets liberate Auschwitz.

January 30, 1945
D6nitz plan failing. Ship Wilhelm Gustloff torpedoed. Great loss of German lives.

January 30, 1945
Hitler's radio speech: He urges Germans to fight to the death and blames his failures on others.

January 30, 1945
It is now obvious that Germany has been defeated and that Hitler's plans have been fanatical and delusional. Germany is outnumbered and has limited resources and production. Yet, German soldiers continue to believe they are winning and continue to fight on to "defend the Reich." I believe German leaders have brainwashed troops and the population to believe that Russian revenge will be brutal, and have used Allied carpet bombing as an example. How could a sane person trust the Fuhrer?

Germany has inflicted suffering and destruction on much of Europe and is now inflicting it on themselves by continuing to fight.

January 30, 1945
Report from German spy embedded in U.S. Pentagon: Some of the scientists working on American secret weapons programs are former Germans who have secretly supplied classified information to Germany. We are told that the U.S. is now testing an atomic bomb so powerful that it can destroy an entire city. Some of the top Army generals and even the SS are advising Hitler to surrender before an atom bomb is dropped on Germany. Hitler refuses to listen.

Germany did have a head start on nuclear research and would have had the bomb were it not for air raids that wiped out German facilities and equipment and destroyed the heavy water facility in Norway.

German sources also report that the U.S. Army-Air Force has secret bases in the Utah desert where large bombers are practicing unusual bombing runs. This location near the West Coast could mean that Japan will be the first target.

January 31, 1945

Wehrmacht- Oder River: Wehrmacht pushed back to Odor. Russians fifty miles from Berlin.

February 2, 1945

As I think back about the V-2 rocket creation, it is really a scientific accomplishment that is, unfortunately, the product of a horrible World War. Our Army research center at Peenemünde possessed three key technologies by late 1941. We had large liquid-fuel rocket engines, a gyroscopic guidance system, and jet-controlled rudders. As chief guidance scientist, I did not reveal the sight variation calculations I have devised that can actually "misguide" the rocket by fractions to make it less destructive to an intended target.

By early October 1942, there was a successful test flight. As Walter Dornberger said at his Peenemünde speech on October 3, 1942, "this is the first of a new era in transportation and space travel." Most of my fellow scientists working on a technology breakthrough are not loyal Nazi "party" members.

The technical problems we solved during V-2 development include tank pressure, combustion chamber design, nozzle coiling, relay contacts, fuel pipe curves, fin design, and graphite vanes used as rudders. Airburst problems caused flight break-up until a tube was designed to strengthen the forward end.

In September 1943, Von Braun was masterful in persuading the high command and Hitler that development of the rocket was "almost" done. Hitler was so impressed that he authorized development in large numbers.

What he did not consider was the high cost per unit and the use of critical resources and labor. We constructed the V-2 in tunnels once Peenemünde was targeted by Allied bombers. Concentration camp prisoners from Mittelbau-Dora were used in the tunnels as slave labor. An estimated 20,000 died from exhaustion, starvation, disease, and being shot by guards. Production exceeded 5,000 rockets.

February 2, 1945

Technically, we use ethanol and water for a boosting fuel to achieve a height of about eighty kilometers. The fuel tanks are expensive alloy and we requisition aluminum and magnesium to build them. The fuel is heated to about 2,700 degrees Celsius in chambers and controlled by 1,200 nozzles. My guidance design included four external fins and four internal vanes, with two gyroscopes, one for the horizon and one for vertical stability. These and the accelerometer for controlling engine cutoff all have settings for following my directions for accuracy or for "near miss." While this highly complex weapon has created technology innovations, it is extremely complicated and, even with the brutal use of slave labor, has been overly expensive and wasteful. For the price of one rocket, I am sure three or four warplanes could be built. However, the Allies control the skies and the V-2's speed is far faster than the fastest Allied planes or artillery.

At the end of August 1944, Hitler demanded that the V-2 calibrations had little effect. My guess is that each rocket averaged two English civilians killed. Ten years of research, a vast expenditure, hundreds of buildings destroyed, and thousands of slave laborers killed; for relatively minuscule results.

My assessment is that each rocket has cost about 100,000 reichsmarks and the total program dating back to the early rocketing lab is about three billion reichsmarks. Most of the money was stolen from Jewish assets or the central banks of invaded countries. However, I suspect that many suppliers and manufacturers profited from our rocket creations and took their plunder to Switzerland and even to U.S. banks. The V-2 project has consumed approximately one-third of Germany's fuel production and most of other critical technologies.

The fuel alcohol for a V-2 launch took thirty, yes thirty tons of potatoes to produce alcohol at a time when Germans are starving. I made sure that the guidance systems were primitive relative to the distance assignment.

Germany has all but lost this horrible war and is using the V-2 as a last (delusional) hope to punish enemies and give hope to Nazi supporters. I believe the V-2 is worthless as a war tool. However, our scientists may have created technology for the next fifty years of rocketry. I personally produced re-calculations for inertial navigation concepts that could be used in years to come.

February 3, 1945

Luftwaffe: One thousand American bombers dropped thousands of bombs on Berlin in an obvious prelude to Russia's advances towards Berlin.

February 6, 1945

Wehrmacht: Oder pull-back. Russia has crossed the Oder.

February 9, 1945

SS concentration camp commanders under orders to "destroy evidence."

February 10, 1945

Navy Report: Still fighting battles in the Atlantic. U-boat losses. Confidential memos relate U-boats escapes headed for South America and Egypt. Refueling secretly aided by Standard Oil of New Jersey and Aramco.

February 11, 1945

Himmler Bulletin: Count Bernadotte of Sweden met Himmler yesterday near Berlin to discuss a release of concentration camp prisoners. While Hitler is resolved to fight to the end, Himmler recognizes that the war is lost and wants a way out. This meeting resulted in an agreement for a Swedish humanitarian convoy to enter Germany. Himmler has banned entry to Ravensbruck. It is my guess that is because he does not want the gassing to be discovered. Germany has now obviously totally lost the war, yet is obsessed with using scarce resources to gas more innocent people.

February 12, 1945

Intelligence Report: The German in the U.S. Administration reports that at Yalta in the Crimea there was a meeting of Stalin, Churchill, and Roosevelt to discuss dividing areas of control when Germany is defeated. Stalin has been pushing his armies to occupy vast territories so that, de facto, he already controls Eastern Europe.

February 13, 1945

Luftwaffe: Allied bombers devastate Dresden. Massive loss of life. Hitler should surrender at once but wants the last German to die with him.

February 14, 1945

Wehrmacht has been battling Russian armies in Hungary for 40 days. One hundred fifty thousand German troops dead. Budapest is lost. Soviets now control Poland, Czechoslovakia, Hungary, Romania, Bulgaria, Austria, and the Baltic countries.

February 14, 1945

SS: Information for top scientists: The Catholic Church is actively working to help Nazis escape justice. South America is often a destination. Argentina's Peron is receiving a substantial payoff to settle Nazis, aided by Cardinal Antonio Caggiano. Bishop Alois Hudal, an Austrian admirer of Hitler, is stationed at the Vatican and is issuing identity papers and Red Cross passports.

Himmler assumes the Pope and American bishops are aware and are cooperating. Assumes the International Red Cross will be completely cooperative. Carl Burckhardt, president of the IRC, is a well-known anti-Semite. The SS plans to detail thousands ofIRC documents and sent 800 Nazis to Argentina. Numerous convents and churches are now housing fleeing Nazis who eventually will go to the Vatican for papers.

There is a broad coalition across Europe, courts, police, and government that is unwilling to act against the Nazis. For example, many of the French are Nazi collaborators acting as Frenchmen in the Vichy regime.

Some South American dictators are welcoming Nazis. The German business community has used slave labor, so is creating a 'myth of innocence" that they believe will protect them from prosecution.

Himmler advises that a special effort will be made to help Horst Wagner reach Argentina. This may require a submarine escape across the Atlantic, with refueling having been agreed to by Standard Oil of New Jersey (for a price). Wagner aided in the murder of at least 350,000 Jews so Himmler holds him in high esteem. Mercedes Benz has a plant near Buenos Aires where Wagner can become "invisible" and where money can be laundered or used to support SS ex? patriots. It is known that many Nazi leaders own land and homes in Southern Argentina at Bariloche. The plan is to create a "German" village.

February 15, 1945

SS: Adolf Eichmann has officially issued a statement as numerous concentration camps are being liberated by the Allies: "I will leap into my grave laughing because the feeling I have. Five million human beings on my conscience, is for me a source of extraordinary satisfaction."

February 21, 1945

Wehrmacht: U.S. forces advancing. Overthrow Orschtez Line.

February 23, 1945

Wehrmacht: Allied/U.S. Army pushes across the Ruhr.

February 24, 1945

The city of Dresden has been incinerated by 800 British bombers. Dresden did not have any anti-aircraft defenses and the remnants of the German Air Force did not appear. This may have been in retaliation for Germany's indiscriminate V-1 and V-2 bombing of English cities. Or, it may have been a way to stop German troop movements. Either way, it is estimated that around 20,000 civilians were incinerated or were blown to bits. Dresden was a city with rampant anti? Semitism that dates back many years. It no longer exists.

February 25, 1945

Diplomatic Memo: Egypt, Syria, Turkey, and other mid-Eastern countries have been on the Nazi/German side and aided the Nazi effort to kill millions of Jews. Now that Allied victory is imminent, they have all declared war against Germany. An obvious desperation move.

February 25, 1945

Luftwaffe: Unable to defend Germany, Berlin is heavily bombed. City is in rubble. Dresden is wiped off the map. Cologne is like a morgue.

February 26, 1945

Personal: Germany's situation is hopeless, but Hitler refuses to end the war. He is now underground at the Chancellery in Berlin. The fate of the German people is irrelevant to Hitler. He wants to use the V-1 and V-2 for revenge by attacking Antwerp and London. Hanz Kammler now controls the V-2. Launch pads are in the Hague and Westerly, Holland, with the missiles directed at London. Amazingly, V-2 missile production has increased, with great loss of life by the slave concentration camp laborers.

February 27, 1945

U.S. Army Radio: General Eisenhower has just inspected one of the SS death camps and has issued a statement. "I have never dreamed that such cruelty, bestiality, and savagery could exist in this world." "It is beyond the American mind to comprehend this inhumanity and destruction."

February 28, 1945

Everything is collapsing in Germany. V-1 and V-2 engineers keep designing new, longer-range missiles, and I keep calibrating their flight paths to go slightly off course.

February 28, 1945

War Production Ministry Memo to the V-2 Leadership Regarding Krupp Armaments, Command of H. Himmler, SS, and A. Speer: "The Krupp family owns massive armaments and munitions factories that have profited immensely in the last wars. We know they have transferred vast sums to Swiss and U.S. banks. With defeat of Germany very near, the Krupp family is leaving and it is very difficult to get finished armaments from them. This devious corporation has promoted wars and German expansionism. Now, most of their facilities have been bombed and the Krupp family is on the run. Do not expect any more material from Krupp."

"The Krupps and the German business community have enjoyed free slave labor we have supplied to them, including from the concentration camps. Now, these businesses are trying to create myths of innocence."

March 2, 1945

Wehrmacht, Netherlands: Still occupies Netherlands. SS contingents continue killing Jews. Allies bombing German troop installations. Dutch resistance is active.

March 3, 1945

Allied bombers looking for V-2 sites at the Hague are way off target and kill thousands.

March 3, 1945

Himmler Bulletin: Bernadotte of Sweden has returned to Berlin to meet with Himmler and get permission to enter Ravensbruck. Gas chambers have been destroyed but the gassing is continuing in trucks. This is inhumane and casts guilt and shame upon all of Germany. The population at Ravensbruck has swelled in recent months as the Army brought women captives from other camps to work as slaves at Siemens Electric Plant, based at the camp.

March 5, 1945

Wehrmacht: Trying to defend the Ruhr. Major battles. Pushed back over the Rhine by U.S. troops.

March 6, 1945

SS Bulletin to Leadership: SS General Wolff has met secretly with Allan Dulles of the U.S.,

O.S.S. in Switzerland. He wanted to negotiate an early surrender and to discuss protection of artwork stolen by the Nazis. Wolff also negotiated Dulles' promise to protect him from war crime indictments.

Personal: The Allies and Germany had organizations to protect and retrieve art. But they did not save people in concentration camps until it was too late. An upside-down world gone crazy.

March 7, 1945

Wehrmacht: Cologne lost to Allies. U.S. 9th Division crosses the Rhine at Remagen.

March 10, 1945

Foreign Report: U.S fire bombed Tokyo. Over 100,000 civilians killed. Japan being devastated by the war in the Pacific.

March 11, 1945

Luftwaffe: One thousand U.S. bombers flatten Essen.

March 12, 1945

SS: Continued execution of Resistance Amsterdamers who are harassing German troops.

March 13, 1945

V-2 Report: Rapid movements of launch pads are hard for the Allies to keep track. However, they are bombing roads and rail, so it is very hard to move missiles that are now open targets.

March 14, 1945

Wehrmacht: Allied bombing cuts rail links. Armies trapped.

March 14, 1945

SS Bulletin, Himmler: The Nazis still control the Ravensbruck women's concentration camp. Although British, Russian, and American troops are advancing and liberating most camps, at Ravensbruck, Germans are gassing thousands of women in a desperate attempt to destroy the evidence of their crimes. Thousands more are being driven like cattle on death marches. It is insane and senseless since Germany has lost this horrible war.

There is word that the Swedish Red Cross is driving busses across bombed-out Germany to try to rescue the ravaged people who have been in camps. We are told that the Swede called Folke Bernadotte, the descendant of royalty, organized this humanitarian effort. Although the Russians have liberated many of the Eastern camps, the Nazis still hold huge numbers at camps on German soil, such as Buchenwald, Dachau, and Bergen-Belsen. The International Red Cross is doing nothing, but Bernadotte and the Swedish RC will take action. Perhaps, it was because Sweden had been neutral and felt guilty of inaction.

March 15, 1945

The Soviet offensive is moving rapidly and may soon reach Peenemünde. Orders have been given to vacate to a research facility in the Harz Mountains in the Bleicherode Mine. Most of the technicians and their families chose to follow Von Braun and Kammler's orders since it meant being captured by the Americans. I am staying here to protect my research equipment, scientific papers, and diaries; and hope that the Russian intelligence experts already know what I have done to sabotage the accuracy of the V-2 rockets. Certainly, my "handler" is aware of the ways I reset guidance systems. Also, by staying put, there may be a chance to reunite with my wife and son who is now 12. The SS has refused photos of either one but assures me that they are alright.

March 16, 1945

Luftwaffe: British bombers destroy Wurzburg. Hitler still refuses to surrender while Germany is decimated.

March 18, 1945

Nazi Bulletin: Berlin hit by 1,250 U.S. bombers. Nothing is left intact. Hitler in underground bunker.

March 19, 1945

"Destroy all German factories." This insane decree is ignored by our rocket group. Mittelwerk and Peenemünde represent great rocket achievements and we refuse to waste great research that might have a life after the war ends.

March 20, 1945
Wehrmacht: U.S. attacks Saar.

March 22, 1945
Wehrmacht: Pushed by U.S. Army. Crossing the Rhine.

March 24, 1945
Intelligence Report U.S.: Six hundred transports drop 1,300 troop gliders behind German lines.

March 25, 1945
Luftwaffe: Allied bombers have attacked Germany for four days. They may have unlimited supplies of aviation fuel, pilots, and bombs.

March 26, 1945
Audio Intercept: Eisenhower orders U.S. troops to cross the Rhine at Remagen and Wonns.

March 27, 1945
Intercept: Eisenhower declares German Western Front is broken.

March 27, 1945
W-2 Kammler: Missile launches suspended. Antwerp evacuated by Wehrmacht. Holland withdrawal. Missiles being moved. Nearing Peenemünde. Plan is to move to the Harz Mountains and existing underground factory at Nordhausen. To this end, vast stores of fuel and food have been moved to Nordhausen-Dora with a plan to accelerate V-2 production and to build more tunnels and factories. Too much too late.

March 29, 1945
With the war obviously lost to the Allies, Von Braun has distributed an SS

memo to all of us; his top research directors. We are advised to escape very soon.

The International Red Cross has issued 25,000 new identity cards. This has been approved by IRC senior staff. Also, the Catholic Church is openly involved in relocating Nazis. As I noted, Bishop Alois Hudal in Rome is running a huge operation in and near the Vatican, and also actively supporting Nazi flight. The Church's program is systematic and intentional.

Destination of choice will include Argentina, where hundreds of high-ranking Nazis have already escaped; bringing with them treasures stolen all over Europe. The Middle East is often named as a haven (Egypt, Syria, Saudi, Arabia, and Iran). Various Muslim leaders will help since the Mufti of Jerusalem is an active Nazi supporter.

April 2, 1945

Von Braun, RE: Kammler: Kammler has taken 500 V-2 experts by train to the Bavarian Alps. Plans to use them as bargaining "chip" with Americans in order to save his own hide.

April 4, 1945

Von Braun memo: Americans approaching Harz Mountains must hide Peenemünde research archives. Herded prisoners at Dora and subcamps being evacuated. Himmler's order to liquidate all camp prisoners is not to be carried out. Prisoners driven on foot; no food or water. Escapees are exhausted and being shot along the way. Allied planes constantly bombing the roads.

April 4, 1945

SS: Orders to evacuate camp at Buchenwald.

April 4, 1945

Wehrmacht: Complete retreat from Hungary.

April 4, 1945

Personal: I have learned for some time that the SS has been hoarding stolen art and other wealth in German salt mines. They are under the impression that after the war they can retrieve these treasures. It is only a matter of time before Allied troops will discover the loot.

April 5, 1945
U.S. Army Intercept: U.S. Supreme Commander Dwight D. Eisenhower has visited the Ohrdruf concentration camp after its liberation. Ohrdruf is a satellite of Buchenwald. He has required his soldiers to view at various liberated camps the shocking malnourished, beaten survivors among the piles of dead bodies lining the road. Even a trainload of dead bodies. Crematoriums, ovens, thousands clinging to life like walking skeletons, warehouses full of stolen goods. Eisenhower plans to bring Allied governments to the camps to bear witness.

April 7, 1945
Wehrmacht: Orders to load three trains with Bergen-Belsen prisoners to use for prisoner exchange with American forces that are rapidly closing in.

April 9, 1945
Navy: Battleship Scheer sunk by RAF in Kiel.

April 9, 1945
Wehrmacht: Defeat at Konigsberg.

April 10, 1945
SS: Allies liberated Buchenwald.

April 11, 1945
Wehrmacht: The Western Front has fallen apart. American forces have reached the Elbe.

April 11, 1945
U.S. Army intercept regarding Mittelwerk and Dora: I have frequented Mittelwerk often in my role of checking V-2 guidance systems. When we heard the U. S. Army communications, it caused me to think back to August

17-18, 1943, when Allied bombers caused heavy damage to Peenemünde. We were forced to go underground for weapons production. The massive tunnels under Kehlstein Mountain were enlarged and became Mittelwerk.

Tens of thousands of slave laborers were used and they worked under brutal, sub-human conditions. The SS set up Dora camp at Nordhausen and subcamps to house the slave labor; which swelled to about 20,000. It is obvious that the Russians and Americans are moving quickly. I have stayed in touch with my technical associates and civilian engineers. They advised me the SS did not want V-1 and V-2 secrets to fall into Allied hands and had planned to gas all of them. Instead, a week ago they all fled into the mountains.

The U.S. Army intercept says Nordhausen has surrendered to the U.S. Army and that the U.S. Army has found many thousands of bodies. These are Mittelwerk slaves that were worked and starved to death. A few survivors also told the U.S. of guards forcing prisoners into a nearby barn and setting it on fire. I am expecting Russians at Peenemünde any day now.

April 11, 1945

U.S. Army radio intercept: The Buchenwald concentration camp has been liberated. Russian prisoners immediately grabbed SS vehicles and weapons and drove to nearby Weimar to murder as many Germans as they could find.

By contrast, the Jewish prisoners held a religious service. The commentator believes this was to defy God and tell him as Jews they chose to remain human. They used the Torah as a "moral shield."

April 11, 1945

SS: Canadian troops liberate camp Westerbork, Netherlands.

April 12, 1945

Personal: As the Wehrmacht continues to retreat, there are Nazi criminals who are frantic to escape justice for their horrible cruel crime and murder. SS officers continue to be "processed" by the International Red Cross, which issued 120,000 documents, and Roman Catholic officials are helping

Nazis. Italy is an escape route to Argentina which is recruiting Nazis. At the Vatican, we know that Bishop Alois Hudal continues to be motivated by his German nationalism and his anti-Semitism.

April 12, 1945

BBC Radio: President Franklin Roosevelt has died at age 63.

April 12, 1945

Washington D.C.: Harry Truman is new U.S. President.

April 13, 1945

Top Secret–Bulletin from Hitler in the Berlin Bunker: Hitler is furious with the collapse of the Wehrmacht that has been holding a strategic line in the Italian mountains as a way of relieving Allied pressure on the western invasion front.

Yesterday a British Jewish Brigade attacked the Wehrmacht that was entrenched on Mount Ghebbio. The brigade evidently engaged German troops in hand-to-hand combat and drove them off of Ghebbio. Hitler is furious that Jews stormed the Wehrmacht defenses and that many of the German troops fled. It is assumed that the Jewish Brigade will pursue the Wehrmacht, which is a happening that Hitler cannot accept.

The Jewish Brigade is composed of Jews from British Palestine, many of whom had escaped the Nazis in the 1930s. Hitler's bulletin laments the fact that had the German North African campaign been successful he could have killed the Jews in Palestine and elsewhere in the Middle East where Jewish populations have existed for as long as 3,000 years.

It is my observation that German manpower has been so depleted that these troops were very young and not well trained. The war is a lost cause for Germany and the retreating troops have more sense than Hitler. All they want to do is save their own lives even if it means returning to a totally destroyed country.

April 13, 1945

Wehrmacht: Retreat at Vienna. Red Army occupies Vienna.

April 14, 1945
U.S. Army Radio: Yesterday, troops have just liberated a train full of concentration camp prisoners who had been held by German troops hoping to use them for "prisoner" exchanges. These slaves are now free people.

April 14, 1945
Wehrmacht: Nuremberg and Stuttgart fall to the Allies.

April 15, 1945
SS: British liberate Bergen-Belsen camp. I am aware of records showing that 50,000 Jews were murdered there and many subjected to starvation, disease, and gruesome medical experiments.

April 15, 1945
SS: U.S. troops liberate camp Colditz.

April 16, 1945
In the past few days, American and British troops have liberated camps Buchenwald and Bergen? Belsen. Since both are death camps, the SS guards have fled, some captured and some lost.

April 16, 1945
Wehrmacht: Trying to defend Berlin against Russian troops. Hitler issuing orders from his bunker.

April 19, 1945
Wehrmacht: Retreating German troops are flooding the Netherlands in a desperate attempt to slow Allied advances. Great environmental damage.

April 20, 1945
Wehrmacht: Russian troops advancing in Berlin; city of Nuremberg falls to U.S.

April 22, 1945
SS: Camp Sachsenhausen liberated.

April 23, 1945
SS: Camp Flossenbiirg liberated.

April 24, 1945
Swedish Red Cross Announcement: "Ravensbruck concentration camp for women still under SS control. Desperate Nazis have gassed thousands and driven thousands into death marches in an attempt to empty the camps. Swedish Red Cross has braved dangerous war conditions to snatch 500 women from the SS and today they have been taken to Malmo, Sweden. The head of this mission of mercy is Folke Bernadotte."

April 25, 1945
Wehrmacht: Berlin completely surrounded by Soviets. Soviet and U.S. troops meet at Elbe River.

April 26, 1945
Wehrmacht: Tank attack. A victory scored at Bautzen.

April 29, 1945
Wehrmacht: German armies in Italy pursued by British Jewish Brigade and U.S. Army have proposed surrender terms.

April 29, 1945
SS: The oldest concentration camp, Dachau, has been liberated by the U.S.; 31,000 go free.

April 29, 1945
U.S. Army radio 157th regimental combat team–message intercept: "We have entered Dachau concentration camp near Munich. There are boxcars full of emaciated corpses, twisted bodies of the living and dead. U.S. soldiers are furious and plan to execute the Nazi guards.

This is a scene of brutality, suffering, and murder. The SS guards near these Dachau death trains have been executed.

April 29, 1945
Dachau liberated by Americans.

April 30, 1945
SS Ravensbruck evacuated by SS and Russian Army approaching. Prisoners abandoned.

April 30, 1945
Personal: Russians have arrived at Ravensbruck and have found piles of starved bodies. Without Bernadotte, there would have been hundreds more.

April 30, 1945
Wehrmacht: Attack by U.S. troops at the Elbe.

April 30, 1945
Wehrmacht: Berlin overrun by Soviets. Hitler is thought to have killed himself. This is the end for Germany and a relief that it may now be released from the lawlessness, brutality, and death.

April 30, 1945
Personal: The world turned a deaf ear on the WWII sounds of suffering. I hope this diary "speaks loud" enough to be remembered. Hitler has destroyed Germany.

May 1, 1945
Nazi Party Bulletin: Admiral Doenitz has formed a new German government. The end is near.

May 1, 1945
Wehrmacht: Soviet advances take Rostec.

May 2, 1945
Wehrmacht: Allies take Weimar.

May 2, 1945
Wehrmacht: German Army in Italy surrenders to Allies, including a Jewish Brigade of the English Army. The Brigade consists of Jews from Palestine and Jews who had fled the Nazis. At Peenemünde, most of the Allied radio dispatches are heard by our electronic equipment.

May 2, 1945
Allied Radio: Yugoslav troops now occupy the important city of Trieste.

May 2, 1945
Polish troops occupy Wilhelmshaven.

May 2, 1945
Germany's defeat is imminent. Because the Nazis have spread destruction and brutality throughout all of Europe, I believe there will be a huge appetite for revenge. At the same time, many of the victorious nations will suffer the hardships of lack of food and basic services.

May 3, 1945
A colleague in designing V-2 guidance systems is Helmut Grottrup. We are good friends and we have agreed to wait for the Russians rather than flee to Mittelwerk.

May 3, 1945
U.S. Army Radio: Werner Heisenberg, the famous German nuclear scientist, has been arrested by the Allies.

May 3, 1945
BBC Broadcast: Concentration camp survivors have been herded onto three former luxury liners in an attempt to hide the hideous evidence of human slaughter. There were about 7,000 prisoners of which 5,000 were on

the Cap Arcona. It is now three days after Hitler is rumored to have committed suicide. These prisoners have survived torture and hunger. British pilots mistakenly have bombed all three boats thinking they were occupied by Nazis trying to flee Germany.

There have been very few survivors of the bombing mistakes. It is very hard to believe that anyone would think that Nazis would "escape" by slow, vulnerable ships, so this sinking appears to be blatant stupidity. Three loaded ships were sunk: The Thielbek, The Deutschland, and the Cap Arcona. Seven thousand died "on the doorstep of freedom."

May 3, 1945

Wehrmacht high command, Ascona, Switzerland: General Karl Wolff has signed an accord that suddenly ended the war in Italy and Austria. Instrumental pressures came from the Jewish Brigade's advances, American forces advances and the diplomatic efforts of Allen Dulles who represented the U.S., O.S.S. This has ended a tedious battle that could have meant the very difficult defense of Italy's mountains and the Brenner Pass.

May 3, 1945

An Army bulletin advised us that the German Army in Italy surrendered yesterday to the Allies. The German strategy of using experienced troops to hold the high ground has failed. This was meant to impede the advance of British and American armies and give the German troops an orderly regrouping to defend Germany. Escape routes were blocked. A key defeat came at the hand of a Jewish Brigade that is attached to the British Army. The Brigade attacked and took German defenses on Mount Ghebbio, which caused a retreat that could not be stopped. M.M.

May 4, 1945

U.S. Army Radio: German troops in Netherlands, Denmark, and Norway surrender to Allies.

May 5, 1945

U.S. Army Radio: Mauthausen concentration camp liberated.

May 7, 1945

Wehrmacht Final Bulletin: German General Alfred Jodi signs the surrender at Reims, France, which means the end of this horrendous war. It will be only a few days before the Russians reach Peenemünde. I will await my fate here rather than try to flee. The diary entries may stop. It is very possible that my expertise in rocket guidance will be of value to the Russians and they will spare me. Since I have confided with my "handler" X the ongoing program to sabotage the V-2 guidance, he may have relayed that to the Kremlin.

All that is left at Peenemünde are my papers, broken machines, and smoldering ashes.

May 7, 1945

Personal: "X" has just advised me that he has been in contact with the KGB. I am to sit tight and wait to be taken to Russia along with my papers, diaries, and equipment. The KGB in Berlin want to talk with me, to make sure I have everything they want. "X" has advised me that my wife had died in 1944 but that my son is alive and will be taken to Russia and will be safe as long as I help the Soviets advance their rocket program. They will not let us have contact but will keep me advised of his growth and education.

The SS had deceived me all along. I have no details about my wife's death. I grieve this personal loss and await my fate at the hands of the Soviets.

May 7, 1945

Wehrmacht: When General Alfred Jodi signed the instrument of surrender at RIMS, it is strange to note that Allen Dulles of the U.S. was present and his role is unexplained. It is also clear that the Soviets were not present, which may make them feel suspicious.

May 8, 1945

Personal: Germany has further and unconditionally surrendered when General von Keitel formally surrendered to Marshall Zhukov and the

Soviets in Berlin. Today is VE day for the Allies. During late 1944 up to the present, there have been about 700,000 concentration camp prisoners. It can never, ever be forgotten that with defeat imminent, Germany kept slaughtering these prisoners, including death marches. Prisoners were shot, beaten to death, starved, and frozen to death. Hitler could have capitulated and saved millions of lives and saved Europe from senseless destruction. What hate and madness can motivate an entire nation to follow the orders of madmen? Germany's guilt and shame will remain for time immemorial. How will these perpetrators of mass murder be punished? What lessons will be learned? Hitler and his Nazis have destroyed a world of learning and culture. Can it ever be restored? Will the world REMEMBER?

May 9, 1945

It is certain that the Allies will be rounding up prominent Nazis as war criminals. Heinrich Himmler of the SS should be the first to go.

May 9, 1945

This may be my last diary entry for some time. Our rocket production office knows that the Wehrmacht has surrendered on this front. Since the V-2 offices are situated at Peenemünde, I will continue to sit tight and wait for Russians to get here. Fleeing, I will only be a target for getting shot. The Russians are well aware of what we are doing, and I know they will want to question and hold German scientists who might be of value for Russia's own rocket research. They may not believe that I have actually been sabotaging the German V-2 program, so my chance of survival at the hands of the Russian Army is to convince them of my strategic value to help them with rocket guidance systems. I believe my handler "X" has told KGB about me.

A horrible chapter in German history now appears to be closing. Forgive them not, Julia, they knew what they did.

ABOUT THE AUTHOR

Ron Kaufman studied European diplomatic history at the University of California, Berkeley in the early 1950s.It was taught by a former officer of the Office of Strategic Services (OSS) who had been active in World War II. Ron went on to receive an MBA in Real Estate Research and Urban Land Economics, and eventually was instrumental to the restoration of the northeast waterfront neighborhood in San Francisco. That involvement took up thirty years of Ron's life.

Ron Kaufman's mother's family was from Lida, Lithuania and emigrated to the U.S. in the early 1900s. His father's family was from Russia and Germany. Ron has devoted all his adult life to serving the Jewish and general communities. The service has included the following: President of the Jewish Community Federation of San Francisco, Marin County, and The Peninsula; a Governor of The Jewish Agency; President of The Jewish Family and Children's Service, including co-founder of the National Association; extended terms on hospital boards in San Francisco and the San Francisco West Bay; and contributing annually to over one hundred different non-profits that serve local and national needs.

Ron is married to Barbara Kaufman (former President of the San Francisco Board of Supervisors); has three children (Steve, Karen, and Nirmada) and four grandchildren (Olivia, Anna, Zev, and Ari.) He has lived and worked in San Francisco since 1959.

www.ingramcontent.com/pod-product-compliance
Lightning Source LLC
Chambersburg PA
CBHW021619030826
48979CB00033B/315
* 9 7 8 1 7 3 5 9 3 7 7 7 9 *